D0360154

BOOKS BY JAMES REDFEARN

Novels

The Rising at Roxbury Crossing

Stories

Latent Images
The Ringmaster

An Appointed Time

AN APPOINTED TIME

— A NOVEL —

JAMES G. REDFEARN

Olde Stoney Brook
Wrentham, Massachusetts

Olde Stoney Brook Publishing
P.O. Box 851
Wrentham, MA 02093

www.anappointedtime.com

This book is a work of fiction. References to actual persons, places and events in this novel are for purposes of providing a historical reference and are used fictitiously. All characters, incidents and dialogue are products of the author's imagination. Any semblance to actual persons, events or dialogue is entirely coincidental.

Paperback ISBN 978-0-9839960-1-9

Interior design by Erik Christopher, *Ugly Dog Digital*

Manufactured in the United States of America

First Trade Paperback Printing
10 9 8 7 6 5 4 3 2 1

In Memoriam

Denis J. Donoghue, Jr. 47th RTT MSP

Robert W. (Skip) Scofield 55th RTT MSP

Those who have crossed
With direct eyes to death's other Kingdom
Remember us —if at all—not as lost
Violent souls, but only
As the hollow men,
The stuffed men.

The Hollow Men
T.S. Eliot

An Appointed Time

Middleborough, Massachusetts

They long-stepped along the embankment, turtled up in sweaters and jackets against the perpetual dampness of the cattail marsh, still and frozen to the edges and capped in a thin veneer of gray ice. The adjacent swamp and woods garnished in a blanket of wet-white snow, the skeleton trees of winter with their long bony limbs rocking back and forth in the chilled bitter wind like withered old men. Behind them, the dust and stone of the power lines. Static electricity bullwhipping the air. Charles Washington Harnett led the way, a .22 caliber long rifle slung across his back with William Coyle, toting another rifle and hiking stride for stride off Harnett's shoulder. And John Coyle, limping badly, twenty feet behind, every fourth step punctuated by the persistent thud of a walking stick. They circumvented the swamp and the hibernating water snakes, the reedy marsh grasses windbent and sallow yellow, the colonies of cattail stands asleep in their purgatory period. Upon the apron of solid ground, the men marched in silent revelation, past the desolate black forest, past the netherworld of the swamp and the entanglement of the underbrush. Past the layers and layers of history and timeless decay. On and on they marched, racing the sun to the horizon and the remaining light of day.

1

Grafton, Massachusetts
Fall 1958

The bus rolled to a stop at the end of the long stone walk outside the building where a pole stood and the American flag blew away like a ribbon in the autumn breeze. On the bus, five young men in old uniforms, smelling like history, smoked and talked quietly or stared out the windows alone with their thoughts. The driver opened the door and the five men came off the bus in single file, duffle bags hung from their shoulders. They were dressed in high boots, breeches and blouses that fit them well. They formed up one behind the other at the thick wooden door and the first in line pounded his fist into it. They stood there at attention and waited for entry.

The old brick building half way up the hill on Route 140 in the town of Grafton had a Colonial Revival design and it often was mistaken for being the residence of one of the town's leading citizens or confused with the public library or the residential dormitory of a prestigious New England Prep school. But the Commonwealth of Massachusetts owned this building and others like it scattered across the state. State Police Grafton served as the operational center and living quarters for the Massachusetts state troopers who patrolled the towns that occupied the rural landscape of Central and Southern Worcester County—the barracks, where troopers lived a military life in a family of brothers and boots learned the values and traditions passed down from generation to generation, descendants of men who conducted one-hundred mile patrols on horseback, frontiersmen who relied on themselves because there was no one else. They were throwbacks, a wisp of dust from an earlier time in American history when men carried their life stories in saddlebags slung across the backs of their horses, hard men loyal to the morals and motives of an earlier country when justice was more often rendered in the moment than before a circuit court judge—the barracks, where junior troopers took advice from their senior counterparts with little argument, and where all listened to the sergeant as if he was standing next to the hand of God.

The commander of State Police Grafton was named after the Father of the American Navy, Commodore John Barry, an Irish immigrant from County Wexford who pirated British commercial ships during the American Revolution. And similar to the Commodore, Sergeant John Barry McGreevey led with a certain panache. He had small hands and a small frame and eyes that gave the impression he had been fighting a misperception most of his life. Troopers who had seen him in action said he had the hand speed and nimble quickness of a young Willie Pep. McGreevey led with a simple dictum—screwing up is one thing, lying to cover the screw-up could be fatal. He preferred to take care of things in-house rather than benignly passing it up the ladder. And if he believed that one of his men had been treated unfairly by the brass, the sergeant like an old gunny might "mount up" and drive to Troop Headquarters to voice his opinion. A sign hung over the station commander's door. It read 'The Busiest and the Best.'

The new boots stood waiting in the large booking room outside McGreevey's office. The walls of the room were halved by a chair rail, the tops of the walls a semi-glossed white, the bottoms deep royal blue. One of the walls had a

6

height chart attached to it. Linoleum covered the floor and while worn in places, it shined. A wooden bench was bolted against the wall. It had two pairs of handcuffs secured to it where prisoners sat, waiting to be processed. The room butted up against the cell block and an odor of disinfectant lingered in that part of the building.

McGreevey's door opened and a seasoned trooper exited the office. A torn piece of piping on the outside of his breeches hung away like a pennant, his leather had a dull black finish and his boots the discoloration of the white stain of sweat. He scuffled along the floor as he walked and his gun belt and holster hung off him like an old gunslinger. And when this large bald man passed, the boots, the leather, the military uniform grumbled and chafed and spoke of things seen that most of them had never seen. The whole physical countenance of the man spoke of hard fought campaigns. And power. He was the SM, the Senior Man.

"Send them in," McGreevey said.

"Alright, leave the duffle bags where they are," the trooper said.

The sergeant sat at his desk, writing an entry into a journal. Two things sat atop the desk, a reading lamp and a photograph of the McGreevey family. A metal crucifix and a framed map of Worcester County hung behind him. A wooden pendulum clock hung on another wall and across from that an orderly arrangement of framed photographs of troopers killed in the line of duty.

He glanced up at them as they entered. "Good morning," he said, "stand easy" and he returned to his writing. After completing his entry, he read it to himself then made an additional notation. And while still writing, he began to talk. "Because this house has no ears, it hears nothing. It cannot speak therefore it repeats nothing. It is not judgmental and it forms no opinion. What happens in this house remains with-

7

in the silence of this house." He lifted his head and put the pen down, "Do you understand?"

"Sir, yes sir," they said.

"You're no longer in the academy. Out here, you address a non-commissioned officer by his rank, a commissioned officer by his rank or sir and civilians as sir or ma'am. One sir will do."

He took a sheet of teletype paper out of the desk drawer and walked the line of boots reading their tags as he corroborated their names with those on the 14A General Order because it wouldn't have been the first time a new trooper on his first day of duty reported to the wrong station.

"Sullivan, Schultz, Miller, Abramson." McGreevey glanced up. "And Mahan. Welcome to State Police Grafton or as we like to call it, Fort Wilderness. You're just what we need—more bodies to help out." He handed each of them a sheet of paper. "Those are the barracks' House Rules. Familiarize yourselves with them and make sure you adhere to them. The state police operates on a seniority system. Which means until another class graduates and new troopers show up at our door, you are responsible for the cleanliness of this house, its cruisers and the field boots of the senior men. Any questions?"

"No Sergeant."

"You have been assigned to ride with a veteran trooper. And at the end of the break-in period, your coach will submit a proficiency report to me, which I will review and forward to the Troop Commander. If you fail to meet our standards during that time, you will be dismissed. And you have no right of appeal. Do you understand that?"

"Yes, Sergeant."

"Abramson, Mahan and Miller will begin patrol at four this afternoon with your coaches. Sullivan and Schultz start tonight at ten." He looked towards the window. "Out there, we treat everyone with dignity. But take no bullshit. We demand the best of you because once you're on your own, you're it. You'll make decisions, important decisions. And you'll often make these decisions with no counsel. Many of the towns in our area either have no police departments or a part time force, usually consisting of a chief and maybe one officer. They may be the local insurance man or a used car salesman with a minimum of training. Your closest patrol can be ten miles away or more. And even when another patrol is in the area, our radio system can be affected by the roll of the land. The signal can be blocked by the Worcester hills or buried in the Blackstone Valley. In other words, your line mate could be right in the next town and not hear your cry for help."

He placed the teletype message on the desk. "Those of you from the cities, if you think you left cruelty and the debasement of the human condition at the city limits, think again. Folks around here for the most part are good people. They'll take care of you once you get to know them. They may be all you have if you run into trouble. But there are some bad actors. And they know that troopers ride alone." He paused. "You may find yourself all alone with one of these boys in some desolate place or in the parking lot of one our gin mills and on the wrong side of a fistfight and you're taking a terrible beating. If given the chance, they will hurt you. Nothing personal, they just don't like being told what to do. Or, you may find yourself on a dark deserted roadway and the person you have stopped likes his odds after sizing you up. And he will shoot you dead with your own weapon. So, each time you leave this building, you best take your assignment seriously."

He stepped in front of one of the new troopers and read his nametag. "I've got good men here in this barracks. Do you know why, Miller?"

9

"Because of their training, Sergeant?"

"Because they take care of one another."

THE SM, PEARLY K CUNNINGHAM led them into the small kitchen at the back of the building. Other senior troopers drifted in and took up seats at the table. They wore t-shirts that complemented the pallor of their skin, and a few of them were burnt to a ruddy shade of Irish.

"What's for lunch, Ma?" Cunningham said.

"Baked chicken," she said. "They look like they could use a good meal, Pearly. Weren't they fed in the academy?"

"They didn't have your home cooking, Ma." He put his arm around her. "We're fortunate to have the best damn cook in the state. This is Mrs. Margaret Healey and she's the only person who can call me Pearly. The name is either Trooper Cunningham or PK and 'PK' only if I know you well enough. Ma has also nursed more than a few troopers through the flu or some other malady. You will always treat her with respect. Take a seat."

More senior troopers filed into the kitchen and sat down while the new boots looked for empty chairs. "Let's go," Cunningham said. "Find a seat."

They jitter bugged around the table until they fell into an unoccupied place. Frank Mahan saw the last empty seat at the head of the table, but he hesitated and a classmate sat down. He found a chair in the corner of the room and brought it to the table, but none of the senior troopers would accommodate him and he stood there holding it with no place to sit.

McGreevey entered the room. "Are you going to eat with that in your hand?"

"Yes, Sergeant."

McGreevey looked at him.

"If I have to, Sergeant."

"What was your name again?"

"Mahan."

McGreevey and Cunningham exchanged glances. The SM turned to the boot sitting at the head of the table. "And who are you?"

"Abramson, sir."

"I'm a trooper, nitwit, not a commissioned officer."

"Sorry."

"What are ya sorry about?"

"I don't know . . . Trooper PK."

A few of the senior men snickered and some of them just stared.

"My friends call me PK. Do you want to be my friend, boot? You have a lot of salt for someone who hasn't done anything yet." He sat back. "Are you comfortable in the sergeant's chair?"

Abramson looked around the table. Older troopers looked back stone-faced, while his classmates glanced at each other uncertainly.

"I . . . I didn't know."

"You didn't ask either."

"No."

"Get up. And give Sergeant McGreevey his place."

The congestive bark of an old dog echoed in the back stairwell and one of the troopers opened the door and a large red and black mixed breed entered, a German Shepherd and some combination of wild feral canine. He sniffed and wandered into the kitchen, moving about the men sitting at the table. A couple of the senior officers patted the dog and he indifferently passed them until he took his place beside Cunningham.

"His name is Charon," he said. "He'll let you know when he trusts you."

Mrs. Healey placed a platter of chicken on the table while Frank stood with the chair in the corner of the room. Abramson circled the table, like a disoriented gooney bird not knowing where to land. Frank put down the chair and took a bowl of potatoes from Mrs. Healey and began to serve the seated troopers. Abramson joined him and they performed the service of waiters until all had their food. Once the meal had been served, Frank and Abramson filled their own plates and stood to the side.

"Look in the pantry, Abramson," Cunningham said, "there's another chair in there." He shifted his seat and they all made room for them at the table.

"Sullivan and Schultz, you've got mess duties at the evening meal."

"Yes Trooper Cunningham," they said.

"Tell us about yourselves," he said, "starting with you" and he pointed at Miller.

FRANK AND ABRAMSON returned to the table after they had cleared the dishes. The senior troopers sat there drinking coffee and smoking. The new troopers just sat.

"Have we saved the best for last, Mahan?"

"My story isn't that interesting Trooper Cunningham."

"How old are you?

"Twenty-eight."

"Twenty-eight?"

"That's right."

"Where have you been Mahan at twenty-eight? Are you married?"

"Yes."

"Were you in the service?"

"No."

"You're a draft dodger, Mahan? A 4-F slacker?"

"I registered when I was eighteen, but I never got called."

"That's because you were a priest, right?"

"How did you . . .? I was never a priest. My first two years of high school, I spent in a seminary."

"You going to give us a sermon? Like Bishop, what's his name?"

"Sheehan," one of the troopers said. "Bishop Fulton Sheehan."

"So what happened?" Cunningham said.

"Just left. Didn't think it was for me."

"You're a quitter, Mahan."

"No."

"What's your first name?"

"Francis."

"Okay, Francis . . ."

"Frank."

Cunningham smiled. "I think I'll call you, Priest."

"So why weren't you drafted, Priest?" A senior trooper said from the end of the table.

"I think." Frank glanced at his classmates. "Because I had a Top Secret clearance from the Government."

"The Government?"

"The Department of Defense and the Atomic Energy Commission."

"Are you a spy, Priest?" Cunningham said. "Care to share any secrets?"

"I don't know any."

"So, what did you do?"

"I worked for a company that tested atomic bombs."

"No kidding." Cunningham wagged his spoon at him. "I knew you were a sleeper. You weren't one of those Commies who sold secrets to the Reds were ya?"

"No."

"Not one of Klaus Fuchs' pals?"

13

"I wouldn't be sitting here if I was."

"Where did they test those atomic bombs?"

"Enewetak."

"Where's that?"

"In the Pacific. The Marshall Islands."

"So, you blew up nuclear weapons?" A senior trooper said.

"I didn't have anything to do with setting off the bomb. I developed film taken of the blast and made enlargements for engineers so they could make their mathematical measurements."

"Did you actually see these explosions?" the senior trooper said.

"I saw enough."

Cunningham dragged on a cigarette. "Be ready to go to work at fifteen hundred hours. Cause guess who's breaking you in?" He blew the smoke across the table.

"Fifteen hundred? I thought the shift began at four."

"Fifteen hundred. You have a problem with that?"

"No, I just thought . . ."

"You've got cruisers to wash."

"Fifteen hundred, got it."

2

They rode into the village at dusk and passed a large brick complex along the Blackstone River its windows boarded-up, the plywood decorated in graffiti. The shuttered textile mill on Route 122, its thick planked floors saturated in oil sat quiet, and its great gate, where trucks once carried raw materials in and American products out, hung shackled and bound by anchor chain. They entered Millville's center where the road split in two, the state highway continuing on one side and Blackstone Street beginning on the other. There, a trough stood since 1866 where weary travelers wetted their horses and a faithful stone soldier stood his post. Behind that, was the Friends Meetinghouse in which the town's business was conducted, religious and civil both.

"You watch what I do and how I talk to these folks," Cunningham said. "Wearing that uniform only counts for so much. They've had some hard times around here since that mill closed, but they're hard-working folks. Earn their respect because without them, you could be up shit's creek."

Two men waited outside the tavern on a bench for the 5:05 Greyhound to Boston, one with a mongrel dog laid out prone by his leg. They watched the state police cruiser enter the village, pass them, drive behind the Meetinghouse and disappear. In back of the building, the police chief waited outside his personal vehicle that served as Millville's cruiser, an unmarked black Chevrolet Bel Air. Joe Renaud owned the village hardware, served as the town's postmaster, was

15

the local constable and the chief of the three man Black-stone-Millville Police Department. All of his business was conducted out of a rambling L-shaped farm house that included his home, an attached hardware store and a barn for storage. At the rear of the barn and under the loft, a converted shed served as the village lockup. Chief Renaud had lived in the unincorporated town all of his life and knew by name and character every living soul within its confines.

"Is he around, Joe?" Cunningham said.

"I seen him working out back of Sam Pritchard's place earlier today. Face all scratched up. Looked like he tried to screw a rooster. They look fresh, the scratches that is." He spat on the ground. "Had a bad case of the tics. Damn near jumped out of his skin when he saw me."

"He didn't take off?"

"Nah, I told him I was dropping off some nails and shelving. Never said anything to Sam either and Sam being Sam, he was joking around with the two of us. So, I don't think Thibodeaux was suspicious of me being there." Renaud looked across the hood of the cruiser. "Who's this? New rookie?"

"Say hello to the Priest, Trooper Frank Mahan."

"Already got a nickname," the Chief said. "What did you do to earn that?"

"It's a long story," Frank said. "Pleasure to meet you, sir."

"I'm breaking him in for the next couple of months," Cunningham said. "When he's on his own, be sure and ask him about his former life."

"Well, welcome." Renaud shook Mahan's hand. "I'm sure we'll get to know each other. If you ever need anything in the Blackstone Valley, you come and see me."

"I'll be sure and do that, Chief," Frank said.

"So, where is he now?" Cunningham said.

"Inside the tavern."

16

"Good. Doesn't have far to go for the lockup. We've got a warrant for him."

The three men walked across the green and Cunningham directed Frank to the tavern's back door while he and Chief Renaud entered through the front. PK pushed his garrison cap back and stood in the entry, his size gobbling up the space around him. He looked about the tavern and moved into the room, brushing the tables and chairs as he passed. The day laborer ate in a booth with his back to the door. A few local boys sat at the bar talking in animated conversation. When the two cops entered, the tavern buzz quieted and Thibodeaux instinctively looked back over his shoulder. He jumped out of the booth and ran, stumbling over a couple of empty beer kegs and blew out the back door. He leaped into Frank's arms, the two men falling together to the ground with Mahan on the bottom, the wind coming out of him in a sudden gasp.

Cunningham exited the door. "That blouse you're wearing, Priest, is dandy for parades and such, but a straitjacket when you're rolling around in the dust." He stood on the top step and watched with amusement as Frank struggled to hold onto his prisoner. "Don't let him go, Priest." He held him in a bear hug, his mouth a gaping hole emitting strange sucking noises while Thibodeaux thrashed and squirmed to separate himself.

Frank cried out.

"Don't you let him go Mahan or you'll be walking back to Grafton."

"Should we help him out?" Chief Renaud said.

"Nah, wait 'til that academy shine gets knocked off him first."

"Okay, your call."

"Better have brought your testicles with you, Priest. I don't need a boot running when the shit hits the fan."

17

When the senior trooper satisfied himself of Frank's tenacity, Cunningham grabbed Thibodeaux by the collar, lifted him up and slammed him back down into the cinder path, driving his knee into his back as he did. The laborer's face was pressed into the dust and black mucus dribbled from his nose. He squirmed and made several attempts to stand before being knocked back down again.

"You're under arrest."

"I didn't mean to do it," Thibodeaux said.

"Well, it's a little late for that now," Cunningham said.

"She said she wanted to make out. I thought, okay. Argh, you're killing me man. Let me up will ya."

Cunningham leaned all of his weight into his back. "Who you talking about?"

"My back you're going to break it."

"What's her name?"

"I don't know. Linda or Susan or something."

Cunningham pressed his knee deeper into his back. "Last time, stupid. Who are you talking about?"

"Please, let me up. I'll tell you everything . . ." Thibodeaux vomited his supper and it bubbled out of his mouth in chunks, lying in a small puddle just beyond his face.

Cunningham pulled his knee out of Thibodeaux's back. "Start talking. Where did you meet this Linda or was it Susan?"

"I picked her up hitchhiking." He coughed up a string of yellow phlegm and spat it on the ground. "Never saw her before."

"How old is she?" the chief said.

"Thought she was eighteen. Asked her if she wanted a ride."

"Is that where the scratches came from?"

"I mean she jumped into the truck." He wiped his nose with the back of his hand. "We shared a smoke, getting on just fine. She gets a little warm and takes off her jacket. And I can see she's not wearing a bra. So I slide my hand under her shirt and she goes crazy, turns into a wildcat." He wiped his nose again. "She gouged my goddamn face."

"Did you penetrate her?"

"What? No, man. The minute she said she was sixteen, I let her go."

"Where did this happen?"

"Up Purgatory Chasm." He spat on the ground again.

"She tell you where she's from?" Cunningham said.

"New York, I think. Said she met some Beats in the city. They're bumming around the country."

"Did you tell her you live in the loft of Slater's Farm, Lover Boy and that you can't keep a nickel in your pocket?" the Chief said.

"Get up." Cunningham lifted him off the ground. "Here you go, Mahan. You earned it. Put the cuffs on him. By the way stupid, we're arresting you on a warrant for stealing weather vanes, you dumb shit." He hitched up his gun belt. "You'd better be sure that you didn't have sex with her."

"I swear."

"And she's not jail bait."

"Jail bait?"

"Under sixteen."

"I think I know where those bohemians are staying," the Chief said.

"After we drop this idiot at your lockup, why don't you take us there."

THEY PASSED THROUGH the opened gate at the entrance to the farm and started up the dirt road when they saw them by the light from the barn. Boys and girls, chanting a *Long John* work song like they were clearing fields. Pushing a driverless

19

car, jump-starting it on the decline. Cunningham stopped the cruiser about halfway up the road and they watched them as the old Ford coup came to life. They heard the doors close and then the whooping and squealing and hauling ass, coming at them fast and wild, pulling a cloud of gray dust behind them. He put on his high beams and hit the siren.

As they came closer, Frank could see the driver, the steering wheel jumping out of his hands, the Ford slapping the ruts and sliding off one side of the road and then the other, the car stopping so close to the cruiser that he could see the expression of inconvenience on the boy's face.

"You're up, Mahan," Cunningham said.

Frank approached the driver while Cunningham and the Chief stood off to the side.

"Get out," he said. "Let's see your license and the registration."

The driver, a boy about nineteen, tall and thin as string, climbed out. "What's your problem, man?" he said.

"My problem?" Frank glanced back at the senior trooper. "I'll tell you what my problem is, give me your license and registration."

"I don't have a license."

"Then give me the registration."

"It's not registered."

Frank spun the kid around, pushed him against the car and grabbed one of his arms.

"What're you doing, man?"

"You're under arrest."

"Ho, ho, ho. Don't you have to have a search warrant or something? This is private property, Mr. Policeman."

"What?"

"This is private property. Why you hassling us? Stop being an ass-wipe."

Frank pushed his head down and pressed it against the car. "How 'bout I wipe your ass with my boot."

"Ho,ho,ho. If you say so, man."

Cunningham cleared his throat so Frank could hear him and he looked back. PK stood with his arms folded, shrugged his shoulders and grinned. He walked over to the car and turned the kid around so that he faced him.

"What's your name?" he said.

"James Pierce."

"And what are you doing here, James?"

"We're staying here at my uncle's farm. We stopped for a couple of days."

"Stopped?"

"Cutting out, man. We're off to find America."

"I see."

"Any road that'll take us."

"Yeah, I get it." Cunningham folded his arms. "I'll bet your daddy is some muckety-muck in suspenders sitting behind a big desk on Wall Street. Or is it a Madison Avenue advertising agency? And you're up with that, aren't you? Because when you finish having your Kubla Khan experience, you'll have a job waiting for you when you return home after your tour of the universe. Or maybe you'll toddle off to Princeton or Columbia, huh."

"So, what's your point?"

"My point?" Cunningham smirked. "You got us this time, professor. Our motor vehicle laws don't apply here on private property. But we're not here for that." He moved the kid aside and looked into the car. A young girl with dewy eyes and long brown hair sat in the back. "You must be Linda or Susan. Why don't you step out here for a moment? I have an idea your family may be looking for you."

21

"WELL THAT WAS interesting, Mahan."

They stood outside the village hardware. Cunningham had his foot up on the bumper of the cruiser with his hands cupped around a lit match.

"I looked pretty stupid tonight, huh" Frank said.

"If that's the worst mistake you make on this job, you'll be alright."

"I should have remembered that the kid didn't need a license on private property?"

"More important. You didn't run or pull your weapon out because Thibodeaux wanted to fight you. You stood your ground." He lit the cigarette. "You survived Day One. Come on, let's get something to eat."

"What will happen to the young girl?" Frank said.

"Oh, they'll drop the runaway charge and she'll be turned over to her parents."

"That's good."

"Yeah, but why do I have the feeling she'll be back on the road before we finish our tour?" Cunningham turned the cruiser out of the Chief's yard. "All these idealistic kids trying to find a new America."

They drove to a little roadside stand, ordered a couple of hamburgers and Coca-Colas just before it was about to close and sat at a bench under colored lights in the picnic area. The senior trooper ate in chunks, ripping at the sandwich like it was his last meal, consuming the food savagely before Frank took a bite of his own. He lit a cigarette and blew the smoke out of his nostrils.

"Do you know how I ended up being your coach?" he said.

"Luck of the draw, I guess," Frank said.

"Nope." He shook the ice chips in his cup. "Sergeant Mc-Greevey suggested I read your background invest. And as they say, done and done."

"Why? Am I under some special kind of scrutiny?"

"You've never stood shoulder to shoulder with a robust man, a best friend who might not live out the hour, have you?"

"No."

"And you haven't had the pleasure of having a best friend shredded and blown apart by an unseen enemy right before your eyes?"

"No."

"Well, I'm breaking you in not because I like riding with boots and babysitting them. I wanted to know what made you tick. You're packaged differently. Most of the new kids today are cookie cutter clones right off the assembly line of military service and/or following in the footsteps of an older generation of cops. You're the new model. You've lived a life, took pictures of atomic bombs for chrissake. You've got a family and you've always been a civilian. There's nothing in your background to suggest what kind of a trooper you'll be." He turned away, cleared his throat and spat into the grass behind him. "Tabula rasa."

"What's that?"

"That's you. Blank slate. Ever heard of Aristotle, Avicenna, or John Locke?"

"Aristotle . . ."

"They're philosophers. They proposed that the human mind in its original state is pure and complete, undisturbed and void of any prejudices. Ready to embrace the experience of life." He shifted his weight on the bench and moved into the light. "The next few months will determine what kind of cop you'll be. Notice I said 'cop.' Because although we wear a funny uniform, our role is the same as all other cops— keep the world from turning to shit. We're clowns in a rodeo, Priest. A distraction. It's all a show."

"What do you mean?" Frank said.

"You'll find out soon enough."

"How long is the probationary period?"

"Until I think you're good enough to wear that uniform and not disgrace it."

"In the meantime?"

"In the meantime, you'll be giving me a refresher course in Criminal Law and other subjects that you took in the academy. And I hope to show you how to use those laws so that they work for you. So you don't continually step on your dick. Knowledge of the law is the best weapon you have out here. It might even save your life."

The string of Christmas lights began to blink on and off. Cunningham turned in the direction of the food shack. "Give us ten, okay." The lights blinked twice and remained lit.

"Where was the academy when you went through?" Frank said.

"Same place. But we were in tents, not Quonset huts." Cunningham pitched the wax paper into a barrel. "How did a civilian like you get through military drill?"

"I had a little in high school."

"In high school, you say. Did you march in the School Boy parade?"

"Yeah."

"Down Commonwealth Avenue?"

"With the old Springfield's, yeah."

"So, you have had a little military discipline."

"A little. So, why did you become a trooper?"

"Good question." Cunningham looked out to the street. "I came out of the Army with no place to go. Some of my friends were killed in the war and others who made it home, well they adapted. I needed the army life, but not the Army. So, here I am. Probably in love with the job more than I should. At least that's what my ex-wives think. At the barracks, I'm comfortable in the military life. In the cruiser, I'm my own boss. And no wife up my ass."

"I'd guess not every woman is cut out for this life."

"You try to explain it. And at first they're okay, then they want more. A house in the suburbs and kids. . ." He lifted his head and listened momentarily distracted by some sound. "I'm not sure I want to bring a kid into this world right now."

"Maybe, you just haven't found the right girl."

"Maybe, I don't know. I tried twice. The second one would holler like a screech owl. But I can do without the drama. It doesn't mean I don't like the company just not long term."

He lifted his head again and then they both heard it before they saw it, a souped-up jalopy, a sheet metal beast, coming in a loud obnoxious statement. It crested the hill and down-shifted, the gears banging inside the box, tires squealing as it took the corner. They watched it spin onto the road across from them. The teenaged driver looked over at them sitting there and he nearly stopped, shifted into first and passed slowly.

Cunningham nodded in affirmation. "Did you see that?

"Yeah."

"That's respect. It's an honor to wear this suit."

"Suit?"

"The boots and breaches."

"Are we going to go after him?"

"What for? If you were his age you'd be hauling balls just like him. Where's the harm, there's no one on this road right now."

Frank glanced at the man sitting across from him. He spoke with pride, but seemed weary, carrying the dull pulse of life's accumulation. A keen mind with a blunted curiosity, per-forming his duty without an exhibited passion. A short-timer with the spiritual absence of an aging cop, at times sharp and scrupulous in detail and other times, free-floating and distracted. Frank wondered whether he chose to break him in to resurrect a lost enthusiasm.

"Do you ever get tired of it all?" Frank said.

"The life of a trooper?" he said. "Nah, but it's similar to Life itself. We bloom at graduation, flower in time with knowledge and experience. And then we tire, and fizzle out like dried-up old men."

"Do you feel like an old man?

"Depends on what day it is." Cunningham looked at him. "I think you're a guy like a lot of people today who need to know the why and the wherefore. I will say that it's getting harder and harder to enforce the law. People seem to want to question everything. But sometimes, there just isn't a rational answer to their question. Now that the war is over, it's like everyone woke up and realized that something is missing. War gave us purpose, a holy sacrifice dedicated to making things right. Now they're itching to find a new purpose."

"Why do you think that is?"

"I don't know. Maybe they want their freedom to live their lives as they see fit. But the problem is that everyone has a different definition of freedom. And truth. The War demanded total consciousness of all. The ultimate reality. "

"We've been living with war or the threat of war for years," Frank said. "What's that make us?"

"Weary, I would imagine. I know I'm tired. I'm a short-timer. But you, Priest, you may see a different America. You can almost sense it coming. Cops will need to be something other than just cops. Nurses and confessors too. Things are changing at a blistering rate. Big cities, suburbia, fast living and everything at your fingertips. Cops will have to adapt. For us old salts, it's about to pass us by. Those kids back there at the farm bumming around the country? They're looking for it, they can feel it. It's like the war opened up a can of worms. I don't envy you new guys or the next to come.

Quiet country roads replaced by Eisenhower's interstate, ripping up farms and forests and tarring them over, bringing all that humanity with it. Questions and more questions. That'll be the new rule. The Rule of Law will no longer be a rule, but a suggestion. And it will be abandoned by the very people who should be defending it. And where will that leave the noble police officer? God only knows." He looked out across the continuous landscape. "But if I know one thing, they can rant and rave and call for our blood, but that's as far as it'll go because they need us to keep the circus playing." He stood. "Alright, that's today's sermon. Let's go."

Frank gulped down the last of his hamburger, balled up the wax paper and dropped it into the trash. He walked to the cruiser where Cunningham stood waiting. They both heard it and turned to the scratching, a nails-on-metal disturbance, a large rat teetering the edge of the dumpster, walking the rim like a tightrope. It reached in and seized a discarded piece of hamburger bun. Cunningham cocked the hammer of his revolver slowly. Leveled the pistol and drew down on the rat and shot it dead. "And that's that," he said. "Sometimes you do get weary, Mahan. But then, something happens, boom and you're off to a new adventure. That's why I love this job."

"I never thought about being a cop," Frank said. "But here I am."

"And that's what makes you interesting. You didn't choose this life, you were called like a vocation. Priest, that's a good name for you."

FRANK DROPPED THE handwritten report into the secretary's box and sat down with a cup of tea. Day One behind him, he thought about the world he now occupied. He envisioned his family, sleeping without him, the warmth of

27

his wife over an hour's drive away. Outside the windows, street lights burned yellow and houses sat somber and quiet. The radio hissed with distant noise and the barracks and the world outside became somnolent in the slow mystical turn of night. He left the kitchen, climbed the stairs to the second floor dormitory and groped along the dark hallway with his hand on the wall. Halfway down, light spilled out from under one of the doors and he heard the soft sound of music playing, jazz he recognized. He continued on to the end of the corridor. A pair of muddy field boots waited for him outside his door. He carried them into the lavatory with a brush and a can of boot polish. An hour later he left them in the hall and climbed into his bunk. He was laying there awake revisiting the day's events when he heard the music and the sluggish heavy footsteps. They stopped outside his room and then they left. A door shut and the music quieted again, embedding itself into the fabric of the building.

3

The desk man hung up the telephone. "Worcester Detox called," he said. "No room in the inn."

"Don't put me in there. Come on, Man." The drunk freed himself from the arresting trooper's hold and opened the door to the lobby. He tackled the man and the two of them stumbled and fell into the holding bench.

"Knock it off, you asshole," the trooper said. "Don't give me a hard time."

"Take me home."

The desk man saw the struggle and entered the booking room. "Your wife and kids don't want to see you right now and you've got to see the judge in the morning," he said. "So, you're going into that cell one way or the other. What's it going to be?"

The man screamed and pulled an arm free and grabbed the desk man's nametag and ripped it from his shirt pocket. "It'll take more than you two assholes."

They overpowered him and brought him to the floor, his body now straddling the open doorway. "Let me up. I'll walk home," he said.

"Stop the bullshit?" the arresting trooper said.

"Real tough guy," the man screamed. "Let me up and I'll kick your ass."

They wrestled his arms behind his back, handcuffed his wrists again and stood him up. He collapsed again and they dragged him across the floor to the cell block. "Assholes," he screamed. They bulled him into the cell on his stomach and the arresting trooper put his knee into his back and removed the handcuffs. "Fucking cop, get off me," he said.

"If we've got to come back here, it's going to get real uncomfortable for you."

"Fuck you."

"Be smart Naum," the desk man said. "Get some sleep."

The troopers closed the door to the cellblock while he continued to scream. He punched the walls and ran full bore into the steel bars, leaping and slamming his body against them, and he howled in a strange and primitive way. His cries inside the metal box rose up and into the bones of the house until they reached the second floor. He continued to vent fifteen minutes or more when the cellblock door blew open with such force that the doorknob punched a hole in the wall behind it.

"Not tonight, Naum. Another night, I might have had my mother's patience. But not tonight."

The prisoner stood facing the corner of the cell. "Go to hell," he said.

"Look at me," Cunningham said.

"Let me outta here."

"Look at me."

Naum glanced over his shoulder.

"You're just not getting what you want. Are you, Teddy?"

"Cunningham." He turned around. "Let me outta here."

"You know I can't do that. And if you remember me, you know I mean business. You're going to lie down and . . ."

"I remember you."

"I've always treated you square, haven't I?"

"Yeah, but . . ."

"And this is when we have problems, Teddy. A battle of wills. And when you've pissed me off, I've done what I promised. Haven't I?"

He glared back at Cunningham.

"So supposin' you lie down and take a nap." Cunningham took hold of the bars. "You get sober and I get some peace and quiet in my house."

"Give me a break, will ya."

"You have a date with the judge in the morning and if you go in there like you are now, it's a pink slip and ten days in the brick buildings. You know, the ones with the ivy on the front and the bars on the windows. So, what's it going to be?"

"Alright." Naum walked to the cell door. "I won't give you guys any more problems. Just take me home."

"I'm not going to stand here and argue with you."

The prisoner and Cunningham stood there separated by the bars. "Can I get some water?" he said.

"That's the first smart thing you've said."

"How 'bout something to eat?"

"Sleep and I'll see that you get some of Mrs. Healey's chow in the morning."

He brought him a container of water. "That's the last I want to hear from you."

"You've always been fair, Cunningham." Naum snuffled his nose. "You know what it's like. You were there."

"Everyone's got problems, Teddy. Get some sleep."

"Can you leave the door to the cellblock open?"

"Yeah." Cunningham opened the door and he heard the low bleedings of self-pity. He instructed the desk man to keep an eye on him and returned to his room.

THE DISPATCHER AT headquarters called out signal 6's on the radio to cruisers as Frank entered the back door to the barracks, the building on the hill now as much a home as a functioning police installation. The disquiet of the earlier

31

hours gone. Snoring drifted out of the cellblock, the telegraph machine chattered and the infrequent radio transmissions became intrusive. An early November wind blew into the Blackstone River Valley cold and unforgiving and it groaned with a winter warning, the harshness of it imposing itself upon the drafty old building. The desk officer sat with his feet up on a chair near a window that rattled with every new gust.

"In from evening pass," Frank said.

"Okay, Mahan." The desk officer turned his head with a transistor radio pressed against his ear.

"What are you listening to?"

"WMEX, the Jerry Williams Show."

"All the way out here? That's a Boston station."

"This time of night if I keep the transistor close to the window, I can hear it."

"What's he talking about?"

"Wait a minute." He moved the radio until he was satisfied. "He's got a guest on, funny name. Malcolm X, whoever the hell he is."

"Is he talking about Elijah Muhammad and the Nation of Islam?"

"Yeah, where would you run into that stuff?"

"One of my jobs. I worked in a TV repair shop on Blue Hill Avenue in Roxbury. Elijah's followers would ride up and down the street in cars, preaching the gospel over loud speakers. I think Malcolm X was a street disciple then, a corner preacher."

"You folks in the cities, all those cosmopolitan issues. We don't have any of that in West Oakham. The only thing moving up and down our roads are tractors and pickups. And an occasional cow or two."

"Did you ever leave the boonies, Tom?"

"Yeah, when I went to Korea. I'm still friggin' shivering."

A cruiser called in its location at a local diner. "Received," the desk man said. "So what's their deal?"

"Black Muslims?"

"Yeah."

"They reject white America because they're denied their equal rights. They want separation from the white man, the white man's religion and the white man's world. They want to create a separate nation."

"A separate nation. What're they crazy?"

"I don't know."

"The city always seemed a little nuts to me."

"That's because most of you country folk all come from the same village in Europe, settle in the same town and you roll up your sidewalks at eight o'clock at night."

"A lot of action in Boston, huh?"

"Yeah, that's one thing the city has, action."

"Nice looking babes, I'll bet."

"Yeah, but there's more than that. Streets full of color from the nightclub neons and movie theater marquees. Bowling alleys and pool halls." Frank lifted the pot of coffee off the stove. "This stuff any good?"

"Good as it gets."

He sniffed the coffee and put it back."You can get a Joe and Nemo hotdog at midnight or a hamburger with enough grease to keep you lubricated for a week."

"You're making my mouth water," the deskman said.

"Did you ever take in a Red Sox game under the lights or the fights at Mechanics Hall?"

"Just once."

"Do you like music?

"Yeah."

"All kinds drifting out of the clubs every time someone opens a door. Western twang and rock n' roll. Blues and jazz at the Black clubs along Mass Ave. with big ass Cadillacs at the curb. Or a strip tease at the Old Howard in Scollay Square. And people, every shape, color and size."

"And action?"

"That's what I'm saying. Ever been to the Basement?

"The basement?"

"Filene's Basement."

"Nope."

"Jesus, where the hell you been? You can get good suits there cheap."

"So, I should take a ride, that what you're saying?"

"It's up to you." He opened the door to the second floor. "But the point I'm trying to make is that it's everything and anything and everyone has an opinion. Including Malcolm X and the Nation of Islam."

The desk man put the radio back to his ear and turned in his chair. "Hey, Mahan? Why would Jerry Williams have a nut cake like this guy on his show?"

"You're listening aren't ya?"

On the second deck, Frank passed PK Cunningham's door and heard the light and silky timbre of Ella Fitzgerald's voice. She was scatting in runs of wordless musical rhyme. He listened and then continued to his own room.

WHEN THE DESK officer shook him awake, his feet hit the floor before he left the room. He came from the second floor, stepped into the lobby and dialed the operator on the public payphone. It was 2:18 in the morning and the winter wind continued to blow off the Worcester hills, rattling and shaking the naked trees. It blew up against the warped wooden door and it squeezed into the building with a high pitch keening. Frank shivered and jitterbugged in place, dancing his feet off of the cold tile while he waited for the operator.

"Collect call to Highlands 2-2330," he said.

The operator asked who was calling and he answered, "Frank."

"Hello?" Sheila said.

"I have a collect call from Frank. Will you take the call?"

"Yes."

"Go ahead, Frank," the operator said.

"Did you call the barracks?" he said.

"Yeah Frank, I did."

"Is everything alright?"

"Joey is running a fever again."

"What is it?"

"A hundred and one." She sniffled.

"A hundred one?"

"It could go higher."

"Jesus, Sheila. My heart is pounding right out of my chest. I thought something happened to you or the kids." He held the receiver away for a moment "Did you call the doctor?"

"Yes."

"What did he say?"

"He said to give him an alcohol sponge bath and a baby aspirin."

"Did ya?"

"Yeah."

He could hear her breathing in small pants. "Sheila?"

"I don't hear anybody there," she said.

"It's the middle of the night." He rested his head against the wall. "Are you alright?"

"I just hope the other kids don't get it."

"What do you want me to do?"

"I don't know."

The teletype machine came to life and Frank could hear the clickety-clack of another message. The paper began to roll onto the floor.

"What time are you going to be home Thursday?" she said.

"Twelve-thirty, one o'clock. If I don't have court."

"Can we do something when you get home? Take a ride?"

"Yeah. I'll need to get some sleep sometime. But, yeah, we'll do something." He rubbed his arms. "I've gotta go. What's Joey doing now?"

"He just fell asleep."

"Get some sleep yourself."

The phone became quiet except for the distant crackle of static.

"I miss you, Frank."

"I miss you too."

"I love you."

He nodded his head. "I'll see you Thursday." He listened until she closed the connection. He hung up the telephone and waved at the desk man to buzz him into the station.

"Everything okay?" the desk man said.

"Yeah, you know."

"Yeah."

He passed Cunningham's room again. The light was still on and the music played expressive and soulful.

4

The cruiser began to roll while Frank fumbled with the passenger door handle. He lost his grip and caught it again, opened the door and tossed the package inside. Now running, the weight of his boots a drag, stumbling and then he leaped into the front seat. And off they went at thirty, fifty, eighty, over a hundred miles an hour, the siren chiseling away at the night's frigid air. They drove off Route 9 and climbed the Worcester hills to St Vincent's, Cunningham beating the Ford past the other traffic, the parked cars and the occasional pedestrian on Vernon Hill.

"Get out of the way," he screamed when two kids stepped off the curb. "Call it in, Priest."

"607 to C-H, two minutes out." Frank held the box with the red crosses close and grabbed the ceiling strap as they skidded around a corner, nearly striking a parked car.

"Received," the dispatcher said. "They're waiting for you at the ER, 607."

"This is the third one of these in two weeks," Cunningham said. "I hope this one's for real."

They climbed the slope of the hill, corkscrewing past rows of three-decker houses. Frank rose in his seat, leaned toward the windshield and saw the hospital bright against the black winter sky. And the closer they came, activity could be seen, members of the medical staff outside the Emergency Room entrance, flittering like moths under the portico, moving in anxious starts and abrupt stops. Two of them, a nurse and a young male doctor.

"Where is it?" the doctor said. "Come on, give it here."

He took the blood from Frank's hands before he got out of the cruiser and he disappeared. The nurse paused, thanked them and then ran the ramp until she too disappeared. Cunningham leaned on the opened driver's door, Frank remained in his seat where the doctor had left him. The two men and the cruiser under the porch, the dome light grinding in the bubble gum machine, the blue light brushing the gray stucco walls of the hospital. The deep throaty bark of a dog somewhere in one of the houses below them.

Frank stepped out of the cruiser and looked up at the sky and thought about the life they might have saved. He shivered in the cold and his breath hung there momentarily before it drifted away. He looked down at the city, its lights burning up through the darkness. "All of these old hospitals seem to be built on hills," he said.

"Often the highest hills," Cunningham said. "I was told once that the medical folks requested that they be constructed on hills because they believed the air was cleaner. Probably to avoid the wood and coal smoke."

Frank looked into the lighted Emergency entrance. "Did you know that retired trooper who died last week?"

"Bobby Martin, yeah I did. I was stationed with him in B Troop when I first came on."

"Did you go to the wake?"

"No."

"But you knew him?"

"Yeah, Bobby was a good guy."

Frank looked over at him and then turned back to look into the Emergency entrance.

Cunningham also looked there and he tipped his head to get a better view. "I don't go to wakes or funerals if I can help it."

Frank looked back at him. "What do you think we should do?"

"Let's go in. They've got my curiosity."

After they were sitting in the lobby for about twenty minutes, the young doctor returned in a fresh pair of scrubs. His face had a resigned gray expression. He removed a partially collapsed cigarette package and a lighter from his pocket.

"You wanted to speak with me?" he said.

Cunningham, who was older and larger than the doctor, held his garrison cap with both hands, gripping it by the rim. "We get a lot of these blood runs and often times, we learn later that it really wasn't the emergency that we had been told. We drive at break-neck speeds, probably endangering ordinary people as much as ourselves. But this one was different. We're just wondering if the patient who received the blood . . . Did it help?"

The doctor pulled the cigarette straight and put it into his mouth. "No," he said. He cupped his hands around it and lit it. "Anything else?"

"Who was the patient?"

"A young pregnant woman."

"Can you tell us anything?"

He looked away and then nodded. He directed them to a quiet corner of the reception area. "The first thing I can tell you is what I can't tell you. I can't tell you what she looked like, I can't tell you if she was loved or if her child would have been president or a thief. But I can tell you about the sound of her husband's wail when I informed him that his wife and son were gone." He straightened. "Like you, trooper, I did my job. With every breadth of my training, my ed-

39

ucation, and my limited years as a physician, I tried to save her life."

"I'm not breaking your balls, Doc but if there was something we could learn here. Five minutes. Would five minutes have made a difference?"

"I don't know. Why? Is it that important to you?"

"For the next time."

"If it bothers you that this girl died. Then that's probably a good thing."

"It's not my first, Doc. I've seen death, held it in my arms. But you hope to learn from each experience. Because there will be a next time."

"On that we agree." He crushed the cigarette into an ashtray and walked back to the ER.

They watched the automatic doors close. "Probably not the best time," Frank said.

"Probably not. But I wonder if he ever considers that we're on the same team."

They stood there for a moment and then left. Cunningham threw the cruiser keys to Frank and climbed into the passenger seat. "Time you got acquainted with this beast."

They started out of the hospital grounds when the dispatcher from Troop Headquarters called. "607 report to the Mendon Police station and meet the patrol supervisor for a large crowd gathered at a local home. C-2 and C-H cruisers are enroute."

"Do you want to drive?" Frank said.

"Nope. I'm going to rest up. We're going to need it."

"Do you know where we're going?"

"Oh, yeah. The Lebeaux Farm. Crazy French Canadians who get liquored up every once a full moon and fight 'til there's only one standing."

"Do you think they'll still need us by the time we get there?"

"Hopefully, they'll tire themselves out so all we got to do is pick up the trash."

"How many are there?"

"The Lebeaux family? They are the Town of Mendon."

5

Charles Harnett sat on the living room floor, rubbing a soft cloth over the barrel of a Winchester rifle. "What did you get, Will?"

"A couple of squirrels, that's it."

"Well, that's more'n I got. 'Bout you, John?"

John Coyle stared into a near-empty refrigerator for a few moments and then turned with a bottle of beer in his hand. "What are you asking me for? You were there." He flipped the refrigerator door and it slammed shut.

"Just askin', that's all."

"What's the matter, John?" Will said.

"Nothing." John took the cap off of the beer bottle with a church key and drank a mouthful of the beer.

"You getting one of them for us or just taking care of yourself?" his brother said.

He turned back to the refrigerator and picked out two more bottles. He walked into the tiny living room where Will stood, wiping down another .22. Handed one of the bottles to him and the other one to Harnett.

"Seem all torn up 'bout somethin', John," Harnett said.

The older Coyle brother ignored the remark and collapsed into the sofa, his legs splayed out in front of him, staring at the wall on the opposite side of the room with a flat vacant gaze. He tipped his head back and emptied the bottle in one long continuous swallow.

Harnett looked at Will with a bewildered expression and the younger brother waved his hand to indicate to let it pass.

"Think I'll put on some music. How about Chuck Berry?" Will said. He stood his rifle in the corner of the room and began to shuffle through his records.

Harnett popped his bottle cap and nodded. "Bustin' in those woods an' swamp for the last five hours and getting' nothin' but a couple of tree rats. Makes you wonder whether it was all worthwhile."

"It's worth it," John said. "Worth every minute of it."

Harnett held the Winchester. "Where do you want this rifle gun?"

John stood and pointed to another corner of the room. "Get the cards," he said. "I'll be right back." He walked out of the little cottage.

"Don't mind him." Will walked to the living room window. "Things been a little lean lately. Makes him uneasy."

"I don't take it personal. A little stud or twenty-one?"

"Either one." Will watched his brother go to the cabin on the other side of the pea stone path. The old man who rented across the way from them stood leaning on a cane in the open doorway. He pointed to a wood pile covered by a tarp. John helped himself to an armful of logs and carried them back to the small cottage. He dropped the wood inside the fireplace and returned to the neighbor's front door. The old man handed him a brown paper bag.

"What do we owe him this time," Will said when John returned.

"Nothing. I told him I would replace the groceries when we went to the store." John placed two quart bottles of Schlitz, half a loaf of bread and an opened can of spam into the refrigerator. "I'll shovel him out next snowstorm."

43

"Did he say anything about the woodpile disappearing?"

"No." John took an empty mayonnaise jar half-filled with change from the counter, walked into the living room and placed the jar on the table. "Maybe, he's figuring we earned that wood with some of the odd jobs we've done for him." He crumbled up sheets of old newspaper, stacked near the fireplace and tucked it under the andirons. "I shouldn't have snapped at you, Charlie."

"It's alright, John. We all have those days."

"No, it's not." He knelt in front of the fireplace. "The winters on the Cape can weigh on you. I miss the summer. The sun baking my bones." He lit the newspaper and watched the flames as worms of smoke rose into the throat of the chimney. "It seems like just when you get used to it, Old Man Winter comes along and sneaks up on you like death."

"But winter's just a temporary thing," Harnett said.

"It's a premonition, that's what it is." John reached for the poker. "No passes on that one."

"A premonition?"

"You can set your watch on it."

"The hardness of winter. The bible would say it's God's way of testing us."

John looked back at him. "Ah, I don't believe that hokey."

"You don't believe in the bible, John?"

"I don't believe in the rules that some bunch of snobs make up to stuff down our throats. And I sure don't believe their stories."

"You believe in God don't ya?"

"I believe in what I can see." John turned back to the fire.

"Bible says you have to have faith," Harnett said.

"Faith? I was a grave digger in the Air Force. Seen where we all end up, the poor and the rich both. Don't see no faith in that."

Harnett took a seat at the table. "What about regrets? Do you regret anythin'? I mean we're all sinners."

John considered the question. He poked at the logs. "I guess there's nothing to regret if no one can honestly remember you. Who do you have to settle with then?"

"Well, we all have Jesus. He remembers us."

"Jesus? They beat Him and hung Him out like a mangy dog. He suffocated to death while his friends ran and hid "

"Still, I would say that He loves you," Harnett said.

"Never knew Him."

He paused like he was considering John's response. "Well, it's what kind of people you are anyways," he said.

"I don't have a quarrel with anyone, Charlie. We're just trying to survive. Just like you. All we want to be is left alone. I don't like being under someone's looking glass. The Government's or anyone else's."

"Amen to that."

John joined Harnett and Will at the table by the window. As they sat there for all their treks into the outdoors, the Coyle brothers never seemed to color. Instead, they had the countenance of a New England winter, hazel eyes amid several shades of white, blue-gray and brown. One would suspect they continually walked in shadow.

"Maybe . . .," John said, "we're just not meant to have a good life."

Harnett thought on that for a moment. Then he split the deck in two and feathered the cards a couple of times. Tapped the deck on its side and began to deal. Twenty minutes later, the men had settled into a warm room and another game of Blackjack.

"I'm out," Will said.

"How 'bout you, John?"

"Double down." He stacked up four quarters onto the table. "All in."

"You ain't even goin' to look at your hole card?" Harnett said.

"Where's the excitement in that?" The older Coyle brother leaned back on the legs of his chair and grinned. "I already know what it is."

Harnett tapped his own down card. "Oh, I wouldn't be grinnin' if'n you could see this." He dealt a single card, a three of spades landed face up on top of John's ten. The elder Coyle stretched out his neck and ran his fingers down the length of his throat. "Lay 'em out," he said.

"Well. I'm showing a lovely lady here and I have . . ." Harnett peeked at his down card again. "Hmm, looks like I'm going to have to match you." He tossed a silver dollar onto the table and dealt himself another card. "Seven of clubs." He turned over a two of diamonds. "Nineteen to the dealer."

John continued to stroke his neck and winked at Will. He grunted and a light snarl rattled out of him. Then he sucked in the air like he was long-sipping on a straw and turned over an eight of diamonds. "Twenty-one, mi amigo."

"Damn," Harnett said. "You countin' cards, John?"

Coyle stared back as if he was looking at him from the end of a long narrow tunnel.

"You'll have to show me how you do that."

"I just knew," he said. "Like I could see it."

"You're a gambling man, John," Harnett said. "Yessir, a Tennessee Riverboat gambler."

MAYBELLENE PLAYED ON the record player and it could be heard outside in the cold winter air in the little village that was located on the Cape Cod side of the Bourne Bridge. The logs had burned down and disintegrated into a pile of gray ashes and hot coals. John slept on his side, curled, face-first into the back of the sofa. Harnett and Will played another hand and as Charlie dealt out the cards, he hummed along with the record. He peeked at his facedown card. "I known you and John 'bout six months now. Never heard you mention kin."

"Don't have any, just me and him." Will glanced at his cards and tossed a nickel into the pot.

"None at all?"

"Our mother died when we were young."

"Don't mind me askin'. What happened to your Daddy?"

"You can ask."

"If it's something you'd rather . . . ."

"Let's just say he was always fighting his own demons." Will crushed a cigarette into the ashtray. "The police found him curled up somewhere, clutching a bottle of shit whiskey."

"The way some men drink, it's a soul's damnation. Like they're trying to find the right pathway to hell."

Will poured a small one into a tumbler and offered the bottle to Harnett. "My mother's friend took us in and put us into Catholic school."

"That who you went to see in Pennsylvania a while back?"

"Yeah, Mrs. Higgins, nice lady.

"Well, it's a good thing you have each other." He poured a swallow of whiskey. "My family, the Harnett's? They're all around. Can't go far in East Tennessee without running into one of the cousins."

"We had a few friends in school, but that's about as far as it went."

"What about cousins, uncles . . . aunts?"

"Never heard from them. I guess they lumped us in with the old man. Mrs. Higgins thought it would be good if we went into the service. Get us out of the city. So we signed up with the Air Force."

"You ought not to be thinkin' that you're all alone. I know the guys at the base think you're good fellas. And you and John got a friend in me."

"We appreciate that, Charlie."

Harnett took another look at his cards and tossed them into the middle of the table where a package of Camels were spilled open. He helped himself to one, lit it and blew the smoke over the table. "How's John's leg comin' along?"

"His ankle you mean. Never healed right, big knot on the side of it. He's constantly in pain like someone's hitting it with a hammer. Everything he does like hiking the woods or making it through the swamp is double-hard. Gets him down at times. Probably what made him upset earlier."

"Whatever happened to the other fella? The guy driving the motorcycle."

"Dead. About the only good thing that came out of that old man slamming into them was the money settlement John got. Otherwise, he would still be miserable at Patrick AFB."

"That heat in July and August can get to you."

"Wasn't the heat, he liked Florida." Will glanced at his brother on the couch. "It was taking orders from people he didn't respect. You know how it is. All it takes is one, a sergeant on your ass just because he doesn't like the way you look."

"Every base's got 'em. Some think I'm just a nigger on a chain. When they start bustin 'em, I give'm my best Stepin Fetchit—Yes'm boss, I'm gettin' to it. Don't even know they're being insulted. But all 'n all, the Air Force has been good to me. And I got a trade if I ever decide to call it quits. Well . . ." Charlie stood. "I should be goin'."

Will turned towards the sofa. "John?" he said.

"Don't wake him. Tell him I'll see him in a couple of weeks. If he wants, we can try that section of woods near

Pine and France Streets. Supposed to be some game up there." He turned to leave.

"Say, Charlie," Will said. I've got mess duty on Christmas Day and I was looking to get it off. Can we do a swap?"

"Sure, I'm not goin' home until after the holiday. If you pull the twenty-ninth for me, I'll work Christmas. That way, I'll be in Tennessee for New Year's."

"Sounds like a deal," Will said.

ON THE RIDE back to the barracks, they spoke of life on the job, the upsides and the down. Frank noted the change in his coach's demeanor over time, less rigid, more apt to trust his opinion. And behind the fierceness and the strength of the man, he saw a wounded compassion.

"We're done here, Priest."

"What do you mean?" Frank pulled into the backyard of the barracks.

"I mean, you're on your own. Your probationary period is over. HQ has decided to cut you guys loose early so the senior men can go home for Christmas. It's the one day of the year when humans try to behave themselves. It should be quiet." Cunningham dumped out two cigars into his hand. "And you're good to go. You've booked accidents, solved a couple of B&E's, broke up a bar fight. The stolen cars." He tapped the cigars against his hand. "What else?"

"The murder."

"Oof, how could I forget that. A goddamn wood chipper."

"Jesus." Frank shivered.

"I would have preferred something cleaner for your first death, like an old rummy who lies down and forgets how to wake up."

"That was one angry woman," Frank said.

49

"Yeah." Cunningham handed Frank a cigar and struck a match. "Light up, you earned it." He opened the window a few inches and pulled up the collar of his reefer coat and sat back. Don't take this the wrong way, but I'm probably as happy as you are that your probation is up. I finally can let go of the fart I've been holding in."

"None taken, SM."

"The batteries are recharged and I'm locked and loaded for a little while longer." He puffed on the cigar and exhaled. "I'm old school, Priest. You've got to show me."

"Yeah, I kinda guessed that," Frank said.

"You did some good things. That kid from Worcester we grabbed near Webster Square, the one who did the robbery? I liked that. You knew he was going to come out, didn't you?"

"Lucky guess. With all those cops in the woods."

"That's instinct. I saw kids get killed their first day in combat because they didn't have any. They needed to live it and they never got a chance."

"Experience."

"Yeah. we've been called out a lot lately—the prisons, Mayor Curley's funeral, guarding the Brink's gang. That's all part of the job. But there's nothing like the independence of the solitary patrol, the testicle test. The job's legacy."

"I've got a lot to learn," Frank said.

"The first and last thing you need to learn is always be fearful."

"I thought you eventually got over that."

"Not if you're smart you won't."

In the months that elapsed since he couldn't find a seat at the kitchen table, Frank had watched and learned and made his share of mistakes. He had developed an older-younger brother relationship with Cunningham. Now he itched to get behind the wheel. He sensed a ritual of change. It was the end of one thing and the beginning of another. The next patrol, he rode alone.

He had settled into the 'two and eight' routine and living two lives with two families, eight days with his barracks family and two with Sheila and the children. He had become the long distance husband and the part time father who had to reintroduce himself each time he returned home.

"Do you like jazz or the blues?" PK said.

"I hear it playing in your room.

"Old habit." He flicked his ashes out the window. "I figured you for an Elvis Presley guy."

"I like Elvis, but I like jazz too."

"Who got you listening to jazz?"

"An old bent negro man. He had nothing but a good record player and he loved to play the blues and jazz. He would listen to that music for hours. It meant something to him. Spiritual I think."

"How did you meet him?"

"Used to sell him nightcrawlers. One day, he invited me to come with him. We'd fish the Muddy River."

"The Muddy River?"

"In the fens behind Mission Hill . . . Roxbury."

"Oh." Cunningham leaned against the door and looked over at him. "During the war, some of the guys would go to the small clubs in Paris. Sit in the back and listen. Little holes in the wall. Said the music was good, made them forget about where they were and what they had done. I went a few times. But to tell you the truth, I think they went there for something else. Something they smoked. Or stuck into their bellies."

"What about you?"

"I drank."

Frank blew out cigar smoke. "So . . . does this mean I can call you PK?"

Cunningham looked over at him and scowled. Then he grinned. The smoke filled the interior of the cruiser. He rolled his window down entirely, closed his eyes and began to snap his fingers in time, humming Peggy Lee's *Fever* just above a whisper.

6

Christmas Day 1958
Buzzards Bay, Massachusetts

A string of colored lights and large golden block letters spelled out "Peace on Earth." The message of Good Will hung over the little village, drifting there freely against a winter's gray sky. All of its stores and businesses, including its only gas station were closed. An occasional car passed through with a family returning from church or on its way to a relative's home. Otherwise, the Route 28 Bypass reflected the reverence paid to the highest of holy days in the Christian year.

Half-way up the hill and two doors down from Schultz's hardware store, the First National Supermarket also remained closed in respect to the day. The supermarket had become part of the national landscape in the 1950s during a decade of prosperity and followed the migration of Americans, who left the cities to take root in sleepy little towns that now defined suburbia. The grocery chain built the Upper Cape's first supermarket earlier in the year, offering a variety of food products that residents had previously acquired only after visiting three or more smaller local stores. Its linoleum floors shined and squeaked, free of the sawdust and the worn wood-planked floors of the smaller mom and pop shops. Self-service shopping had come to the Upper Cape and excited residents from as far away as Mashpee regularly strolled its aisles in the pursuit of variety and value.

The First National's ceiling-to-floor windows advertised "Holiday Specials" that smaller stores could only dream about. Aisles and aisles of canned foods, several kinds of bread, cereal and eggs made shopping easier, quicker and convenient. A well-stocked warehouse at the rear of the store kept the multiple rows of shelves filled to capacity. And all of this product and all of the energized customers who shopped there created a healthy flow of cash.

"We should try it," John Coyle said. "What do you think?"

In the farthest corner of the asphalt parking lot, a solitary automobile sat, its engine running, blue smoke drifting from its tailpipe. Inside the 1953 Ford Ranch wagon, Coyle sat straight in the passenger seat and looked into the mirror that was attached to the back of the visor, raking back his tight brown hair with a comb. Because of his disproportionately larger upper body, one would imagine that as he sat there John was six feet or more in height. But in reality, he stood at a little over five foot eight inches, a ruler's width taller than his younger, slimmer brother. William Coyle lay slumped against the driver's door, an unlit cigarette, hanging from the corner of his mouth and stared out through the windshield at the supermarket with a shine produced by a night's worth of drinking.

"I think it's a good place to start," John said as he tucked the comb into his shirt pocket. "We've been in there enough times to know the layout."

"All right, if that's what you think." Will leaned closer in his seat toward the windshield, resting his chin on the steering wheel like he expected to see more of the store's interior from that advantage.

"I'll take care of the safe. You grab some food. Something we can carry out easily." John rubbed his hands together and blew on them.

"I'm thinking, a nice juicy steak," Will said.

"Yes indeed, but make it fast, no messing around. We want to be back to the house before the police set up any roadblocks." John placed his hand under the dashboard. "What's wrong with the heater? It's throwing cold air."

"The thermostat. I told you it overheated twice on me last week on the way to the base."

"So tomorrow, we jump into a getaway car that will overheat before we get out of the village?"

"Don't worry about it. I picked up the part yesterday. A few minutes under the hood and she'll be good to go."

Physically similar, the brothers appeared youthful, lean and life-worn hard, the difference being Will's lighter sandy-colored hair and flushed complexion. They had freckles across their noses and white alabaster skin, long and wiry muscled arms, they were built for endurance. Will stood round-shouldered and John jutted his chin out defiantly at the world. Both brothers looked out through eyes made vacant from a lifetime of disappointment. The older brother had the calmness of a reflective pool, never indicating the turmoil that lay inside. He never showed his anger that is if he ever truly became physically angry. John Coyle epitomized the stoic man, the lifelong survivor, the personality of a glacier. But he could be moody or sullen and often calculating. He spoke flatly and distantly, always occupied by some kind of thought or other, trying to figure out how to get the edge. He might fidget or squirm a little and glance away upon making eye contact. Some described him as shy. Others would say he was coy.

Since the day their mother died, Will looked to John for direction and liked being included in his older brother's schemes. John had the ideas and liked being in control, one step ahead of the competition while Will tended to be affable, easy going and disarming and if he was excited, his voice could break into a high pitch crackle like a teenager in puberty. But while charming and engaging, his off-putting personality masked a hair-trigger penchant for violence. The younger Coyle could be the more dangerous brother, a knife, thicker and smoother on top with a razor sharp cutting edge underneath. But while seemingly different personalities on the surface, they both could execute violence dispassionately. They were impulsive, free of consequence and deadly as cornered rattlesnakes.

John thought, "It was just a good idea" that they should become modern-day versions of the notorious outlaws of the Old West. Robberies would be their new source of income. And so from this Christmas day onward, the Coyle brothers looked for easy targets and always kept their guns close at hand.

Will leaned back and readjusted the Camel in his mouth, struck a match and cupped his hand under it. "So, you're sure, huh?"

"That's it, the honey jar. That place should have more dough than any other business on the Cape. I'll bet it hauls in around $1000 or $2000 bucks a day. You've seen it. There's days when you can't walk down the aisles without bumping into someone. Just think what it hauled in before Christmas." John reached into his jacket and pulled out a pint bottle of Jim Beam. "And think of what we can do with that. Go on the road. Maybe drive out West, see the Pacific. Tomorrow we'll be the first customers when they throw open the doors. Get 'em first before they go to the bank."

"And what if they give us a hard time, start yelling or something," Will said.

"It's all in the preparation. Remain calm and they'll remain calm, think and act professional. Stay cool. Tell them nobody will get hurt if they do what they're told."

"And what if someone tries to be a hero or wants to make a beef?"

"Don't waste valuable time on them. If they don't do exactly what you tell them to do or they start yelling or something." John waved his hand. "Hell, they'll be so scared, they'll gladly give up the money."

Will's knee vibrated involuntarily against the steering post. He blew cigarette smoke into the windshield. "And the police?"

"If they get in the way, we got to take care of ourselves." He held his hands up. "Remember what I told you if you get caught. Put your hands in the air with a gun. Maybe two. And when they get close shoot."

Will said, "Do it to them before they do it to us."

"Yeah." John unscrewed the cap off the liquor bottle. "The accident money is gone. Another couple of weeks, and we'll be out on the street." He drank a mouthful of whiskey and passed the bottle to his brother. "You want to live on Airman 2nd Class's pay? You can move back on base if that's what you want."

"No."

"We're in the cold soup line, Will. It's almost 1959, people expect things. They expect more and they're getting it. We served this country and what did we get? We're scrounging around like a couple of dogs."

"Then we do it."

"It's going to be alright, Willy boy" John said. "This is a small town with nice polite people and nice polite police. They don't want any trouble."

"Alright."

"Besides, nobody will care, it's not their money. It belongs to some big corporation and they can afford to give up a few dollars to the poor." John saw a local police cruiser pass. "Come on, let's go before we attract some attention. They watched the cruiser until it went out of view. They pulled out of the parking lot and drove in the opposite direction.

The elder Coyle looked out the rear window as his brother made a turn. "This time tomorrow, we'll be gangsters."

Northborough, Massachusetts

IT CAME OUT of the sun and he blinked. A whiplash of light snapped off a reflective surface, a piece of metal or glass or something. Maybe off a car. Maybe a '56 Ford sedan, color blue. It disappeared, swallowed whole by the woods at the back of the rest area on Route 20. Vanished, gone like a sub slipping beneath the surface. Aqua blue, he guessed.

"602 to C-2," he said with little force and almost apologetically, knowing that it was the only transmission heard on the radio in the last hour and that the desk man was probably in the kitchen fixing himself a turkey sandwich, carved from the bird that Mrs. Healey had prepared for the unfortunate junior troopers working on Christmas day.

He drove into the empty rest area and stopped at the beginning of the dirt trail that ran behind the parking lot and dropped in elevation so that a car driven into the trail could be completely hidden from view. He made another transmission, hoping that the troop dispatcher or another cruiser heard his location. "602 to C-2. Checking a vehicle, a blue Ford sedan in the rest area on Route 20, Northborough." The radio crackled static and indistinguishable white noise.

He entered the dirt trail and saw the Ford below him, its driver's door open and a man sitting behind the wheel. A winter wind whistled and it chilled him as he stepped from the cruiser. He listened for something, the man's voice, the metallic click of a cigarette lighter or the cock of a pistol. For a moment, he glanced back at his cruiser and considered calling in again, but instead, he continued to the vehicle with the Connecticut plates.

The driver leaned across the front seat and reached into the glove box. Exposed wires hung from under the dashboard and the interior of the car had a trashed lived-in appearance. Frank unbuttoned the snap on his holster and approached the Ford, almost tip-toeing his way to the driver's door.

"Put your hands where I can see them," he said.

"Whoa, it's cool man." The driver sat up like he was balancing himself on a ledge, snuffling air into his nose with short little bursts. He lifted his left hand in an exaggerated manner, spreading it wide, thumb to little finger, in plain view and held it near the dashboard. "Here's my hand," he said with sugar, looking back with a fixed smile, a golden tooth and the eyes of the dead. The hand had the spoon-shaped polished fingernails of a ten dollar hooker and he rattled the hand like he was shaking a tambourine, enticing Frank's attention to the dashboard. "I got my license right here," He smiled broadly, the gold tooth now fully exposed. "It's right up there in the visor, officer." He looked closer. "Oh, I mean Mr. State Policeman."

Frank's revolver seemed to find its way into his hand by instinct, not by academy training and not by his three months of service, but through the realization that he could die right here in this out-of-the-way place. "Don't move," he said and he opened the door completely.

The driver rested his left hand on the dash. "What's the problem, man? I ain't looking for no trouble. Just sitting here, listening to the music." He spoke with sing-song comfort in his voice. Maybe, it was the sound of that voice or the artificial smile. It could have been his eyes. Frank wasn't sure. He looked closer and saw the slightest tremor in his right hand, the partially hidden one, hovering above an old towel on the front seat. The man moved like a magician, a slight-of-hand misdirection, a diversion. Now you see it, now you don't. He moved for the towel.

Frank pushed the .38 against his skull. "I can't miss from here," he said. "Put your other hand up on the dashboard. Mr. . . ?"

"It's cool, man. It's cool. Name's White, Julius White. Which hand?" He turned over his left and showed the palm. "What's going on?" he said as he withdrew his other hand, the one near the towel, back into its hiding place.

Frank felt it like razors cutting his skin. He shot-poked White's head with the barrel of the revolver. "Put your right hand up on the dashboard with your left!" He could feel the rage, the violence of survival, demanding that he eliminate this threat to his life.

The man placed his other hand on the dashboard, but not with intimidation, the two hands side-by-side now, him looking back no longer with artificial sweetness, but with hate.

"Now, slowly back your ass out of the car while you continue to grab the dashboard."

"I'll fall on my face," he said.

"And you make sure that I can see both of your hands at all times." Frank stepped back and allowed him to place his first foot on the ground. "Stop," he said.

"I'm not a fucking circus performer."

"Shut up." As White balanced on one leg, Frank slapped the cuffs on his wrists and pressed him into the door. He grabbed the back of his trousers and held him up while he patted the towel. Felt a solid object and tossed it aside. A .45 automatic pistol lay on the seat like it belonged there in its usual place. "That for me?" he said.

"What's this shit? Don't know what you're talking about." White squirmed and began to turn. "What's the matter, man? You afraid of a skinny-ass nigger?"

Frank clubbed him to the ground and held up the automatic. "What were you going to do with this? Shoot me in the back?"

"A man can't protect himself?"

"Get up!"

"That's my gun, my property. What you arresting me for?"

"That's the easy part. I'll bet by the time I'm finished going through the car, I'll have a laundry list. Frank lifted him up by the cuffs and walked him tip-toed to the cruiser. As he opened the door, White wiggled to a halt, turned his head and grinned, the golden tooth like an exclamation point. "Could have had your ass if I wanted you. Fuckin' big man."

He body-slammed him into the side of the cruiser. "Well, guess what Mr. White! I've got you. Merry fucking Christmas." He pushed him in the door, closed it and walked around to the back of the cruiser, out of the sight of the prisoner. A high-pitched ringing sounded in his ears. He stood there and leaned against the cruiser's trunk, tasting metal, waiting to regain control over his now alien body, the rage demanding that he shoot this cocksucker right here, right now with no witnesses, this piece of shit who would have slapped that silver-plated .45 against his temple, scattered his brains into the woods and walked away with an ending smile on his face as his own life leaked into the soil.

He slid his hand through a gap in his shirt and held his scapular. He stood there for awhile until he sensed the world around him once again. He exhaled, collected himself and walked to the driver's door just in time to hear his number called.

7

The towns along Route 140 seemed like a tour of Norman Rockwell's America. Woody hills, tranquil pristine ponds, quiet rolling fields and the white corrals of small New England farms. But in the hour's drive from the barracks to Randolph, he never saw any of it. Frank drove alongside the bucolic landscape numb and mentally exhausted totally oblivious to the beauty that lay feet beyond his moving vehicle. He continued to replay the encounter with Julius White or Julius Caesar or any of the other aliases the man gave while being booked.

"Well, smartass, you're going to sit here in a four by eight foot metal box while I take my time, finding out who the hell you are," Frank said. "So who's got who?"

On Route 128, he suddenly became aware that he was close to his home. With the ending light of day, the western end of his little white cape reflected the muted tone of the waning sunset. He drove into the driveway, shut off the engine and sat there, trying to remember where he was, trying to remember what Sheila had bought each of the kids. And he tried to put Mr. White behind him. He took a deep breath, opened the door and sat there with one boot in the drive. "That asshole could have had me," he said.

He stood and listened to the sounds of suburbia. Muted laughter and children's excitement leaked out of the houses up and down the street. A woman next door laughed the exaggerated hearty laughter brought on by a couple of after-dinner drinks.

His kitchen door opened and Sheila stood at the threshold with one of the boys on her hip and the other two kids wrapped around her legs. They waited while he stood in the driveway, his ditty bag slung over his shoulder. Finally, his older boy broke from the doorway and rushed to meet him. Frank smiled, put on his excited father's Christmas face and took his first sure step for home.

SHE SAT ON his lap, snuggled into him on the couch with her head against his chest. The kids had finally given up and surrendered to sleep upstairs. Johnny Mathis sang, "Let it snow" and the light from the Christmas tree dripped down the living room wall like a Jackson Pollock painting.

"Your chest feels like it's going to explode," Sheila said. "Like there's something inside you trying to get out. What's going on?"

"Nothin'. Just an interesting day at the office."

"For a new trooper, you seem to have more than your share of interesting days."

"It's the job, Sheila. Everyone's in the same small boat."

"You know how I felt when you first considered 'The Job'," she said.

"Yeah, you weren't jumping for joy."

"Well, we're both in this thing right now. So, don't turn me off."

"I'm not."

They sat there, Sheila staring at him and Frank looking at the tree. After a few minutes she said, "You're not going to tell me, are you?"

"What do you want to hear?"

"What happened."

"I'd rather keep the two worlds apart."

"I don't see you for days at a time. And when you're home, you're really not here."

She played with his hair. Then kissed him.

"Still not telling you."

She traced her finger along the rim of his ear. "I just hope you're not going to become *that* guy."

"What guy?"

"The guy who never turns it off. The guy who never knows when to come home. Like Bobby McDonald." She leaned away. "Where did he end up?"

"He was Boston Homicide. They were up to their ears in the gang war murders."

"Where did he end up?"

"Mattapan."

"Alcoholic bed?"

"Psych Unit."

"See what I mean?"

"I'm not Bobby or Boston Homicide." Frank saw the expression, the deep reflective pooling in her eyes. He kissed her and ran his hand under her nightgown. "How about now? Am I that guy?"

"I worry, that's . . . ."

"Sshhh."

"And just about the time when you're your old self . . ."

"Sshhh."

". . . you leave."

She lay back and he dragged his fingers into the valley of her legs and her thighs fell open to his touch. His hand moved there, like water, sensing her life blood, tracing the silky white highways to the place where life begins. She touched his face. "Let's go into the bedroom."

He lifted her up and carried her to their bed while the pressure behind his eyes and across his forehead receded.

She was warm and moist to his touch and he laid his head on her naked stomach and stroked her. His eyes closed and he felt himself falling away from the anger and his explosive self. Falling into her.

8

Buzzards Bay
December 26, 1958

Nathan Lavin was a practical man—a child of the Depression and block-long soup lines, a veteran of World War II and now a responsible adult in the age of Consumerism when Americans pursued goods not out of necessity, but because an advertiser sang a siren's call. Where their parents paid in cash, postwar Americans bought now and paid later. Credit drove the robust American economy. Cars replaced tanks and refrigerators replaced bazookas. Automobiles, purchased on time, sat in the driveways of homes financed with low interest loans from the Federal Housing Authority and the Veterans Administration. Obsolescence had become the driving force in the American economy as last year's discarded model sat on enormous hills of junk in discreet out-of-the-way dumps, hidden on the outskirts of every American town. Mr. Lavin fretted about this new Jazz Age that seemed more interested in merrily acquiring the next best thing than in the rhetoric that spilled out of the mouths of politicians in Moscow and Washington, daring each other like a game of chicken to take the first spiraling step on the destructive path to Armageddon.

The practical minded manager took solace in the safe and comfortable cocoon of the corporation. The First National supermarket provided security for him and his family and it seemed to be a good all-around fit with the salary that he received, the $5000 Life Insurance policy, five paid sick days and seven paid vacation days. It was a simple arrangement when he thought about it, work for the corporation every day, make it profitable and everyone benefits in the long run. Then enjoy your sunset years, compliments of the First National profit sharing plan. "Security" was the new buzzword in the United States whether Americans built fallout shelters or planned for the days when having their morning coffee might be the most important thing they did all day.

The manager of the supermarket towered over most of his employees. At six foot, three inches tall with a flat top and an angular body that had little extra meat to spare, most people guessed that Mr. Lavin was a former basketball player. In fact, he missed being selected All Cape Cod only once in his four years of high school. He ran his store by the principles that he had learned in the Army, a no-nonsense, but fair approach. He expected three things from his employees: show up on time; be polite to the customers—"Welcome them as if they were in Mr. Warsofsky's butcher shop around the corner or Miss Shipman's confectionary across the street"— and dress professionally, shirt and tie under the issued blue smock.

He protected the store as if it was his own. More than one boy got tossed from the First National by the ear after being caught pilfering a box of cookies. Some of the townspeople described him as reserved, teenagers thought he was rigid and a pain in the ass, but most of his customers thought of him as a competent manager who provided a clean, pleasant place to shop for quality food at the best prices on the northern side of the Cape Cod Canal.

The doors to the First National remained locked as Lavin prepped his clerks and readied the store for his customers. His Assistant Manager made up three hundred dollar envelopes with $10's, $5's, and $1's for the registers near the front entrance. He assigned two of his clerks to product inventory after the busy pre-holiday week of shopping. The remainder of his staff stocked shelves and prepared their work areas for the day. Lavin inspected the aisles for cleanliness. An hour later, he checked his watch and at precisely eight o'clock, he walked to the front of the store and unlocked the doors.

ON THIS BRILLIANT morning on the day after Christmas, William Coyle drove the '53 Ford wagon down Main Street and coasted by the grocery store with only a glimpse of John Coyle's face exposed in the passenger window. He slumped in his seat with his head tucked in behind his shoulder. "There she is," he said. "Like a piece of ripe fruit, just waiting to be picked." He slapped Will on the shoulder. "Did I tell you? Look at that. Eight o'clock on the nose and they're opening the doors." Will drove another sixty yards up the hill, passed the post office and turned into its parking lot. He backed into a space and shut off the engine.

"Do you have your backup?" John said.

"Right here, in my pocket."

Two young boys dressed in cowboy outfits ran passed them, wearing gun belts and holsters and armed with toy cap guns, slapping their thighs as they ran, encouraging imaginary horses to out gallop one another. They dodged a couple of pedestrians and ran out of view.

"Put your gloves on." John rolled up a couple of foot-long lengths of rope and stuffed them inside his jacket.

"You going to be able to run if we have to?" Will said.

"Don't worry about me. I'll outrun you."

"What about your leg?"

"Let's go."

"Wait. What about masks?"

"No one knows us."

"But we've shopped in that store."

John sat back in the seat. "Ah hell, these people are simple Cape Cod folks, not city tigers. Relax, this'll be easy pickings. In 'n' out, won't even know what hit them." He opened the passenger door. "They don't know us with all the people that come into that store."

The brothers got out of the car, stuffed their hands into their jacket pockets and started down the hill.

MR. LAVIN PUSHED on the side-by-side front doors to ensure that they swung open and walked away. He hadn't reached the first register when he heard the clap behind him.

"I got you, Philip," said one of the cowboys.

"Naw, you missed," said the other. He shot his gun and when only one cap fired, he yelled, "Bang, I got you."

The first boy clutched his chest and fell to the floor, his toy gun skidding across the polished surface to where Lavin stood.

"Out you two," he said. He lifted the "dead" cowboy off the floor. One of the clerks grabbed the other boy by the collar and handed him off to Lavin who brought them to the front door and extricated them. "This is a place of business. Find somewhere else to play."

The Coyles quickened their pace and moved down the hill quickly, but just before they reached the bottom, the store manager stepped out of the door with the cowboys in tow. John grabbed his brother's arm and they came to a halt. They heard the manager say, "Find somewhere else to play." He turned to reenter the store. "Come back here and I'll boot you in the ass."

"Let them settle down," John said. He watched the two young boys cross the street, one of them, rubbing the back of his neck. He looked through the grocery store window and saw unmanned registers. The clerks were busy with other duties away from the entrance. "Come on," he said, "Looks like the place is quiet." They rushed the front doors and pinned them locked. John rummaged in his pocket and found a note, which read *Will Open at 8:30*, and pinned it to the glass. Will sprinted up the main aisle while John moved toward a raised booth with a .32 caliber pistol pushed out in front of him.

"This is a holdup," he said with detached politeness. "Drop to the floor. All of you."

Some of the clerks ran to the back of the store in a confused disoriented way as if they weren't sure how they should react.

"What the hell is going on here today?" Lavin said. He stepped out of the booth. "Is this a joke? Get the hell outta here before I call the cops."

One of the employees tried to escape to the men's room and John fired a shot over his head and then three rapid shots into the ceiling. The employee stopped short and raised his hands. For an instant, he considered the power of command and the instinctive response associated with human survival. And he relished in the rush that it gave him. He was not a failed man, John Coyle had found purpose.

"This ain't no bluff," he said in a dry conversational tone. "This is a holdup."

"Are you boys crazy?" Lavin said to him. "I'll have you arrested." He stared at John and saw a boy unnaturally calm, almost transfigured, separated in time and place from the violence of the robbery. And he recognized the empty wells of John Coyle's eyes, the unmistaken loss of life. He had seen it in France near the end of the war when he separated from his unit and turned down an unfamiliar alley and found himself in a standoff with a fourteen-year old German soldier. He remembered the stark realization that someone so young could hold mastery over his life, a youthful executioner, never introduced to the concept of negotiation who knew only how to apply seven pounds of pressure to a trigger. The recognition of power greater than one's own, akin to falling into a hole in the universe and not knowing whether you will come to the Light or to the god of Blackness.

John backed the manager up against the outside of the booth. "Stay here, please," he said. He entered and removed one cardboard envelope from the safe, containing hundreds of one dollar bills. He then walked to one of the registers and removed one envelope of money from a draw. A gunshot sounded at the back of the store.

Red Means, Mr. Lavin's assistant, had not fought in France or Germany or North Africa, had never encountered a standoff like his manager until Will Coyle pressed a snub nose .38 into his ribs and the offended Mr. Means instinctively lunged for the weapon. Later when asked by the police to describe what they saw, Lavin said, "Thought it was a joke at first. Two clean-cut boys, early twenties, courteous, smooth-cheeked, baby-faced, about five foot six to five foot nine. Wouldn't be surprised if they were brothers. The bigger boy walks with a limp. Almost felt sorry for him until he fired a shot that went right past Sweeney's head and stuck into the bread counter. Then I knew it was for real."

But when questioned by the police, Red Means said, "They walked in through the door being all nice and everything. I was getting to edge in on the little guy, when he suddenly turned and fired at me. Jesus, he went all Jesse James on me." And when asked for a second time what he saw, Means responded, "A two inch snub-nosed pistol, itchy-fingered, trigger-happy guy."

"Is that it? the investigator said. "What did he look like?"

"I was scared see, but I think he was scared too. I didn't think he'd have the guts to pull the trigger. He fooled me."

71

"Yeah, I understand that. But do you remember anything else about him."

"No, that's it."

When he heard the shot at the back of the store, John moved toward the center aisle. He looked down the aisle and saw his brother at the end, standing over an employee who was holding his leg.

"I'm all right," Will said. "This guy tried to take my gun. He won't do that again. Isn't that right, mister?"

"Aw, Jesus, God!" Red Means said.

"Quit your bellyaching."

"Round them up," John said. While he was distracted, Lavin darted for the telephone and John jerked a shot at him, the bullet ricocheting off the floor behind the fleeing manager and struck him in the foot. He stumbled against a partition and lay against it upright and frozen. John took the store manager by the arm and brought him to where the other employees had been herded near the walk-in freezer.

Will opened the door and pushed the manager and four other employees into it. "Go on. Get in there," he said. The wounded clerk remained on the floor.

"What's your name?" John asked.

"Means." The employee rocked back and forth, holding his left leg.

"Get up and get moving, Mr. Means." John lifted him up and pushed him into the freezer.

Will removed his gloves and stuffed them into his pockets. He found a shovel and jammed it against the handle of the freezer to keep it from turning.

"I don't trust that," John said. "If they rattle the handle, they'll liable to get out before we get away." He took a broom, snapped off the head and pinned the handle between the door and a support post to prevent it from being opened.

The brothers picked out some groceries, walked to the entrance and John removed the note from the glass. He unlocked the doors.

"Wait," Will said. He ran to the telephone and took out the speaker.

They pushed open the doors, stepped out into the brilliance of St. Stephen's day and climbed the hill to the post office parking lot where they threw their jackets and groceries into the trunk and drove away at a proper speed. And on the following day December twenty-seventh, Airman 2nd class William Coyle, dressed in his fatigues, reported for duty.

9

Lines rolled up from the bottom of the ten-inch RCA. The
revolving image, the black lines and the stark light created a strange mood in the darkened room where John Coyle
sat, watching an episode of *Maverick*. He got up from the
couch and adjusted the rabbit ears. Stood back and a more
distorted image played on the screen. And with each correc-
tion, the picture worsened, snow and eventually only voices
came from the metal box. He lifted his arm while he held
onto one of the ears and a perfect picture appeared on the
television. He moved the antennae to the same proximate position and found an acceptable image.

Outside, the papergirl dropped her bike and her carrier's
bag on the frozen grass strip that separated the pea stone and
the cement walkways in front of the cabins. A black and blue
winter sky hung over the buildings and the fixtures outside
the doors glowed in dingy sulfurous light. The wind blew between the buildings and she pulled her coat up close around
her and zippered it. She tossed a rolled-up copy of the *Boston Globe* at the old man's door, then walked across to the
cabin on the opposite side, knocked and watched the curtain
in the picture window move, hang momentarily and then fall
in a chatter. The door opened the width of a two by four and
through the narrow opening, a man's face peered out. Behind
him a small black and white television played, appearing to
the young girl like a cave's entrance in the darkened room.
The door closed and she heard the chain strike the wooden

molding after being lifted out of its track. It opened fully and John Coyle stood in the entrance. He smiled at her as though it took all his effort.

"Mr. Coyle," she said. "Do you want the paper today?"

He reached into his pocket and held out a five dollar bill. "Yes, indeed," he said.

"I'm sorry," she said. "I don't have enough change."

"Don't I owe you for some other days?"

"Just one."

"Then let's call us even."

"But that's more than you owe."

"Well, that's for giving me the paper when I didn't have the money to pay you."

"Thank you." She handed him the newspaper. "Some people will take a paper, but they never pay me. My father says I should always get the money first."

"He's right there." He stepped out to the walkway and into the yellow light. "Can't tell the good people from the bad today."

She slipped her carrier bag over her head and slung it across her back. "If I'm short, the company takes the money out of what they owe me."

"Sometimes," John Coyle said. "You can do the right thing in this world and you still can't win."

"I guess so." She studied his face.

"Hmm, I see they had a robbery in Buzzards Bay?" he said as he scanned the newspaper headlines.

"Yes. And nothing ever happens around here."

"True," he said.

"Oh, it's nice and all," she said with a trace of doubt on her face. "But I can't wait to be old enough to leave."

He looked at her and smiled, pleased with himself. "Sometimes, there's just no other way," he said in a strange casual voice. "You have to take care of your own life."

75

The girl shivered in the cold. "I don't mean right away."

"But eventually, you have to do what's right for you," he said. "Even when other people might not agree."

She picked up her bike and turned it towards the road. "I should be going."

"Don't be concerned about the robbery."

"I won't. Thanks for the five dollars." She began to pedal toward the road. When she reached the end of the drive, she looked back. He was still standing there, staring at the front page of the newspaper. She watched him for a moment like she was marking him in that place, reading in the doorway.

A door slammed shut. Coyle lifted his head and he looked between the rows of small buildings, the complex mottled with pools of yellow light. He listened for a few moments and then looked around, his glance ending at the entrance down by the road where he saw the papergirl ride away. He tucked the newspaper under his arm and turned, satisfied with himself.

Inside the cabin, he spread out the newspaper on the kitchen table and put on the overhead lamp. The account of the robbery was on page one and he read it to himself with great satisfaction. *They were a crazy pair. But they knew what they were doing.*

He continued to read the inside story with a particular interest in the police strategy. *The state police set up roadblocks on all the major roadways on the cape.* He laughed at the thought of them running around crazy and shutting down the bridges to the mainland while he and Will sat in front of a cozy fire, drinking bottles of Narragansett. The article lifted him up with pleasure until he read the first sentence in the last paragraph. "Authorities report finding a good fingerprint at the scene." He sat back in his chair and calculated. After a few minutes, he left the cabin and walked to the office where he got change from the clerk. He entered the booth outside, dropped a nickel into the slot and dialed the telephone.

Otis Air Force Base
Bourne, Massachusetts
"AIRMAN WILLIAM COYLE. Call the operator. Airman William Coyle."

Will heard his name over the loudspeakers. He hoisted a hamper full of dirty laundry, rich with the sweat of grease monkeys who kept planes in the air and vehicles moving down the road, the coveralls saturated with fuels, motor oils and solvents. He boosted up the hamper to the height of the dryer door and heaved the clothes into the enormous tub in one fell swoop, sprinkling the clothing with lighter fluid. He stood there, staring at the laundry with a cigarette, hanging from the corner of his mouth. The building shook and the windows rattled as another plane thundered down the runway.

It seemed to Will that someone had been telling him what to do all of his life. A life that never had been shared, a life never requested as a born child. But if raised under his own hand, it might have been a life that he desired or he trusted. He just existed at the pleasure and for the pleasure of others, always at their beck and call—foster parents and social workers, nuns and sergeants. And leering camp counselors who came at night. "John has it straight. They found my fingerprint. So What?" It was time to take hold of it, to laugh when they wanted, to cry only when necessary, and to burn in a glorious fire until fate snuffed out their candles. He had no ill feeling toward the United States Air Force. It had fed him and clothed him these last three years. But his brother had come before him and had lived in the military world and knew that it served him little when he returned to civilian

77

life. He needed the satisfaction of self, to test the boundaries, to feel the excitement of confrontation, to survive and go to ground if necessary. He needed to test the limits of his existence. "Who needs to be a laundry worker when there is all that easy money just laying around?" He flicked his cigarette into the dryer and walked out of the Quonset hut into the winter night.

The glow from the flight line lit up the end of the base behind him. An F-86 sat at the end of the runway, blowing fire from its tail. He heard the release of its brake, saw the settling down and then the fighter flashed the length of the runway and disappeared into the night sky. He left the business end of the base, the sights and sounds of conflict and battle, and passed into the sleeping darkness of the living quarters, the elementary school and the post exchange. He stood in the middle of the street outside a row of small wooden homes built after the war for families living on base and listened to the peace and quiet.

Then the younger Coyle began his trek down the long access road toward the glow of the guard shack and a new life on Civvy Street while sirens wailed in the distance.

"Airman William Coyle. Call the operator. Airman William Coyle."

"I know, I know," he said.

THE ELDER BROTHER held the curtain away from the window just enough to see outside and the night that waited for them. A cold wet December camp under a pale winter moon, an eerie landscape in mist, the familiar waterfront community now strange and alien. "Is the tank filled?" he said.

"All ready to go." Will tossed his uniform onto the bed. "Good bye, Uncle Sam. Nice knowin' ya." He changed into civilian clothing and tossed a few changes of clothes into a laundry bag.

"Check the refrigerator," John said.

Will found a half a loaf of white bread, some baloney and a full bottle of RC Cola.

John pulled on a pair of slacker pants and a sport shirt. "Did anyone see you when you left the Base?"

"No. But I left them a present to remember me by."

"I told you to leave quietly. Give us time to get out of here."

"Wasn't much. Fired up a pile of laundry." Will rattled with satisfying laughter. "Burning my bridges, so to speak."

"I was hoping we'd be long gone by the time the cops matched the fingerprint to you. That was a dumb move."

"All right, alright."

"You cost us twelve hours, at least. They wouldn't have missed you until you didn't show up for Charlie's shift to-morrow afternoon." John pulled a few shirts from the closet and stuffed them into a laundry bag. "Let's go."

"What about the other stuff?"

"Leave it." John flipped the mattress and pulled the label aside. Reached in and retrieved a wad of cash and stuffed it into his pocket.

They traveled the deserted and monotonous road alone, the station wagon penetrating the dark confessional of the night, the light from the Ford's headlamps blunted by a sheer curtain of thin fog. They approached the Bourne Circle, the bridge with its lamps in vertical line behind it, rising up and over the canal like a radiating cathedral in the sky. At the foot of the bridge, a state trooper sat in his cruiser with his head-lights directed across the road. John slid down in his seat below the level of the window, holding a snub nose against his chest. Will shifted the Ford into second gear and steered it around the rotary, entering the 360 degree perspective and the inquisitor's incriminating light, the interior of the station wagon illuminated, everything open to the light's interpretation and subject to its authority. Separated from his older brother, Will now alone and vulnerable to the interrogator. *Come on. I don't have all day. Sit up! Look me in the eye when I'm talking to you. Tell us what happened. We know you're not the brains of the operation. Do you want to make a confession? Johnny can't help you now.*

He turned the steering wheel and reached for the .38, found it wedged into the seat, pulled it close and felt its comfort. *Did you hear what I said, William? Sister Reginald is waiting for you in the principal's office. What happened to you? You were such a good kid.*

He remembered his mother's hand, small and wrinkled, and how she often buried it in her apron pocket, clutching the tissues she used to blot her tears and wipe her nose. He pictured her in the bedroom small like a frightened animal, a saint in bones, her beautiful face, falling into its skeletal cavities, her head tilted up wordless, gasping on her last breath with the priest bent over her, making the sign of the cross in oil.

Will stabbed the brake pedal and turned the wheel like ticks on a clock. His brother remained in a slumped position and watched him. He stepped on the accelerator and the station wagon jerked forward.

"Don't panic," the elder Coyle said. "Keep driving."

"I think he recognizes us."

"Look into the light and wave to him."

"What?"

"Give him a big wave like you go by here every night."

Will looked into the light with a small plastic smile and waved. "I'm no rat, mister state policeman," he said through clenched teeth in a cracked falsetto voice. The trooper lit him up with his spotlight as they passed directly in front of the cruiser.

"Let's take a run at him!"

"Has he moved?" John said.

"No, I don't know."

"Then, keep driving."

They rode onto the bridge's apron and began the climb over the canal. He glanced into the rear view mirror, rolled down the window and breathed in the damp bitter night, sucking the freakish winter air into his lungs. "Get ready!" he said to his brother, anticipating the blue light of the cruiser.

"Keep the same speed." John opened the cylinder of his pistol, checked it and snapped it shut.

They climbed to the top of the bridge, enveloped in an obscure haze that reflected their lights back at them like they were travelling alone in their own space and time. Will, his hands steering with small calculated adjustments drove with his chin level with the wheel. At the peak of the carnival ride high over the water, he glanced into the mirror and they began to descend on the mainland side of the bridge, finally breaking free from the insecurity of the fog and the confusion of the white light.

"I don't see him," he said.

They reached the bottom and he let go of a long breath. He lit up a cigarette, pulled on it deeply and blew out a rope of smoke. They drove away from the Cape with restored confidence, the butt of the cigarette now hanging defiantly from the corner of Will's mouth.

John motioned to the revolver on the seat. "Would you have used that gun?" he said.

Will flicked his ashes into the tray. "If I had to."

John put his head against the door window and closed his eyes. They traveled in the company of trucks, riding the station wagon amongst a herd of tractor trailer behemoths hugging the Massachusetts coast, and crossed over the state line two hours later, arriving at the Ancient Mariner Motel in Portland Maine as the monotonous gray of another New England winter day lifted up and out of the Atlantic.

A GRIZZLED OLD man dressed in a plaid shirt with a two-day stubble sat on a high stool behind the counter. He dozed with his arms folded, propped against the wall like he had been thrown there. A single low-watt bulb burned in the table lamp in the corner of the small dingy office that was dressed out in cheap artificial wood paneling. Dried-up brittle linoleum covered the floor and it was curled and split at the ends where it met the walls. The bell over the door rang when the Coyle brothers entered and brought in the bleak winter night with them. The clerk opened his eyes, but remained attached to the wall.

"Do you have a room?" John said.

"Yessir," the man said. "How long ya plannin' on stayin'?"

"One night. How much?"

The man rubbed his arms. "It's cold out theah."

John leaned against the counter with no expression.

"That'll be seven dollars."

"Seven dollars?"

"Yessir.

"For each?"

The man stood and slid a registration card and a pen in front of John.

"Both of you, but I'll need some identification."

"What for?" John said.

"It's the law." The clerk looked at the laundry bags, hanging off their shoulders. "You boys in the service?"

Will spoke from behind his brother. "What's it to you, mister?"

"Don't mean anything by it. But we give servicemen a discount."

"He's in the Air Force," John said.

"Then, it'll be five dollars."

John paid the clerk. "Say, that train station we passed? Can you catch one to Bangor?

"Ay, the Pine Tree. Leaves at 5:45 in the evening and gets in about 9:30. One of the last of them runnin'." He handed John a room key. "Seems like the railroads are givin' way to the highways."

"Where's this room?"

"Round back, number 137. I figured you might want some privacy."

"Why's that?" Will said.

"Well, in case a couple of the local girls come looking for company if you know what I mean."

"What makes you think we're interested?" John said.

The clerk looked down at his hands. "No reason. The girls are clean if you're worried about that."

"We're not worried about any of that, mister," Will said.

"If it's money. We take care of our servicemen."

"Listen mister, all we want is a room," John said.

"Well, it's almost daybreak and that room is quiet."

"Thanks for the discount," John said. He opened the door and looked back. "We're not queers in case you were wondering."

They left the office and drove the station wagon to the rear parking lot, locked it with the two .22 caliber rifles inside and tossed the keys into a trash container. The brothers toted their laundry bags into the room, locked the door and jammed a chair under the door handle. Will stretched and yawned. He removed his shoes, collapsed onto the bed and

83

fell back into the pillow. "Are we taking the train to Bangor?" he said.

"Yeah. We can hide away there among the woods for a time." John sat down on the other side of the bed. He remained there, long after Will fell asleep, long after the cold black night closed around him, sitting there quietly dissolved into the culture of the room, the dingy curtains, the shabby threadbare rug, the cheap furniture, and the soiled garish paper on the walls. He sat there a long time and anticipated the thing that had eluded him all his life.

10

Frank dragged himself up the barrack's stairs, carrying the weight of a night shift and found a piece of wall to lean against at the rear of the booking room where Sergeant McGreevey was holding roll call. The sergeant stopped in front of two of his men and looked over his glasses at the shiner on one and the fat lip on the other.

"All settled then?" he said.

"Yes, Sergeant," said fat lip.

The station commander turned to the trooper with the black eye. "Let it go. Do you understand me, Sibley?"

"Yes, Sergeant."

"Next time you two go drinking make sure you bring a referee." He stepped back from the line. "Dismissed." As the Day shift filed out, McGreevey motioned to Frank. "Got time for a half a cup?"

"Yes, Sergeant." He joined McGreevey at the kitchen table.

"That guy you brought in on Christmas Day? The one in the rest area with the .45?"

"Julius White?"

"Yeah. His real name is Joony Hall. Runs dope from New York to Worcester."

"That lying bastard. He didn't have any drugs on him when I locked him up."

"You caught him going the wrong way."

"That's why he had a lot of cash on him that he couldn't explain."

"And why he has a high-priced attorney representing him. When Mr. Green shows up, he's in the game for the long haul. You'll see him again."

"Was the van stolen?"

"No." McGreevey stirred his coffee and then allowed it to cool. "There's more," he said.

"Oh?"

"At yesterday's hearing, Judge Whitlock didn't buy your probable cause for locking him up before you found the gun. He threw out the charges."

"He threw out the charges? I'm telling you Sarge, this guy would have shot me if he had gotten the chance."

"It's easy to be critical when you're looking at the facts while sitting in a library."

"Maybe he should try walking up to a car hidden in the woods."

McGreevey picked up his coffee. He drank the coffee and then set it down. "I was stationed with Alje Savela at C-1."

"I didn't know that. What kind of guy was he?"

"Good guy, mature. Made lots of stops, similar to yourself."

"Where was he killed?"

"122 in Barre, outside the center. Shot seven times with a nine millimeter." McGreevey dropped a package of Camels onto the table and removed one. He held the unlit cigarette between his fingers. "He was sitting in his cruiser, writing a violation. Never had a chance."

Frank watched him search for his lighter.

"The courts seem to be more interested in scrutinizing what a cop does today than whether the guy he brought in might be guilty as hell. But for the record, I don't give a damn about Judge Whitlock's rules. You're sitting here with me right now, alive and having coffee. That's a good thing. And it's the most important rule of all." He lit the cigarette. "Mr. Hall doesn't have a gun license so he's not getting back the .45."

"I hate the idea that this guy is walking away."

"He's not going anywhere. Several towns have paper on him. And you'll run into him again. All good things do come to the righteous."

Frank put his hand over his mouth to stifle a yawn.

"You should get some sleep." McGreevey stood. "Don't let it get to you." He pulled on his blouse and began to button up the front. "This will all be here when we're long ago and far, far away." He clipped his cross strap to the Sam Browne. "I see you've been checking motels."

"They're interesting places, seem to attract a special class of character."

"Be careful. Make sure you call in to the desk man. Motels are like Cracker Jacks. You never know what's inside until you open up the box."

"Okay, Sarge."

McGreevey leaned into the communications room. "Boomer?" he said to the desk officer.

The desk officer lifted his head.

"I'm out to the District Court to speak with Judge Whitlock about his rules."

"You think it's going to make any difference?"

"Probably not. But you got to let them know there's only so much shit we'll take."

Mashnee Village
Cape Cod, Massachusetts
HE DIDN'T BELIEVE the scuttlebutt when he heard it. But there it was in black and white.

A/2C William J.E. Coyle, AF 13550001, officially dropped from the morning report of the 551ˢᵗ Field Maintenance Squadron

And he didn't believe it when he was told by a couple of guys in the Field Maintenance Shop. AWOL—gone. A fire and something about sticking up the First National store. The master sergeant asked him about him, thought he might know his whereabouts since he and Will were pals. Then a couple of days later, the police showed up and took him to the station. Asked him why he never came forward. They accompanied him to his house, 'bout scared his wife to death. Where he gave them two snapshots, one of William in uniform and a rare one of John, smiling shyly.

The chain on Charles Harnett's bike rattled against the guide as he peddled up the drive to the compound of cabins at Mashnee Village and parked outside the familiar place where he had spent many off duty days, playing cards or preparing to go hunting at their favorite spot near the old abandoned house in the Middleborough woods. He liked those boys because they treated him fairly, as an equal. They respected him as a man. The wind blew off the bay and it blew the island dust and sand around the yard and between the buildings; it had pitted the door of the Coyles' cabin. Gray, water-soaked and rolled-up newspapers stood stacked against the door like cordwood. Harnett tipped his head and defended his eyes from the grit. He leaned against the building and rapped the door with his knuckles. The pulverized sand dust blew into his ears and he could feel granules in his mouth. He turtled his head inside his jacket and pounded the door again. He remained in that lean-to position, waiting for a response that he knew was never coming. Saw the sand collecting on the threshold and on the cement lip where it met the door, and in the pea-stone bed. He cupped his hands around his eyes and pressed his face into the window at a place where the curtains were separated. He could see the end of the sofa and an edge of the television. A pile of their personal belongings lay in the middle of the floor. Another gust of wind blew up and tiny sheets of sand and dust danced across the drive. He listened to the wretched grit scratching at the front of the cabin. And he heard the despondency and the desperation in their voices.

11

Massachusetts Correctional Institute at Walpole
Walpole, Massachusetts
March 1959

Outside the twenty-seven foot walls and the taller guard towers, the stillness, the reflection of the night and all the ghosts that belonged to it evaporated in the early morning sun. The audacious day in Walpole began when ribbons of red and orange arrived and settled into the woods like circus light dancing among the standing trees and firing up the field beyond them. There in the open land, fifty-five heavily armed troopers stood. Their shadows laid out before them like rows of sullen graves. They mustered in the field with little sound, the air moist with condensation and they stood at the ready, silent as smoke.

Inside the metal shop, wire restraints hung around the hostages' necks like choke collars and rebel convicts yanked on the wire leashes when the six captured prison officials refused to walk on all fours like dogs. They humiliated them, taunted them with fourteen-inch shanks cut out of sheet metal, nicking them with the edges if they didn't crawl fast enough. The warden and the chaplain, who had came to negotiate, and the other hostages were dragged across the shop floor and dropped into chairs, stacked back to back in the middle of the room. They sat there with their wrists secured behind them, bound with bailing wire. The wire handcuffs cut deep into their skin and for some, they were sliced to the bone. The hostages bled from their wrists and from the wounds on their faces and necks where they had been cut with the knives. Blood and sweat fell together and the odors of urine and vomit fermentation hung in the air.

Sitting on the floor under windows that opened to the yard, eight inmates assigned to the metal shop who took no part in the break, suffered the same humiliating experience as the prison officials. They sat on both sides of a heavy metal door, barricaded with machinery used by the correctional institution in the manufacture of license plates. On the other side of that door, the big yard and the first calculated step to freedom.

The general population remained in their cells and taunts from these locked-down prisoners flew from the tiers in epithets. Continuous bitching reverberated like white noise in the big yard where whispers at one end were heard clearly across at the other. The threats, the promised threats and the hyena laughter rang out in tortuous rants. "Hey baby, goin' to pay for fucking up my day. Better hope you get slammed." Tough-talking cell soldiers locked safely away made obscenity-laced threats to the rioters, certain individual guards and other locked-down inmates. Some of them complained about the living conditions or the food and others about the lack of gate time. Some cheered the escape attempt with deviant erotic taunts. Large tattooed hands wrapped the bars and mirrors hung out beyond them like road reflectors. The highways along the tiers trashed with litter in sympathy or in opposition to the standoff. In some of the cells, the walls were finger painted with feces. And within the expanse of the big yard, wolf laughter howled defiantly.

"I'll tell you what I want," Martin Feeney said in the metal shop. "I want a car brought to the door and I want it pronto. You got that?" He slammed the receiver down and stood in front of the prison officials, jiggy and calculating, one of his legs jumping involuntarily. He swallowed dry and walked to the sink where he filled his hand with water, sucking in the liquid and wiping his face with the residue. The leader of the escape attempt leaned against the sink with his arms folded, saw what he had wrought and smiled with grim satisfaction.

Feeney had spent most of his adult life incarcerated in the state's penal institutions. He had participated in several inmate uprisings and break-out attempts. While being transported to court, he had bolted from a prison van in Jamaica Plain. And in the few years when he was a free man, he spent his time earning his way back to the maximum security prison. In prison vernacular, he'd been jumping out all of his life. His five associates came from similar backgrounds, had long criminal records and were incarcerated for murder and other violent crimes.

Just before daybreak, the rioters grabbed an unsuspecting milkman making his morning deliveries, put a captured guard's gun to his head and ordered him to drive to the first gate of the trap. Feeney threatened to blow the milkman's brains out unless the gate was opened. Instead, the tower guard fired a warning shot. He fled the area and had the truck driven to the wall where he and his other escapees put a ladder on the roof and attempted to climb over it. But the tower refused to kill the juice in the electric fence even when Feeney threatened to send up the captured guard to the wire. His well-thought-out plan had 'shit the bed' and now he was cornered in the prison's metal shop with fourteen hostages and no place to go. He moved to one of the fold-out windows that faced the yard and listened. Outside, military commands echoed like shrill whispers and boots beat the macadam like a distant drum. He ran his hand over his face.

His gang of rebels, snowed on prison julep, yammered and yapped like mindless hyenas while he attempted to calculate his next move. "Dummy up, will ya. I can't think." He scanned the faces of his hostages. And then he had a revelation, an epiphany. He positioned himself in front of the chair where the prison chaplain sat, an early wound dry as jelly on the priest's forehead and fresh liquid wounds weeping high on his cheek and across the bridge of his nose.

"Whore of Babylon," he said. "How about a shower? A baptism of sorts to cleanse you of your sins."

"Let up on him, Feeney," Warden Frank said. "You're just digging your hole deeper."

"How deep can we go, Warden?" He looked at the priest. "What do you say, Father?"

"God loves you."

"Knock off that crap."

"You served Mass in the chapel."

"Is there an easier way to get a drink around here?"

"Let the others go, Feeney," the priest said. "They've done nothing against you."

"Don't tell me who's done what to who!" He vaulted to the other side of the room and opened the spigot on a barrel of paint thinner, drew off a gallon of the chemical and dumped it over the head of the priest. He rubbed the heels of his hands into his eyes and stuck his fingers into his ears, pushing the flammable liquid into his canals. "Is it becoming clearer, seeing what needs to be done?" He picked up a container of gasoline and filled two glass jars.

"Feeney!" the warden said. "If I'm not back in thirty minutes . . ."

"We need a miracle!" Feeney stuffed the glass jars into the priest's jacket pockets. "Let's see what you can do."

"Feeney! I've ordered them to attack and shoot to kill. They'll welcome the chance to put a bullet into your brain."

He stood back from the priest and stared at the warden and then looked around the room. "Showers for all of them. Open the spigots." The other rebels filled buckets with the

93

chemical and poured it over the heads of the other hostages. The turpentine ran freely from the spigots and long ribbons of the chemical slithered across the floor and settled around their chairs, the sweet smell of pine gum and licorice hung in the room.

"You'll be the first to go, Reverend. Can you hear them calling, the legions of Hell, those tortured souls?" Feeney charged the folded-out window and screamed, "Hey, are you listening out there? The next sound you're goin' to hear will be the priest squealing when I grill him. Grill him like a hundred an' eighty pound stuffed pig. Unless I get a car outside this door in five minutes to take me and my friends out of this hell-hole, or so help me God, I'll grill him. Are you listening out there? He'll stink like a tar baby."

"Don't do this, Feeney," the priest said. "For God's sake, have some compassion."

"Compassion?" He lit a match. "Any compassion I had was left inside my mother's womb. Never seen any compassion."

"You're a punk, Feeney," the warden said. "And you'll always be a punk. There's no car coming for you. Only ones coming for you are the state troopers and they can't wait to get their hands on you."

"Let's see if you're still talking tough, Warden when I put a match to you. Because after the priest, you're next."

Feeney lit a cigar he had found in the shop's office and then tossed the lighted match onto the floor near the hostages' feet. The warden reached out with his shoe and Feeney looked back with amusement as he pawed at the burning match. He leaned his head into the window's opening again. "Looks like we're going to have lots of pigs for the roast. Because they're all lathered up and ready to go. Only it ain't going to smell like a pig roast. No Sunday ham dinner here. Just burning flesh." He raged at the partially opened window, punching the pane with his fist until the glass cracked. "What's it going to be?"

He knew they stood only feet from the building, felt them, believed that they would kill him and he waited for someone to respond. Shivered and made quick little pigeon movements with his head and leaned further into the window's opening, inhaling the free air of the yard. "I've got a match in my hand and in two minutes, the Reverend is going to be raised to the Lord Almighty. Fire-raised! And his death is going to be on your conscience unless a car is brought up to the door." He waited again, but still heard no response. Pulled his head in and glanced at the clock on the wall. "One minute and forty-five seconds," he screamed into the window opening.

Frank Mahan loaded his magazine, dropped the last shell into the chamber and ran it home. He pulled down on the straps of his gas mask, breathed deeply and tested it for leakage. Felt for the flap on his holster, ensured that the button was in the hole, checked the safety on the shotgun and pulled his cross strap tight. Scrupulous rituals and nervous anticipation, busy time re-mapping the plan, imagining the steps, opening the wall, blowing the door, taking out the ringleaders. He wiped his free hand down the side of his breeches, switched the shotgun and wiped the other. The other members of the squad similarly fidgeted and readied themselves in much the same manner.

Fifteen yards behind them the remainder of the force stood at ease, uncomfortable in their horse-blanket reefers with shotguns pointed to the sky. Behind them fire trucks and firemen running out hoses. The troopers' trips to the penal institutions had become commonplace as with other prisons throughout the country. And over the years when they marched into these institutions, the rioters, hostage-takers and break-out artists knew that the time for negotiations had expired when the horse soldiers arrived. The dogs were out, clear the yard.

And the troopers knew this also. Their mission was simple—restore the institution to its lawful authority. And while they knew in their hearts that their life's work was honorable, each time they marched out of a prison, they left a little piece of themselves behind, a little less whole and a little less compassionate, like domestic soldiers. The conflagration at Walpole and other institutions carved them hard and left them less forgiving.

The corporal turned away from the building and faced the squad. "Get ready," he said. A correctional guard stood next to him. "We're not waiting any longer. Not like the Cherry Hill fiasco. If they don't surrender immediately, we've got orders to shoot the bastards. Look for the hostages as soon as you enter the building and get them out of there. It's not going to be pleasant for them. This is the second time for Father Hartigan and Deputy Thompson." He stepped around Frank. "After we take out the door, you and Guard Robertson here will enter first, identify Feeney. And if he doesn't have his hands in the air, if he isn't indicating that he wants to surrender, take him out. Don't waste any precious time on that asshole."

Frank nodded.

"It'll be smoky in there. So, make sure you see him good. Officer Robertson, you know which one is Feeney?"

"Yes."

"Okay, let's go."

The Assault Squad with a contingent of prison guards moved quickly across the yard to the metal shop and waited for a command. An audience of state police brass, local politicians and prison officials stood as spectators at the back of the yard. The dull gray house of misery became quiet, the locked-down prisoners ceased their chattering, the constant bitching suspended. A quiet and dangerous moment enveloped the yard.

Frank stared at the heavy metal door and fingered the safety on the shotgun. Metal doors—passageways to fury, total anxiety, the threshold to life and death, the barrier between order and disorder. In the door, he remembered the project and the Housing Authority that always built things to last. Large metal doors on strong buildings constructed with brick and mortar, steel and cement, industrialized home fronts. The yards, with chain-link basketball courts and stone picnic benches, the shape and size of football fields paved in green asphalt instead of grass. Where dogs ran in packs. Someone behind him coughed and he heard his own measured breaths, felt the rising and falling of his chest. Long anxious exhalations of anticipation heard in the ranks of armed still men. He remembered the echoes of distant children and the nimble footwork of quickly moving shadows, darting across the macadam and between the project buildings, a small closet of a bedroom at the end of the hall and the warmth of a streetcar, idling in the car barns at the end of the line. Fists on the door in the middle of the night. He remembered—

He slaps the dust from my back and turns me away from the Colburn brothers. Tears and dirt streak my face. I'm shivering. He wipes the blood from my nose with the sleeve of his shirt. I want to go home, I say. He lifts my hands. Keep them right there and punch, he says. Don't stop punching. Every time you hit him, I can hear him. He doesn't like it. He doesn't like getting hit. I'm making him madder, I say. He looks at the crowd of boys that has formed a circle around us and he grabs my shoulders. What are you goin' to do, run chicken? Is he goin' fight or not? the older brother says. Yeah wait a minute, he answers.

The air raid signal sounds and I stick my fingers in my ears. It pierces the neighborhood and its apocalyptic wail shreds the afternoon. The younger boys in the crowd grind their teeth, the older boys ignore it. On the sidewalk next to the abandoned lot, a mother steers her two children into the drug store. Across the street, the barber pulls his shades. An automobile stops at the curb. I want to go, I say. Please . . . Alright, he says. And I'm running. He can't take the siren, he says to the Colburn brothers. It hurts his ears. We'll finish it another time. The brothers sniff and smirk to each other. They walk out of the vacant lot with attitude. And the siren continues to wail.

"Thirty seconds!" Feeney screamed from the window. He stepped in front of Reverend Hartigan and pulled him out of the chair. "They're coming, I can smell them. Looks like we're going to Hell."

"You don't have to do this," the priest said.

"Don't I?" he howled. "One way or the other, padre."

"God is merciful."

"Shut up!" Feeney struck a wooden match along the side of the box just as the phone rang. One of the other escapists picked it up and gave it to him. He stood there with the lit match and he listened for just a moment and then he interrupted the caller. "You're not going to screw with me any longer, Commissioner! The priest is standing right next to me!"

The windows blew into the room, pieces of glass smaller than the size of BB's, a terrible coming. The wall, the cement, and the rebar, the destruction under a powerful force, giving way and leaving a large gaping hole to the outside. One side of the shop seemingly imploding and folding unto itself. A machinegun spit bullets into the metal door, tearing it off of its hinges. There was a momentary lapse of noise, an unnerving calm and then the door imploded with a terrorizing mechanical rumble, pile-driving the barricade back into the room. A rioter threw a Molotov cocktail into its space and now fire burned where the door had stood. A cloud of dust and spent gunpowder wafted into the room, an odor of hot sweet metal and dirt hung there like gray destruction. Tear gas, CS canisters hissing and pin wheeling across the floor, too many for the rioters to toss back. They filled the room with noxious chemical, overcoming both rioters and hostages, scorched their eyes and lit their skin on fire. They covered their faces and gave muffled yelps, coughing and gasping for air, their skin and every orifice a torrid sensation. They became blinded by the tear gas and ran helter-skelter with their eyes closed, falling over one another in an attempt to escape. The flammable paint thinner ignited, the metal shop floor burning like a lake of fire, the room lost in black smoke, hanging in the air like Hell's night.

"AT THE TOP of the news . . ."

Sheila half listened to the radio while she checked her son's book bag. "Where's your arithmetic book?"

"Oh, it's upstairs in my room."

"Get your coat on, you're going to miss the bus." She raced up the stairs.

"State police have mounted an assault into Walpole prison where fourteen hostages are being held by six inmates in the prison's metal shop."

Jack started up the stairs. "Ma!"

"What?" Sheila half way down turned him around. "Here's your book. Get out to the bus."

"Dad's at the prison."

"What?" She pushed him along to the kitchen door.

"The state police are attacking the prison. It's on the radio."

"Don't worry, it's probably a drill." A horn sounded out in the street. "That's your bus." She guided him out the door and waved to the driver. She watched him struggle up the stairs with his overloaded book bag, saw his concerned face in the window as the bus pulled away. She waved again and closed the door. Sat down at the kitchen table and listened with her eyes closed.

"Just before dawn, six convicts took several prison officials hostage, including Warden John Frank. About an hour ago, troopers launched an assault that began with two loud explosions. WBZ reporters are at the prison and we hope to have more information at the top of the hour."

MARTIN FEENEY HAD hold of the priest with one hand and the telephone receiver with the other when the light disappeared and the wall began to groan. Then came the explosion like the world and all within it was returning to original dust. Canisters spilled across the floor, aerosols releasing volatile chemicals that scorched every inch of his exposed skin, his lungs burned like he was being consumed from the inside. He released the priest and pulled his t-shirt across his mouth. Everything he knew about the metal shop vanished instantly. Collapsed onto his knees, the gang leader crawled about the floor with his shirt across his face. Other rioters and hostages fell victim to the assault and collapsed on top of him. He wiggled free and crawled blindly to escape the terrible conditions, trapped by the smoke, the fire and the screams of hysterical men, the heat and flames of the burning floor driving him in a panic to the back of the room. And when the hellish conditions began to abate, he opened his eyes and two alien men in gas masks stood above him.

"Stand up!" Frank said to several men through the canister of the mask. "Which one is Feeney?" Before Guard Robertson could answer, one of the rioters identified him with a tip of his head. Frank thrust the barrel of the weapon at him, held it there and pulled his shirt away from his face. "Are you Feeney?"

"I surrender," the gang leader howled. "You can't shoot me."

"That's him," Robertson said.

"I have no weapon."

Frank held the shotgun on him.

"I want my lawyer. I want my lawyer. Lawyer!"

He drove the butt of the shotgun into Feeney's chest and knocked him backwards. Then dragged him to the blown-out section of wall where the corporal and other troopers were lending assistance to the hostages.

"Feeney," he said.

The corporal fell upon the gang leader, slapped him down and kicked him in his lower back. "Get up," he said to him. "Strip down, you asshole." Other squad members rounded up the remaining rioters and put them against the back wall. "Strip yourselves bare-ass," he said. He waved in the firemen and they entered and began to hose down the floor. "Put your shoes on," he said to the rebels. "Hurry up!"

Six pale alabaster men in the company of blue troopers moved in somber funereal procession across the yard, steering towards the hole and solitary confinement. They walked humpbacked with their heads down in a wretched distress, croup-coughing like barking seals. And naked to a man, their hands cuffed behind their backs, their faces streaked in black tears, some with the backs of their thighs stained in brown excrement. Broken feral men with dried-out voices and a mechanical concoction in their mouths and a taste of ash. They passed a military tank, its engine idling, shivering the ground and shaking itself like a great metal beast. The remainder of the troopers stood off in the yard at odd angles

101

and glanced at the parade as it passed, while they collected or cleaned their equipment, wiped down their weapons and held up bottles of saline to their eyes.

A prevailing breeze with moist tepid air drifted down into the yard and it carried the fragrance of early morning spring, an earthy and cherry blossom release, the last of the trailing smoke drifting away from the yard into the morning brilliance. A saw played outside the metal shop as trusted inmates began the cleanup and repairs. Hospital ambulances ran the hill with injured hostages. The troopers climbed out of the bowl of the institution, scuffling the ground with their heels in an exhaustive, informal bone-weary cadence. They reached the first gate of the trap and a voice, heard clear in the hollow of the yard, called out from the top most tier. "You're not just any punk, Feeney. You're my punk now."

12

Bangor, Maine

John and William Coyle sat on opposite sides of a double-sided park bench, John with an unfettered view of the Penobscot River, William looking out onto Main Street where a thirty-six foot fiberglass statue of Paul Bunyan stood smiling down at him. An old man sat at the end of Will's bench. He had both of his hands resting on a cane and his head was tilted back.

"It sure is large, isn't it," he said.

"How come they put it up?" Will said.

"You're not from around here, are ya?"

John turned away from the river and looked back at the man.

"I wasn't born here if that's what you mean," Will said.

"If you'd been from around here, you would have known that that question has been asked a few hundred times at city council meetings. And reported in the Bangor News a few hundred more. Folks here don't just put things up. They have to have a reason and then they think on it a while. Talk about it until they forget what the original question was." He looked around as if to ensure that no one was eavesdropping. "And then they argue over it some more."

He turned towards the water. "About a hundred years ago, Bangor was the lumber capital of the world and that river a six-lane highway. In the spring, logs free-floated downstream to sawmills. Later, ships sailed upstream and carried

103

off the wood and things made from wood. They carted off bricks and leather too and every other imaginable thing you could think of. Even harvested blocks of ice floated down that river to the world. Then the paper men bought up the forests and, well that was the end of that." The man sat back satisfied with himself.

"You didn't answer his question, mister," John said. "Why did they put the statue up?"

"History." He spat onto the ground. "A while back, the city celebrated its one hundred and twenty-fifth birthday. And the town fathers wanted to remind people how Bangor came to be." He pointed up to the enormous lumberjack. "Bangor people are a tough lot, hard-working, independent folks and they thought that Paul Bunyan suited them well. That's why they put it up."

John gazed up at the grinning leviathan. "I can see that."

"They wanted to remember the good town history. Not Bangor's violent past."

"What violent past?" Will said.

He looked out to the street. "Maine's bloodiest gun battle happened right out there on Central Street."

"Who was doing the shooting?"

"The Brady gang from Indiana and the FBI."

John turned towards the street.

"Public Enemy Number One was shot dead by the FBI and state troopers. Right there, in front of Dakin's Sporting Goods."

"When was that?" John said.

"Columbus Day, 1937. Al Brady and Clarence Lee Shaffer took their last breaths on that street."

"You seem to know a lot about it," Will said.

"Everyone around here knows about it. You ask anyone. It's like it happened yesterday." He spat into the dirt again and rubbed the soil with the toe of his shoe. "I was on my way to Dakin's that day to buy brass polish. Thinking about it later, it's a good thing I was late."

"How close were you?"

"Close enough so I could see the coins falling out of Brady's pocket when they picked him up out of the street. Used to keep one of those coins in a jar on my bureau."

"Wished I'd been there." John stood to get a better view.

"Were they all killed? Will said.

"James Dalhover was in the store trying to buy a machine gun when he was captured. They brought him back to Indiana and electrocuted him."

"What were they wanted for?" John said.

"Robberies. They lived off them, two hundred stickups in two years. Anywhere they thought they could get money or guns. And four murders. Shot three cops and an Indiana state trooper." He took a handkerchief from his back pocket and blew his nose. "Supposedly Brady told someone he would make John Dillinger look like a piker."

John listened with great intent with one foot up on the bench. "Must have been pretty good shots." He smiled in spite of himself.

"I heard they ambushed a couple of those policemen," the old man said.

"What were they doing here? All the way from Indiana," Will said.

"I guess they thought no one would recognize them. They could buy guns without any suspicion because of the huntin'. But I ask you, automatic pistols, firing clips and Tommy guns and you say you goin' huntin'? That just didn't sit well with folks. Must have figured we were just country bumpkins."

"How did they get the drop on him?" John said.

"Well." The old man raised his cane. "Brady was sittin' in the back seat of a car right at that red brick building, waiting for his two sidekicks. A black Buick. He didn't know that one of them had been captured and the other shot dead. Two agents snuck up on him and got the jump on him. They ordered him out of the car with his hands up. He was cryin', 'Don't shoot! Don't shoot! I give up!' He had his hands in the air like he was about to surrender and he slid along the back seat to the door. One of the agents opened it and just as Brady put one foot on the ground, he leapt into the street with guns blazing. Shot the agent." The old man's cane shivered in his hand. He lowered it and rested himself on the handle.

"What happened then?" John said.

"Bedlam. Bullets everywhere and some of them awful close. Felt one buzz right past me." He moved his hand in front of his face. "Zip, like that. I jumped behind an automobile with my head down between my knees and my fingers in my ears. The soda clerk at McCarthy's drugstore told me later that those agents and troopers up on the roofs opened up on him. And he dropped like a Thanksgiving turkey." He spat again. "There was blood on the cobblestones. It leaked into the joints and it settled next to the trolley tracks. I had awful nightmares, dreamed my bed sheet was soaked in blood."

No one spoke for a while. Then the old man stood, his weight shifted over the cane. "Well, I should be goin'. Nice talkin' to you boys."

"Thanks for telling us the story, mister." Will said.

The old man began to shuffle away when he turned back to the Coyle brothers, Will seemed to be studying John, the older brother fixed on the place where Brady had died. "Not for nuthin', but he's buried in the Mount Hope Cemetery just up the road a piece in an unmarked grave. There's a wooden sign that'll direct you to where he's at if you're interested. No one ever did claim his body."

JOHN KNELT ON ONE knee and pressed his fingers into the dew-laden shade grass and the moist dirt that covered the slanted earth. He ran his thumb along the tips of his fingers, rubbed the earth into his skin and it stained them with the color of the living soil. "They ought to have put a marker here. This man put the backwoods of Bangor on the map. Who would have known about this place or what he had done unless there was a marker."

"I've been thinking," Will said. "We should be moving on."

John sat back on his heels. He picked up a length of tree branch and traced a circle on the ground. "I'll bet he came from the same stock as us." He tapped the point of the branch into the circle. "We're just meant to go a different way."

"Did you hear what I said, John?" Will stood behind his older brother and looked about the cemetery. "I think we should be going before people start getting suspicious."

John stood and tossed the branch aside. "Yes indeed, Will. Time to go home."

13

The door to his room blew open, slamming into the wall behind it.

"Let's go, Priest!"

He lay there unsure if the person yelling in the room was part of his dream or not. "What?" he said.

"Here, drink up." Cunningham handed him a half-filled shot glass.

He sat up in the bunk and propped himself on one elbow. "What is it?"

"Holy Communion."

"What's going on?" He drank a small amount of the whiskey.

"We need to be going to Sonny's."

Cunningham scrabbled around in the near dark until he found the light switch. "Anderson got jumped. And someone is about to take a thumping." He stood over Frank's bunk, dressed in combat boots and voluminous gray sweatpants that hung from his hips in waves. His uniform bunny hat sat on his head with the ear flaps airborne like Rocky the Flying Squirrel. He pulled off Frank's blankets and stood him up. "You're the last one." Tossed him dungarees, a sweatshirt and a pair of socks. "Let's go. It's ass whipping time. Can I hear an Amen?"

"Amen." Frank said with little enthusiasm.

"A little louder. Can I hear you say A . . . men!"

108

"All right, alright. A-fucking-men."

"Let's go, C-2." Cunningham left the same way he entered, throwing one of his fists into the door. He disappeared and then the back stairwell echoed with his voice. "Mount up."

Frank could hear the others in the kitchen shouting, the back door slamming, obscenities filling the stairwell and a vehicle being started in the backyard. More slamming, more obscenities and the howling of vengeful troopers about to pay back some ignorant bastard who made the mistake of striking a brother. He gulped the last of the whiskey, slipped a sap into his back pocket and jumped the stairs three at a time.

Hours past closing time, Jerry Lee Lewis' *Breathless* grinded out of a juke box at Sonny's roadhouse bar on Route 146 in Sutton when the eight troopers emptied out of a VW Bus seized from a beatnik who decided to do some dope while he teetered on a guardrail. Harley and Indian motorcycles were stacked at the entrance and one with black rawhide handle grips blocked the door. Cunningham removed a short club from his back pocket, smashed its headlight and kicked it over. He stepped inside the bar with Anderson next to him and he squinted into layers of smoky haze. Seven gang members of the Outlaws Motorcycle Club sat at the bar on stools, 'one percenters' in black leather jackets, engineer boots, and dungarees cuffed at the bottoms, spilling off the stools with their jeans hanging just below the cracks in their asses. Long-neck brown bottles filled the spaces in front of them. Their loud alcoholic and testicular laughter overrode the rock n' roll, their voices filling the tavern with the power of exclusive ownership. In a corner of the room, their old ladies sat at a table and watched the troopers like conjuring cats.

"Is that them?" Cunningham said.

"Yeah," Anderson said. "That little cocksucker at the end is the weasel who chucked the boots into my face and ribs."

When the troopers entered, the bikers ceased speaking, glanced at each other and then looked to the corner of the bar where one of the gang members was separated from the others. He sat slumped, his body in the tucked position with his feet on the foot rest, his knees splayed out to the sides. A black leather jacket hung from the back of his stool. Long sideburns framed his face and he wore a crushed stovepipe hat cocked to one side of his head. Both of his hands gripped the bar rail, the middle fingers tattooed with the letters FTW. A couple of the Outlaws looked back at the troopers and then returned to their drinking and stories. Cunningham poked the biker at the end of the bar and he jumped off his stool, pressing his face into PK's chest.

"You got a problem?" the biker said.

"Who's the head man?"

No one responded.

"I'm going to keep asking until someone claims ownership."

The Outlaws continued to drink and talk among themselves.

"Okay," Cunningham said. "Let's try this. Which one of you bums belongs to the Harley parked by the front door. Let me correct that. That was parked by the front door."

The man in the stovepipe didn't move. "What's it to you?" he said.

"Because I'm the meanest mother fucker in the jungle and I just smashed the headlight on that bike and then kicked it over." Cunningham watched him flinch, saw his jaw jump. Saw his fingers clamp down tight on the rail. He slapped the first biker aside and stood in front of the Outlaws' leader.

"You got a problem with the world, right," Cunningham said.

"That's right. I saw enough goons like you in the war. You're being used, Man."

Cunningham tapped the top of the stovepipe. "Who you supposed to be, fuckin' Bill Sikes?"

"No, your mother."

"I don't need an incentive, asshole. Do you know who you fucked up tonight?"

The biker stood. "We fuck up a lot of people."

"Yeah. Well, you made a mistake tonight."

The biker glanced at the injured Anderson, his face swollen blue and the blood in his hair now like dried jelly. "Looks like he got fucked over pretty good."

"That's one of our brother troopers."

The bartender threw up two short clubs and an ax handle onto the bar.

He gazed up at Cunningham with a long plastic smile. "So what do you want to do about it?"

It began quickly. Cunningham shot his open hand into the biker's Adams apple. And keeping one hand on the man's throat, he grabbed him by his belt and ran him tippy-toed across the room, whipping him ass-first into the wall. Before he could rise, Cunningham stomped his face with the heel of his boot. A tall reed of an Outlaw shattered an empty beer bottle over his head. His knees buckled and he put out a hand to steady himself. When the biker lunged at him with the broken bottle, Cunningham sidestepped and hooked him with his fist and the Outlaw fell to the floor in a shudder. One of the gang reached for a club on the bar and Frank brought his sap down on his hand and fingers. Laid him out with a blow to the side of his face. The biker's gamely bitch screamed like a Banshee and flew at him all bony angles. She landed on Frank's back and rode him hard into the bar rail, bit down on his ear and dug her long fingernails into his eye sockets, screaming something about her old man. He

111

stumbled backwards and backpedaled across the floor on his heels until he drove her into the wall behind him, the breath coming out of her in a large liquid bubble, followed by spasmodic retching and a torrent of vomit that dribbled down the back of his neck. The two of them sat there propped against the wall with Frank on top and she jellied up beneath him.

Hoss McCaffrey bulldozed two bikers, head-locked them and drove them into the side of the pin ball machine, the bells rang twice and the lights flashed 'Tilt.' JJ Murphy fell into a short plug of a gang member and punched him like a speed bag until the weasel at the end of the bar snuck up behind him and cold-cocked him. Murphy fell over and the weasel laid his boot into him until Anderson found a chair and brought it down across his back. He screamed something at the biker, but it was lost in the noise and confusion of the battle. The weasel laid there folded on the floor with his head propped up on the bar's boot rest.

Bodies began to pile up and navigating the floor became a hazardous venture. Combatants slipped and fell into the sticky mix, pulling one and then another down into the shavings, dust, spittle, blood and spilled beer where they continued to punch and gouge each other. Two of them locked in a contested wrestling hold, stumbled together across the floor in a tango until one of them found the footing to drive a knee into the other's crotch. Bottles whistled through the air. One of the Outlaws stabbed a trooper in the hand and each time the trooper punched the biker, his blood sprinkled the biker's face. The fight blew up against the jukebox and Elvis Presley's *Blue Suede Shoes* hiccupped each time someone hit the machine.

The bartender grabbed the ax handle and took a step to enter the fray. But when he realized that the troopers were cleaning out the Outlaws, he decided to escape. Bobby Johnson saw him and busted him anyway across the neck with a short club.

The weasel rose again and got to his hands and knees. He crawled to the exit, but when within feet of making his escape, McCaffrey spotted him, grabbed him by the collar and garrison belt and flung him into an overturned table. "Is this where you wanted to go?" he said. The biker attempted to rise from the filth of the floor with flecks of wood shavings stuck to his face, got to one knee and fell back where he lay in a heap.

Frank now painted in blood across his forehead and over the bridge of his nose, his knuckles split by teeth, and gouges of skin missing near his eyes and ears, rose and reentered the battle, clubbing down a biker who was about to lay out his roommate as he entered the bar.

"Where you've been?" he said to Jimmy Kelly.

"I just got back, the deskman told me where you guys were," he said. "Holy cow, you don't look too good, roomy."

"Pick out a body you don't recognize and hammer it." A strange lopsided feeling overcame Frank. He wobbled back and forth and then fell against the overturned table where the weasel lay. He landed in a sitting position on top of him and sat there in a stupefied gaze.

The bikers gave up the fight and began to retreat from the bar. Cunningham walked to where the gang leader lay propped against the wall and lifted him to his feet, handed him his leather jacket, placed his stovepipe hat on his head and led him to the door. "Be safe," he said to him. Frank stared at the somber parade of dungaree legs as they stumbled past. One pair of legs stopped where he was sitting, moved Frank to the side, picked up the weasel and carried him out. A pungent sugary sweetness came next when the perfumed old ladies passed. One of the bikers' bitches dropped back and kicked him. The loud rumble of exhaust pipes rattled outside. Then a thin receding sound.

"Jimmy. Jimmy Kelly. Set up some beers," Cunningham said. The senior man sat at the bar with his arms sprawled back over the counter. He removed the bunny hat, shook it out and replanted it on his head. "I pity the poor bastard that has to do a day shift today."

"That would be me," Bobby Johnson said from the corner of the room. "It's going to be a fireman's schedule, PK. Wait for the alarm."

"I'll cover you with the sergeant."

The remainder of the troopers limped to the bar, bone-dragging tired and sat heavy on the stools with cold bottles of beer on their necks or the sides of their heads. A few of them were laid out on table tops. They lit up Camels and Lucky Strikes and the smoke in the small tavern rose and lay in the air with the stench of beer, sweat and the smell of rank human beings. Music blared from the jukebox and they spoke in top-of-the-lung waterfront voices.

"You look like shit, Priest?" Cunningham said. "What are you doing today?"

Frank's head rolled to one side against the top of the overturned table, one eye rising up to a vibrant shade of black and blue. "SDO," he said in a small dry voice and then he cleared his throat again and spat a combination of phlegm and blood onto the floor. "Somebody kill that jukebox, will ya."

"You better find an excuse to stay at the barracks Buddy Boy so you can clean up your act before going home to the little woman."

"Jimmy Kelly, any tomato juice over there?" Frank pulled himself up into a sitting position. "Kill that jukebox."

"And what advice would you give poor old Frankie, PK?" Jimmy said.

"Well, there is such a thing as keeping a wife."

"Said by the guy who's been divorced twice." Jimmy handed Frank the tomato juice and a chunk of ice that he pressed into his eye socket.

"Well, Priest can do what he wants, but I'd have a really good story," Cunningham said.

Frank sipped the tomato juice, sat there slumped against the table top. Then a sudden thought caused him to jerk up straight. "Ah jeez, it's my anniversary."

"Ho, ho, ho. You're in deep shit, Frankie boy," Jimmy said.

"I do owe the corporal a couple of reports. And we were in a bar fight. She just doesn't need to know the particulars. Jesus, please, I'm begging you. Kill that jukebox."

Someone finally ripped its electric cord out of the wall.

Cunningham lifted him to his feet. "Come on, Priest. We need to get you into some kind of shape. I'll give you a lift home after we clean you up."

"You don't have to do that."

"Not a big deal, it's on my way. Besides, I feel some responsibility for getting you screwed up."

"Say, why did you help that asshole to the door?"

"The head biker?"

"Yeah."

"Because of the shoulder patch on his leather jacket. Forty-second Rainbow. My Division."

They sat or stood in various positions of surrender, quiet and stiff in the sulfurous light of the roadhouse bar and watched the arrival of the new day, making its appearance on the other side of the highway. Cars passed, their headlights burning into the cool and colorless polluted air. Then came the light, the horizon in orange and the day became official. They pushed all the debris into the center of the room and limped outside like walking dead.

115

JJ Murphy put up a hand to shield his eyes from the glare. "Turn out that light, will ya."

Cunningham lifted the bartender up from the floor and propped him on a stool. He stuffed dollar bills into his shirt pocket and walked out the door. "What a glorious day," he said.

Portland, Maine

THE DETECTIVE LOOKED out the window of the motel office and watched the tow truck leave with the 1953 Ford Ranch Wagon hooked to the rear of it.

"They were nice enough boys," the clerk said. "Didn't give me any trouble."

"Anything else you remember?" the cop said.

"Well, sir. I do remember that one of them was in the Air Force. Like I said, they were here only one night and I only spoke to them when they registered for the room."

"Did you see them carrying any weapons?"

"Guns? No, can't say that I did. I would have remembered that."

"How about calls? Did they make any calls from here?"

"There are no telephones in the rooms. Once they checked in, I never saw them again."

The cop opened the office door and flicked his cigarette outside. "You never tried to open her up, huh? Before calling the Portland Police, I mean."

"I might have if I'd known there were two rifles in the back."

"And tell me again why you didn't report the car sooner."

"They were two decent boys and they must have had a reason for leaving the car here. They might have been out of money. Down on their luck. I didn't think it proper to be causing them more misery. Especially servicemen. They have enough misery."

"Right. They didn't say where they were going or leave a forwarding address, did they?"

"No, sir. I thought they'd show up eventually."

"Okay. If you remember anything else, call me at this number." The cop pushed a business card across the counter and turned to leave.

"I would have called sooner if I had an inkling that they were wanted."

"I'm sure you would have." The cop closed the door behind him and left.

The clerk waited until the cruiser drove out of the parking lot. He placed the train schedule to Bangor back on the counter and tossed the business card into the trash.

Philadelphia, Pennsylvania
WHILE THE POLICE recovered the Ford station wagon at the Maine motel, the Coyle brothers arrived by train in Philadelphia, dumped their arsenal of weapons into a station locker and jumped the subway to 1539 Erie Avenue where they viewed a furnished second floor apartment in the rear.

"You're brothers?" Mrs. Hinkle said.

"Yes."

"I thought you might be. You look alike. How about seventy dollars?"

John stepped out onto the back porch and inhaled the city, the neighborhood and the place he called home. He felt comfortable again. "You can smell spring coming."

"It won't be long. Change is in the air."

"So, it's been unoccupied," he said. "A couple of months, huh?"

117

"Yes." The landlady stood at the kitchen doorway. "But as you can see, it is a very nice apartment and it has a beautiful view."

"Sixty-five dollars."

They walked back inside the apartment.

"You'll take it for sixty-five a month?"

"Yes," John said.

"Alright. Who is going to sign the book?"

"I am," Will said. He began to reach into his pocket. "I have my Selective Service Card."

"That's not necessary. After all, you seem like nice boys. You're not gangsters, are you?"

"I would hope not," John said.

"So, I keep you fellas straight, you're John and your brother is Gilbert?

"Yes."

"Thank you, Mr. Kessler. I'll get you the keys."

Mrs. Hinkle left the apartment and John watched her walk across the street to her home. "Nice apartment, tucked away and quiet." he said.

"What makes you think this is a good place to stay?' Will said.

"I don't know, a hunch maybe. It's just a place."

"How long do you think we'll be here," Will said.

"We're back home. So, for as long as we want."

14

S heila sat forward and placed her elbows on the table. She stared at his eye and the other injuries to his face. The restaurant was half filled and the sounds of the staff scurrying about and diners settling in could be heard in the room.

"It's alright," he said.

"Does that have anything to do with Pearlie K sleeping on the couch last night."

"I couldn't throw him out after he drove me all the way home."

"Of course not. That's not what I meant though."

"Come on, he doesn't have someone like you waiting for him. It was the least I could do."

"The least." She reached over and brushed his hair back to examine the bruises. "But one of us is not going to survive this, Frank."

"It's not always like this, the last six months have been crazy."

"Let's hope so."

He leaned over and kissed her. "Happy anniversary."

"Happy anniversary."

"Ten years, do you regret it?"

"And miss all this?" She drew a circle in the air around his face.

"I remember when your father summoned me to the house. He and your uncles, sitting on the porch with a wash tub full of empties. I figured I'm dead."

"Well, being pregnant and not married. And just turning eighteen."

"Yeah." Frank nodded. "They were alright, though."

"They liked you Frank. That probably saved you."

"It was your mother and her sisters who saved me. They came out on the porch just as your Uncle Dave stood up."

"They thought I was too young."

"Yeah," he laughed. "My friends thought I was robbing the cradle."

"Who?"

"Tommy, Eddie . . ."

"Eddie? What number marriage is he on? He should talk." She took a mouthful of her drink and winced.

"How come you ordered a highball? That's pretty strong for you."

"I felt like something different. Something new."

"But the hard stuff?"

"I'm a big girl. I can try something new now and then. Besides, I'm feeling very relaxed tonight."

"Yeah?"

A single candle sputtered in the middle of the table. She glanced across the room. Most of the tables now filled, conversation percolated throughout the restaurant. In the opposite corner of the room, a piano played. She drank the whiskey and ginger slowly this time and she felt the alcohol skating through her body.

"You should wear a tie more often," she said. "It looks good on you."

"Thanks." Frank buttered a roll.

"The suit gives you a whole different persona. Carefree, not so . . . military."

"Persona? Working the crossword puzzles?"

"You know what I mean."

"What? Ordinarily, I'm a curmudgeon?"

"Curmudgeon?"

"You think you're the only one who reads or does crossword puzzles."

"What are you reading?"

"The Man in the Gray Flannel Suit."

"Really?" She fingered the rim of her glass. "I'm impressed."

"You think all we do is read Playboy? Lots of guys at the barracks . . ."

"Here we go. Fifteen seconds into the conversation and we're talking about the guys at the barracks. Can we escape the state police for one evening?"

"Sorry. When I'm at the barracks, I talk about you and the kids. So, you and the guys have something in common. You're both sick of me yammering on about the other."

"Oh, I see. Whomever you're away from, you miss?"

"Nah, you and the kids mean more to me than anything. But . . ."

"But what?"

"I live in two different worlds. You've seen it. Every time I leave one and go to the other, it takes a little time to get acclimated again. That's all. It's like living a double life."

"Like Herb Philbrick."

"He led three lives. Two are enough for me. Besides, I'm not chasing down Commies."

"Well, the point I'm trying to make is that you look good in that suit and tie," she said.

"You look pretty good yourself. That waiter wasn't eyeballing me when he served the drinks. I thought he was going to fall into your lap."

"He wouldn't look twice if he saw me at seven in the morning with my head up in curlers, wearing my big fluffy robe and trying to get the kids off to school."

"That's how I keep you all to myself."

121

"Oh I see, dumb, pregnant and all dressed up in a brown paper bag. Home on the range. That it partner?"

"Nah, just plain enough to keep the wolves away." He looked down and began to straighten his silverware. "I appreciate what you do, you know." He looked at her. "Doing everything yourself while I'm away, the house, the kids."

"Keep talking and you might be looking at a promise," she said. "By the way, the plumber fixed the toilet."

"Talk about ruining the moment. I could have . . . How much did he charge you?"

"We needed it fixed, Frank. We've got one toilet and three kids."

"Yeah, I guess that would be asking too much."

She sipped the whiskey. "You happy?"

"Of course." He tipped his head to see her face past the candle.

In the six months he had been on the job, she thought that Frank had remained the good husband. Different though, maybe a little more edgy. And distant at times. What's new, Frank? Ah, same old stuff. And recently she realized that she had changed too, more independent, more self-sufficient. But still a housewife with three kids and a part time husband, a bride of the state police.

"You remember when you signed on with the job, I wasn't thrilled," she said.

"I remember."

"I was concerned about the barracks system and you living away from us."

"Yeah, but I . . ."

"I was the good wife. We adapted and made it work, didn't we."

"Oh, oh. Where is this going?"

"I realized something the other day while I was looking at the obituaries."

"Obituaries?"

"Jackie Scales."

"Jackie Scales? What about him?"

"He's dead."

"Jesus. He's younger than we are. What happened?"

"A car accident on the interstate."

"Another one. Ike's new highway system is great and everything. But the accidents, the speed. The turnpike had six die in one accident the other day."

"Frank, I'm trying to make a point here."

"Sorry."

"It just makes you think." She straightened the napkin in her lap. "I'm thinking of getting a job."

"A job?"

"Before you say anything . . ."

"I don't know."

She sat straight.

"Geez, Sheila, you're driving me nuts. Where you getting these ideas?"

"I worked before we had kids, Frank."

"That was different."

"I like getting dressed up. I like the challenge. I like being told I am worth something."

"You're worth something."

"Gee, thanks for the endorsement." She looked away.

"What kind of a job?"

She turned back to him. "Travelers Insurance. They have a new office in Braintree."

"Doing what?"

"Clerical to start."

He placed his elbow on the table and dragged his fingers across his forehead. "Hmm."

"A small office and I don't have to go into Boston. It's two shifts a week."

"What about the kids?"

"They have a mother's shift." She leaned closer. "The personnel director told me . . ."

"You've already spoken to them?" he said with a slightly raised voice.

She looked around the room and with a lowered voice said, "I met with him when I filled out the application."

"An application? Sounds like you've already made up your mind."

The waiter refilled their water glasses and turned to her. "Would you like another drink, Miss?"

"Yeah in a second," Frank said. "Give us a few minutes."

After the waiter left, she said, "I wanted to talk with you first."

"I don't want to be out in Grafton, worrying about you."

"Why would you worry?"

"I don't know. Maybe I'm old school, I like my wife at home."

Sheila looked down at the rug and the depressions left by her high heels. "I never wanted you to work," he said. "You're the mother." She looked up at him. "I could do what some of our neighbors do. Afternoon cocktails and gossip about whoever isn't there. I didn't have a frontal lobotomy when I gave birth."

Frank leaned back and looked past her. He stayed in that position for a few moments before he put his elbows on the table. "Are you going to be able to handle a job, the house and the kids?"

"Yes. And you know why? Because it's going to make me a better wife and mother. I can use my brain again. Feel like I'm doing something productive."

"And what if you become pregnant?"

"It's 1959, things are beginning to change. Do you know that they're working on a pill to prevent pregnancy? Women can have careers if they want."

"I know the Church isn't keen on the pill."

"When a priest carries a baby to term—well, that's when he can tell me what I can and can't do with my body."

"Boy, you've come a long way since St. Mark's."

"Well?"

"I'm thinking."

"Businesses are waking up to the fact that a mature woman is more stable and reliable than a young girl who's looking for a husband so 'she can settle down'."

He nodded. "Sometimes, I come home after being away and you're irritated. And I'm irritated. And we say things to each other that we regret later. And then I'm leaving again." He looked at her. "If getting you out of the house makes you happy then that's what I want."

"Do you mean it?"

"Yeah."

"I could bring in a few extra dollars," she said.

"What about the kids? Job takes enough from this family."

"I can schedule my days. All they care about is that the work gets done. One shift the day you get home while you're sleeping and the kids are in school. My mother can watch them for the other shift."

"How come Travelers is so accommodating?"

"They don't have to hire a full time person," she said. "It's cheaper for them."

"We could use the money."

"I was going to buy the kids' Easter clothes with it."

He tapped his glass. "One condition. If the kids need you, the job goes."

"Deal." She reached across the table and they shook hands.

He began to butter another roll. "So what about that promise you spoke about earlier?"

She held her arms out. "Do you like this dress?"

"Yeah, it's nice."

"Well, I'm drinking a highball, feeling very warm and fuzzy. And there is nothing between me and the dress."

He drew in a breath like he was sipping through a straw. "Ooh."

15

Philadelphia, Pennsylvania
April, 1959

They climbed out of the Wister Street subway station. Walked the two blocks to LaSalle College, made their way to the Administration building and asked for Mrs. Higgins. While they hadn't seen her since their arrival in Philadelphia, the brothers genuinely respected her and hoped to say hello. They also hoped that she might be a source of cash as the money from the First National robbery was about to run out. When told she had taken the day off, they changed their plans and stood off from the large student parking lot and waited.

"Just hotwire one," Will said. "That one."

"I don't want to take a chance someone may discover it missing and report it to the cops while we're still driving it around," John said. "We take the owner too, then there's no one to report it."

"We'll be here all day."

"Who screwed up the First National job by leaving a fingerprint?"

"You not going to let me forget that are you."

"I'm just sayin'. Let's do it right."

"Is that guy over there watching us?"

"Where?" John looked around the lot. "Relax, will ya? No one knows us here except Mrs. Higgins and she hasn't seen us." John stood erect and stretched to see over several

127

cars. "See that guy over there. If he goes for a car, we'll grab him." The man continued to walk through the lot and exited the campus.

They slouched behind a tree in a grove that created a green barrier between the parking lot and the campus proper. They were lean and pale, desperate and edgy from a lack of food and the self-imprisonment in the two room apartment. Their slacks and shirts hung off them like clothes thrown over kitchen chairs. They watched the students pass, some of them talking and joking, some of them with their heads buried in text books. Wisps of images of another life quickly moving in and out of their view into buildings with religious statues erected outside and flowers planted at the bases.

"Here we go," John said. A two-door blue ninety-eight Olds drove to an open space not far from where they stood. A man in his twenties, wearing a worn suit stepped outside the car and stood by the open door. He leaned inside to retrieve his books and they were on him before he stood again.

"Hold it right there," John said to him.

The driver turned. They looked like bookends to him, being about the same age and the same size. And matching expressions of two people who just didn't consider consequences.

John stuck the .32 revolver in his face. "Don't do anything stupid," he said." Get into the car." He pushed the man into the back seat and climbed in behind him. Will jumped behind the wheel. They drove out of the city and found a quiet road where John ordered him into the trunk.

"Why don't you let me go," he said. "You don't have to put me into the trunk, you have the car. I'm in the middle of nowhere, I don't even know where I am."

"Because I said so," John said. He pressed the gun against the man's stomach. "Get in the trunk." The man climbed in and John held the lid. "What's your name?"

"Gallagher."

"Your first name?"

"Ralph."

"You married Ralph? Kids?"

Gallagher nodded. "Married. I don't have any children." Mucous trickled out of his nose and he wiped the corner of his eye with the back of his hand.

"Come on, let's get going," Will said.

"Do you gamble, Ralph?" John said.

"What? No. I don't make much money. I'm paying for school."

"I'm not talking about money, Ralph. I'm talking about your life."

"What?"

"Come on," Will said.

John pulled on the trunk lid. "You won't be in there long, Ralph. Just don't give us any trouble. Got it?" Gallagher stared in a plea as John closed the lid.

WILL SLOWED AS they passed a sandwich shop. "How about that one?" he said.

John leaned forward. "We can do better."

"Jesus, John. We've been driving around for . . . It's six o'clock."

"I know, I know. I'm trying to find an easy target with a lot of cash." He drummed his foot against the floor boards. "Pull over, I got enough for a sandwich and a bottle of milk. I think better on a full stomach."

They drove to a wooded park and found a secluded area. They let Gallagher out of the trunk and gave him a piece of the sandwich and a swig of milk. "Thanks, I appreciate that," he said. "Sure is hot in there. It smells of gasoline."

John turned away and leaned against the Olds. He stared into the emerging lights of the city below them while Will kept an eye on the prisoner. He studied the ebb and flow of the life at the bottom of the hill, the glare, the shadows, the noise of the car engines and automobile horns, the elevated railway rattling and squealing against the curve of the rail. And after a few minutes, he snapped his fingers. "I got it," he said. He turned to Gallagher. "Back in the trunk."

The temporary release from his imprisonment and the audacity to imagine his freedom rattled Gallagher, and he became emotionally distraught, a knee-jerk reaction, out of his control without a synapse of contemplation. Suddenly, the seriousness of the moment and the possibility that he could be hurt or even killed hit him hard and it triggered an involuntary reaction. He jumped in place in a spontaneous reflex like a body hiccup, the expression on his face like he had been slapped or punched. "Look you guys, let me go. I'm not going to do anything stupid. My wife . . ." He began to sniffle. "My wife is going to be worrying where I am. You guys don't need me."

John looked at him and held him in a gaze of animal curiosity.

"Do what he says," Will said. Gallagher wept and climbed in and they started down the hill to the lights of the city and back onto Wister Street.

"It's almost 7 o'clock," Will said.

"Take a right here."

They turned and followed the colors of neon half way down the block.

"This is it, Willy Boy. The bonafide big cheese, Schmid's Tavern."

"Isn't that a wise guys' bar? They'll have guns."

"Yeah, so don't we."

They double parked the Olds at the entrance and ran for the front door, Will exploding into the tavern with guns in each hand and John a few steps behind. Five men sat at the bar and another three sat at a table, playing cards in the dense air of cigarette smoke. A color television played soundlessly at the back of the room with some game show. The tavern prior to the brothers' entrance had buzzed in quiet conversation. They disturbed this low human activity like a clap of thunder.

"Everyone on the wall!" John yelled.

The patrons, a few of them with mashed-up knuckles on the backs of their hands, some with unnatural noses and some with hard scarred faces, turned with mild curiosity and looked at the two boys pointing the pistols at them. One of them said, "Get the fuck outta here kid before you get hurt real bad."

John fired a shot into the ceiling. "This is a holdup," he said.

There were two bartenders working and one bar man was drawing a beer. The other bent over to retrieve a pistol under the counter. John pointed his revolver at him and pulled the trigger and the hammer fell, the firing pin falling against an empty chamber, the metal on metal misfire like an exclamation point. An opportunity for the embarrassed thugs hung there for a disquieting moment, but in that moment, the younger Coyle vaulted to a chair and used it to spring to the top of the bar, both arms locked out straight, guns sweeping the room like searchlights. "These will fire, mister," he said. The bartender stood straight and placed his hands in the air. "Get on the wall," Will said to him.

John pushed a slow moving patron face-first into the wall and told him to pin his hands up as high as he could. Will emptied one cash register into a pillow case then he did the same to a second. He cleaned the top of the table where the

131

men were playing cards and then politely asked each of the customers to deposit their cash into the pillowcase. He turned and saw one of the patrons slide a hand inside his jacket. "The guy at the end of the line is reaching for something," he yelled to his brother.

John raised his pistol to the man's head. "I'd hate to have to shoot you, mister."

"Do you know who I am?" the man said.

"No."

"I'm someone you don't want to fuck with. I own this joint."

"Yeah?"

"Yeah, and you picked the wrong place, kid. So why don't you turn around and get outta here and maybe I give you a running start."

"Sorry, can't do that." John pulled a snub nose .38 from the man's jacket and tucked it into his belt. "Thanks."

The man stared at John Coyle, his tongue curled up and touching his upper lip, fixing this alabaster punk with the brown hair in his mind, seeing him with a bullet hole in his head, a shallow grave under one of the overpasses of the state highway. "You're a dead man," he said. John stared with no expression.

The amount of time the Coyle Brothers spent inside Schmid's Tavern and the manner in which they conducted their business gave them a bad-ass reputation, in and out within three minutes. But their attempt to escape fit the machinations of a couple of bungling amateurs. The Olds sputtered and choked when Will flooded the engine. And when the patrons realized that the "dead men" who had just robbed the tavern were still sitting in the middle of the street, they ran at the car with assorted weapons and surrounded them, hammering at the Olds until John stuck one of his pistols out the window and cranked off a round. The car started in an explosion of blue smoke and they left in a ten-foot strip of rubber, a beer bottle bounced off the trunk as they sped away. John watched the men in the street through the rear window and he saw one of them write down the registration number.

Once back on Wister Street, they casually drove out of the area, stopping at every stop sign and traffic signal they came upon. They visited the tenement on Armat Street behind the Band Box Theater where they had shared a one bedroom apartment with their paranoiac alcoholic father about the time their mother had died, the rising and the falling, the dis-association from life, the periods of starvation and the early forays into hunting to survive. And the longer they sat there, the longer John had to talk Will back into the car with a cig-arette lighter in his hand, deciding whether to burn down the house that tortured him with so many memories. They drove to their apartment on Erie Avenue, left the Olds running on the street, dropped off their guns and counted the money. The pillow case contained $156 and they celebrated their success with glasses of cold milk. A few minutes later they returned to the car, drove the short distance to quiet Hunt-ing Park, flipped the keys onto the front seat and casually walked away, drawing the cool Philadelphia night air into their lungs. In the trunk, Ralph Gallagher cried not because he might never see his wife again, but because he had failed to kiss her goodbye.

HE ENDURED ANOTHER hour of terror and thought his life might be near its end. But when he no longer heard the men who'd kidnapped him, a flicker of hope gave Gallagher cause to believe that he might actually survive this ordeal. He found the tire wrench in the trunk and pried the lock. He stepped from the vehicle rubbery legged and unhinged, sat down on the edge of the curb, amazed by the night, the sky and its depth, the odors and the sense of coming spring. Sat there for fifteen minutes or more appreciating his life. Then he stood and shuffled to a public telephone to tell his unlikely story.

16

He drank his coffee in the dark. Frank sat alone on the quiet highway with no one save himself and those great metal beasts that carried America's goods to far-off destinations. The absence of human clatter and the busyness of day struck him and he both regarded and respected the mystery and obscurity of the moment, its lack of pretension. He thought of his family and Sheila. Of her lying with him, her flesh and his flesh, her welcoming. How they had scrupulously submitted to Church law, avoided the temptation to consume each other like two animals until their honeymoon night. How they broke their celibate promise. And how he felt neither guilt nor shame, entrusting their love and their passion to a natural order.

The radio crackled. "C-2 to 602."

"602," he said.

"Would you check a disabled car on the side of the road, Route 146 southbound near the Douglas State Forest exit."

"Received, en route." Frank closed the thermos, dumped out the last bit of coffee, pulled onto the divided highway and started south, the road a carnival ride through a tunnel of twenty-foot ledges on one side and the black state forest on the other. Commercial rigs owned the American road in the middle of the night and as he raced beside the wall of ledge, these eighteen wheel behemoths hugged the shoulder and flashed their headlights as he passed.

The car sat off the breakdown lane with its red turn signal blinking. He could see it in the darkness from a quarter mile away as he crested the hill, the light from that distance appearing like a warning harbor beacon. He turned on the dome light as he approached, lit up the car with his high beams and the spotlight. The vehicle listed slightly towards the woods and it straddled the breakdown lane and the grass embankment. He thought he had seen someone standing near it when still a distance away, but when he approached, the car appeared abandoned, a solitary thing surrounded by night's darkness.

"Anyone here?" Frank said. He walked to the driver's side and shined his flashlight into its interior. A few odd pieces of men's clothing were scattered across the back seat. An opened bag of potato chips was on the front seat and the chips had been crushed as if someone had sat on them. Empty beer bottles lay on the floor. He walked to the rear of the vehicle, saw the registration plate, and shined his light down the passenger side. Swept the shoulder and the embankment and the woods where the light's illumination fell away and disappeared.

"Hello," he called.

A breeze brushed the top of the trees and he could hear the leaves chattering. Heard a sound close by, not a cry so much as a gentle whimper, turned away from the woods and he heard it again in the vicinity of the car. He lit up the interior once more and now saw a school bookbag on the floor partially covered by trash.

"Come on out," Frank yelled. "I know you're out there."

The first blow struck his elbow and he instinctively pulled his arm back, dropped his flashlight and it rolled away. Someone punched him on the side of the head then kicked him, striking his knee and again near his groin, the pain, sharp and sickening. And then he saw the man with a club poised

136

to bring it down again. He flailed at the air and found his attacker, drove his head into him and knocked the club away. He clutched and grabbed and pulled himself close, smelling the breath of beer and the man's last meal. His foul odorous clothing reeked of dust and animal urine.

The man attacked in a clumsy oafish way while making wild feral sounds. His strength was brutish and when they hand wrestled, Frank could envision him lifting heavy bags, grasping and tearing at things. He pulled at Frank's uniform, ripping away first his whistle and then his badge. He fought for separation, but Frank held him close.

"Goin' to kill you," he said.

In the light of the cruiser they fought, their shadows dancing in a strange surreal way And they fell as one across the car's trunk with Frank underneath, bent over and flat on his back. His boots flailed and skidded in the sand and he lost the power of his legs. And each time he attempted to wriggle a hand free or rise, the superior strength of the man pinned him against the trunk again. He finally created an arm's distance and Frank saw him, lanky and broad shouldered, dressed in bib overalls and a checkered work shirt like signature pieces worn every day of his life. He had a high forehead and a stubble beard with a monk's haircut. He slapped at Frank's face and plunged the heel of his hand into the bridge of his nose again and again. Frank was losing control and he became dazed.

Two tractor trailer units passed in tandem within feet of the car and the draft rocked the vehicle back and forth. The clamor of their engines tearing at the night and the draft of air that accompanied them became a constant reminder to him. He forever associated that sound and the force of those trucks with the pull on his holster, the lifting of the holster's flap and the movement of his revolver. The strength of that man's hands, he would never forget.

137

He was dazed and weakening and he heard his attacker say again, "I'm goin' to kill you." The man grabbed his hair and slammed his head into the vehicle's trunk and Frank felt the .38 sliding against the leather.

"God!" he said. "My gun."

THE SEMI SKIDDED and the truck moaned. The engine downshifted in a violent rattling, the thirty-foot trailer skipping and swinging away from the cab and then returning home. The rig stopped just beyond the disabled vehicle, the acrid odor of burning rubber and locked-up brakes hung in the air. Frank pushed against the hand that continued to pull at his gun, took another blow to his face and tasted blood in his mouth. He could sense the cylinder clearing his holster.

Suddenly, his attacker moaned and fell on top of him, his blood dripping into Frank's face. He rose again. And Frank saw the trucker behind him rising up large and menacing. He brought down the pipe and his attacker jellied. He collapsed on top of him once more, pinning Frank against the trunk.

The trucker removed him and he fell into the breakdown lane, curled on one side and shivering, the blood pooling beneath his head. Frank cuffed the man's wrists and treated his wound.

"Think I heard something in there," the trucker said. Frank pointed to the trunk. "Yeah." And the driver began to walk away.

"Are you leaving?"

"You don't need me any longer." The trucker spat onto the highway. "And I don't need the problems."

"You heard something?" Frank said.

"Like a whimper."

"Do you want to give me your name?"

"No. Just remember when you see us out here."

Frank saw the tow truck cresting the hill.

The tow truck driver popped the lock and opened the trunk. Curled inside a young girl dressed in her school uniform cowered. Her hands and ankles were tied, a dirty rag in her mouth. She gazed out from the trunk pale and hollow-eyed with an expression of profound loss. He stood there on the highway stunned by her despair, the night and its immense silence.

GRAFTON SHIMMERED AT daybreak when Frank entered the town. He rode west with the brilliance of the new day laid out before him, the sun lighting up the still wet trees as if they were draped in tinsel. The light glazing the dew-laden grass. Farmers waved to him as they led their animals from barns, their chimneys pulling the odor of wood smoke. He climbed the hill and turned into the drive, parked the cruiser at the gas pumps and began to fill the tank. PK Cunningham, dressed in coveralls knelt in his garden with one of Mrs. Healey's pots beside him. The dog lay in the sun a few feet away and watched him. The senior trooper looked up and then turned back to his business. Frank replaced the first aid materials and washed the cruiser. He parked near the garden, packed up his ditty bag and stood outside. The sun warmed his face and he stared up at it and let it soak into him.

"I'm hearing good things about you," Cunningham said. He looked closer and saw the damage from the fight.

"That so?" Frank said, his eyes still closed.

"That's so."

"Well." He turned away from the sun. "Whoever is making that assessment wasn't out on 146 last night."

"I understand." Cunningham stood with a bunch of snap beans in his hand. "You're not the first cop that maniac tangled with and you're not the first trooper to know what it

139

means to ride alone." He broke up the beans into smaller pieces and dropped them into the pot. "Is she okay?"

"Physically. But it'll take a while to get that monster's image out of her head."

"She's safe. That's all that counts."

Frank took a deep breath and blew it out. "If it wasn't for . . ."

"No one need to know about that," Cunningham said. "Who cares how that man fell. The truck driver doesn't have any desires to come forward. So let the truth stand on its own. That pervert kidnapped a little girl, assaulted her, and probably scarred her for life. And you made the arrest and freed her from her misery. Nothing else matters."

"I guess so."

"You could have killed that son-of-a-bitch and the town would have thrown you a parade. Did anyone wave at you when you came through the square?"

"A few people, yeah."

"Well, there you go."

Cunningham picked a sunflower from his garden and carried it with the cooking pot to where Frank stood. "Who cares if you had help. The most important result is that you were the last man standing. It is he who writes the definition of winning and therefore gives the accounting. But if you're dead, there is no accounting. You win or you leave it for the next time. And you know there will be a next time. So end it one way or another."

Cunningham handed the pot to Frank. "Here hold this." He returned to the garden and picked up his tools. He walked back to where Frank stood. "Don't let your scruples suffocate you, Priest. There are things that go on, things that aren't written down anywhere. Aren't even spoken about outside the barracks. Things that have to be done, plain and simple for the next man. There is history here." They walked across the backyard with the dog trailing close behind. Cunningham stopped at the rear door before opening it. "When that man is arraigned at the District Court this morning, there will be no vacant seats. They'll be filled with cops."

17

Philadelphia, Pennsylvania

Exactly one month after they walked away from Ralph Gallagher and his stolen Oldsmobile, subway bandits John and William Coyle exited the Wister Street station again and walked four blocks to the Savings & Loan on Wayne Avenue in the blue collar Germantown neighborhood. The S&L was in close proximity to La Salle College, less than a mile from the park where they had shared a sandwich and a bottle of milk with Gallagher and an even closer distance to Schmid's Tavern. All of these locations a few subway stops from their Erie Avenue apartment.

The brothers burned through the $156 take from the wise guys' bar on rent, canned food and the daily number. Their refrigerator sat almost empty save for an opened jar of peanut butter and a half filled quart bottle of milk. With each passing day, they exhibited a gradual deterioration and it evolved over time since they first had tasted the call of the hunt at the First National grocery store. They ate little and they were lean and hungry. The thought of confrontation intoxicated them and they were edgy and at times, short tempered with each other. They had found new purpose, the need to test one's mortality, a rush greater than sex. They maintained a celibate and monastic existence and never considered the companionship of a woman. Will now as delusional as his brother, willingly accompanying him on his journey down a rabbit's hole. He exhibited a similar black state of depression

142

that could only be satisfied with a violent brush with death. The euphoria, the anticipation, the intoxication of the 'next time' was addictive. They were the boys from Armat Street who planned to write their own story.

"It's still there, John." Will said. "They didn't move it since the last time we were here."

John folded his arms and looked across the street. "It must be loaded."

"How many times are we going to stand here and stare at it?"

"What's your hurry?"

"I say we move on it. Or we look for something else."

"Preparation . . . best day, best time." John continued to watch the building. "Do you see that?"

"Where? Oh, yeah."

The beat cop opened the door to the S&L, waved to the manager and walked out. Continued his way along the sidewalk and entered a variety store on the corner. A few minutes later he reappeared with a newspaper under his arm. He turned the corner and disappeared."

"That's why we've been waiting here." John looked at his watch. "Ten thirty-three."

"Okay, you made your point," Will said.

"Remember the old man in Bangor who told us about Al Brady? They were waiting for him." John looked up and down the avenue. "Hang out here. I'll be right back." Will slumped against the street lamp, his foot propped up on the pole. John limped across the street and stood by the S&L, looking about and glancing in from time to time. After a few minutes, he shoved his hands into his pockets and limped back to where Will stood.

"Well?" Will said.

"Yes indeed, banks and armored cars. It's time we made some real money, top dollar. If this one's not loaded, I'll eat my shirt."

"What's it look like?"

"It's smaller than I expected, but an easy layout. Two girls behind the counter. Manager in a side office on the right. Safe right behind the girls. Doesn't look like there's anyone else."

"No guard?"

"No."

"Sounds easy."

"That's what I'm saying. A piece of cake."

"So, when?"

"End of the week. People need to cash their checks."

"So what do we eat in the meantime?"

"We'll heist more milk. I've got money for oatmeal. But that's about it."

"Alright," Will said. "Let's get out of here before we're seen hanging around."

"What are you worried about?"

"I just keep thinking about Massachusetts."

"Why? We're a long way from Massachusetts. Besides, if they were looking for us, we would have heard from them by now." John looked across Wayne Avenue at the S&L one more time. Saw himself vaulting the counter, the girls petrified and trembling.

A FEW DAYS later, John walked into the apartment. The room smelled of the pungent odor of gun cleaning solvent. Will sat at the table with a rod and a patch and he ran it through each cylinder of his .38 and then the barrel. John stood with his back against the sink, gazing at the floor and the shadows created by the late afternoon sun. He drummed his fingers on the lip of the sink. Will pulled the rod from the barrel and laid the pistol on the newspaper that was spread across the table.

"You're stinking up the joint," John said.

"You take care of your weapons," the younger brother said. "I'll take care of mine. My guns don't have an empty chamber when I need them."

"So I forgot. I take care of everything else, don't I?"

"What did she say?"

"She's giving us an extra week to scrounge up the rent money."

"What did you tell her?"

"I told her we're broke and waiting for a money order that our father mailed a few days ago from upper state New York."

"That's pretty good, seeing he's dead."

"She gave me another finif to tide us over."

"I don't know that I like that," Will said. "She's going to get wise."

"What else could I do?" John walked to the porch and opened the door. "It's going to change, we just need a good score day after tomorrow." He picked up a stack of pawn tickets and began to peel through them, dropping them on the table one at a time. He looked around the room. "Not much left here to trade. Besides, Uncle's only giving me a two-to-one rate."

"Pass me the Carnation," Will said.

"Where's the milk?"

Will nodded to indicate rows of empty bottles stacked against the wall. He walked to the sink and filled a glass two-thirds with water.

"Couldn't you've left me a little?" John said.

"I'll get more in the morning."

"Where's the paper?"

"It's on the chair."

"Those tellers won't give us any problems. I'll do the talking." John scanned the newspaper for the daily number then tossed it on a pile of discarded papers in the closet.

"Anything?" Will said.

"No." John sat down at the table. "The landlady asked me if we had any milk stolen. Said the police have been checking porches."

"What did you tell her?"

"I told her we get it at the store. She said people have been complaining about missing bottles of milk. You think anyone saw you?"

"No." Will stirred his glass deliberately. "I guess we better double-up from now on."

"That's what I figure."

18

June 5, 1959

Sydenham Street reminded the Coyle brothers of what they didn't have and what always lay around the corner from them—the emerging American middle class life. Warm comfortable homes, ownership, small patches of green grass, hedges and flowers, places where real families lived. Tree-lined Sydenham Street intersected with blue collar Erie Avenue and its three and four story tenements. The brothers lived on the second floor of one of these tenements, became comfortable there and ensconced themselves into the fabric of the neighborhood. To their neighbors, they were polite boys who just lived quiet lives. But in the privacy of their apartment they were outlaws, converting their living space into a terrorist's bunker, stockpiling it with guns, hundreds of rounds of ammunition, gas masks and enough volatile chemicals to blow Sydenham Street and Erie Avenue all the way to Pittsburgh. Where they existed on a Spartan diet and prepared for battle—they spoke of robberies, survival tactics and mayhem. And when they left for extended periods of time, they booby trapped the apartment door with a loaded sawed-off shotgun.

Will looked out the rear window to Sydenham Street and the predawn night. Haloes of yellow street light hung over the neighborhood and the street glistened in the sheen of the morning dew. The air was warm and moist and the day began with the promise of another unseasonable round of heat.

147

He had a good view of the truck and he watched the driver exit the vehicle and deliver two more bottles of milk to a porch. He returned to the truck and moved again, standing behind the wheel as he made his way up the street.

"What do you think?" John said.

Will shut the window. "Let's go."

MILKMAN WARREN SAUNDERs had been working this route for four years and had never remembered losing more than one or two bottles. But in the last two weeks, he had complaints of more than twenty bottles stolen and the foreman had called him into the office. The supervisor informed him that the company had never lost so much product over such a short period of time and that he could expect unannounced route inspections.

John Coyle, his left hand in his pants' pocket slouched in an alley that ran between Erie Avenue and Sydenham, watched Saunders move in rhythm up the street, drive a short distance to the next pair of duplex homes, jump out with a carrier filled with bottles and run the milk to the porches. First the east side and then the west, back and forth until he reached the intersection with Butler Street. Then the milk truck stopped and male voices resonated near it with garbled conversation and an underlying murmur that resonated in the quiet neighborhood.

"Hey, Jimmy how's it going?" Saunders said from his truck.

"Ah, alright," Jimmy Kane said.

"What, you didn't miss us? Living the life of Riley. Sitting in a cruiser for ten days."

"Nah, it's not that. My kid just had his tonsils out. Five years old. Jesus, he's sick. Just lays there."

"Don't worry about it. My kid threw up pans of blood when he came out the operating room," Saunders said. "He'll be okay. Everyone has his tonsils out and everyone gets sick. It's that damn ether."

"But when it's your own and they're so small."

"I know, but give him a couple of days and you'll be givin' him a whack in the ass for gettin' into somethin'."

"Yeah, you're probably right."

"Say, listen. My boss is all over my ass because we're losing a lot of milk."

"Out of the truck?"

"No. Someone's been lifting it off the porches. "

The beat man put his foot up on the bumper and tied his shoe.

"If I have another week like last week, I'll be looking for a new job. And I like this one."

"Okay, I'll keep my eyes open," the cop said.

"Thanks, see you tomorrow." The milkman pushed the stick, Kane stepped away and the truck turned the corner.

At the other end of the street, John Coyle leaned one way and then the other, looking past the parked cars and the trees to get a better view. "He's gone," he said. "He was talking with someone, probably one of the neighbors."

"Kinda early to be gabbing with someone isn't it?" Will said.

"It must be five. Some of them are already up. Make it quick."

A few minutes later, Margaret Taylor thought she heard someone on her porch at 3716 Sydenham and called upstairs to her husband who was preparing for work. "Did you hear that?" she said. She retrieved a whistle that she kept on a hook by the entry and looked across the street to Eva Northrup's home. Per the prearranged plan she had with her neighbor, Margaret stooped down to her mail slot, filled her

149

lungs with air and prepared to blow the bejesus out of that whistle to alert Eva that the milk thief was there. Eva would use her telephone to call the police. But Margaret hesitated. She stood and ever so slowly pulled her curtain aside and looked out. She didn't see anyone on her porch and the street was quiet. And she wasn't going to be responsible for waking the neighborhood. So, she stood there and watched and listened.

In her Erie Avenue apartment, Sarah O'Brien started her day the same way she started all of her days. She rolled her wheelchair to the back kitchen door, opened it, looked up the alley to Sydenham Street in the obscurity of the pre-dawn darkness and offered up her suffering to God and prayed for relief from her difficult existence. She fingered her rosary beads and contemplating the suffering of Christ, began the second decade of The Sorrowful Mysteries.

With Margaret Taylor's milk in his canvas bag and a third bottle in his hand, Will Coyle started down the street to where his brother waited for him. The bottles grinded against each other and he held the bag close to stifle the sound. Someone coughed behind him and he turned. Four houses back, the beatman flashed a porch with his light, behind the hedges, down the sidewalk, and then around the car at the curb, moving through the neighborhood while painting it in light. Will saw him and jumped behind the bushes in front of 3712 and curled himself small.

Jimmy Kane moved down Sydenham with more purpose than the ordinary drag at the end of a midnight shift. The milkman is right, he thought. Every kid has his tonsils out and they get sick. Give them a week and they're raising Cain again. He paused at 3712, brushed it with the light and moved on to its mate at 3710. He continued this routine until he reached Erie Avenue where he stood in the middle of the street, lifted and relieved, consoled by the milkman's good words. He postured with his hands behind his back, turning and taking in the silence of the moment and he gazed into the sky as if he recognized the immense vastness of the cosmos for the very first time. A dog barked and he looked up the street. It was then that he noticed the changes to his route and made entries in his notebook—*3702-3704 painted brown. Yeah, I like that. That's what I would have done if I owned it. And that one there, on the right, it's occupied again. A vacant house is just problems.* He admired the street and thought that it could be on the cover of LOOK Magazine. He stepped out smartly, began his last swing and wondered if the boys at the station would open up a tavern to celebrate his two year anniversary on the job. *Two years, where did the time go. Jeez, everyone has their tonsils out. My boy is going to be fine.*

John saw his brother come down the stairs, but then he disappeared. He saw the cop walking down the same sidewalk and flashing his light onto the porches. Reached into his pants' pocket and slid out the .32. The cop coming closer. He pushed his face out of the darkness, slouched against the building with the gun behind his leg and watched the beat man complete his rounds. The cop stood at the end of the street not more than twenty feet away, looking up and making notes. Will was out of sight. The patrolman began to move again and John saw him walking in the middle of the street, heard him whistling as he swung his flashlight back and forth. And as he moved farther away, John also lost sight of him, just saw the light, sparking up here and there like heat lightning, exposing the entry of a home, sweeping a sidewalk or splashing off the metal of a parked car. Then a shot sounded. The beam of light jolted into the black and blue sky and it disappeared.

He heard him coming up the middle of the street. The younger Coyle saw the light, heard the shoes scuffling

151

winter's leftover sand. He fled the cover of the bushes and jumped the stairs, the bottles of milk clanging in the bag against each other and he fell in a heavy-footed stumble against a parked Buick. The bag dropped and one of the bottles broke. The milk leaked out of the bag and it began to pool where he squatted.

Kane ran towards the noise. "Come out with your hands up." He fisted the handle of his revolver without removing it from its holster.

The milk continued to leak out of the bag and Will knelt down in the liquid to make himself small. He heard the patrolman coming. Pulled the .38 revolver from his pocket. The footsteps so close, he could see the cop's light, falling just beyond the end of the Buick. "Come out with your hands up or I'll shoot," Kane said. Windows lit up on the street as if in response to the order. Will stood, his hands over his head, one with a bottle of milk, the other with the .38.

"What're you doing there?" Kane said. He moved closer.

"I couldn't sleep . . . the heat."

Kane shined his light and saw the bottle. "What've you got there?"

The muzzle blast lit up Will's face and the shot resonated throughout the neighborhood. A porch light went on across the street. More shots sounded. More flashes. A dog barked. Then another. In the alley, John Coyle waited and readied himself.

The first bullet entered Jimmy Kane's stomach. He teetered with his hand over his abdomen and fell against the fender of the car, the blood pumping through the hole in his shirt and staining his fingers red. "Oh, my God!" He felt sick and unhinged. Then angry. *Why didn't you see the revolver? A milk thief shot you?* "Hands up!" Then a second bullet struck him in the right arm. "Stop!" The patrolman stumbled towards the rear of the car. Will hounded him around the

Buick in a trail of white footprints and shot at him like two kids playing cops and robbers. He fired again, striking the cop in his left arm and Kane yodeled in a high pitched clamation. Then he shot him in the back, the bullet tore through his organs and exited his chest. Kane drew his weapon and fell against the passenger side of the car, the gun clanking against the fender. It hung limp at the end of his arm. He collapsed onto the sidewalk on his hands and knees. His cap fell into the gutter. He coughed and blood ran out of his mouth, his body twitched in a terrible convulsion. Coyle fired one more round. The bullet struck him again in the back and he fell, sprawled face down over the edge of the sidewalk, the revolver still in his hand, the flashlight rolling away and lodging itself between the Buick's tire and the curb. Will stood over him, holding the bottle of milk and stared at his ashen face. Kane shivered, his eyes opened, turned up glazed and mottled. He tried to speak, but his lips moved silently. Blood drooled from his mouth and it gurgled in his throat. "You screwed up everything," Will said. "I wouldn't have had to do it." The wounded patrolman moved his hand along the edge of the curb and touched Coyle's shoe in a desperate reach for life. Will recoiled and jumped back. A pool of blood began to form under the patrolman. It leaked away from him and some of it mixed with the spilt milk. Air rushed from his mouth in a long repentant sigh and he lay still with his cheek on the lip of the curb. A shrill whistle blew out from one of the houses.

Will knelt on one knee next to the dead patrolman, "You shouldn't have come back," he said. He saw the expression on Kane's face. His mouth was open and he looked back in wonder.

Margaret Taylor saw him, saw him fire the gun again and again. She thought she would be sick to her stomach. But she opened the mail slot and blew the whistle until the sound

153

screeched in her ears and filled the street with a scream. She blew it with all of her breath. And when she exhausted herself, she took another deep breath and blew it again.

The man was running fast and the neighborhood dogs were barking. Lights came on in the houses and there were voices. Loud voices. A whistle pierced it all. From the alley, John saw the man coming. He was running fast, under the trees and in and out of the streetlight. And splitting the shadows and making his own shadow. So much so that John couldn't tell whether he was the cop or his brother. He aimed his .32 up the street in the direction of the oncoming runner and decided that if it was the former, he would drop him. Drop him dead.

Sarah O'Brien was praying her last Hail Mary in the decade when she heard the gunshots, the anguish of the police officer and the terror in his voice. And she saw the devil himself as he ran under the streetlight at the beginning of the alley with a gun in his left hand and a canvas bag in the other. He sprinted past her opened door and vanished into the darkness.

Will emerged from the fabric of the street, exploding out of the background of the tidy little neighborhood and ran down the alley past Sarah O'Brien's open door, never seeing his older brother. John remained in place with the .32 pointed up the street, laying in ambush for the pursuing cop. The whistle blew again. He remained in the shadows for another minute and when no one came, he slipped away from all of it, the noise, the confusion. That damn whistle and the howling of dogs.

ON SYDENHAM STREET, the day divorced itself from the night in noise and anger. Sirens, shouts and police radio transmissions echoed in the street of row houses. Blue and red lights reflected off them in color and newspaper photographers lit up the morning with flash bulbs and strobe lights. Curious bystanders gathered near number 3712, smoked their cigarettes and crushed the butts into the street not far from the body. Wives followed their husbands out onto the porches and cautioned them as they left for work. Some teenage boys reenacted the killing, claiming they saw the whole thing, but when the cops asked them what they had witnessed, they said, "nothin'" and slipped away. A drunk staggered jiggy up the sidewalk and he wandered from side to side. When he reached the scene, he leaned against a picket fence outside one of the row houses. He spoke in gibberish and his body jerked convulsively. "The Russians did it," he jabbered. The crowd laughed and the cops pushed back and walled them off from the scene. They swore at them, told them they'd be back, and promised that every mother's son would see them. They cursed the day, raised up Jimmy Kane and carried him away.

IN THE APARTMENT, John stood with his back to the sink, making small circles in the air with a glass jar and he watched the colorless liquid swirl, mesmerized by its lazy turn. Ambient light leaked into the room from behind the drawn shades. Furniture barricaded the front door. "I'm thinking we should lay low," he said. Will shivered in his underwear and flinched at the ordinary sounds of the house. He changed into a clean pair of slacks and stuffed his blood stained trousers and shoes into a brown bag. Then he skittered through the rooms jacked up and electric, piled up weapons and ammunition for a possible siege. He went to the front window. "They come in, we'll blast them." He collected the sawed-off shotgun and boxes of 00 buck from the bedroom. "Five times I shot him," he said. "Five times. He wouldn't go down. He screwed up everything." He opened the cylinder of his revolver, dumped the spent shells into his hand and stuffed the expended rounds into his pocket. John placed the glass jar on the counter next to another bottle of colorless liquid. And he thought on it. He would get them out of this. He just needed time to think. Will walked to the window at the rear of the apartment. He pushed the curtain aside with the barrel of the shotgun and looked up the alley.

"I say we leave," he said.

"The streets are full of cops," John said. "Why make it easy for them?"

"What are we going to do?" Will returned to the kitchen and began to pace.

"We've been in tough places before and we'll get out of this one too. Let things settle down out there."

"He screwed up everything," Will said. "The Savings & Loan job. Everything."

John filled two small glasses.

"Why did he have to come back?"

"He had no say."

"What do you mean, he had no say. He could have walked away."

"No, he couldn't."

"Why?"

"It was his time. That's all."

"And what about us."

John looked at him. "We're at war." He handed one of the small glasses to his brother.

The brothers stood in the darkened room. Someone across the hall coughed. Two floors below, the muffled cries of a child. They stood there in silence in their reckless desperation, drinking shot glasses of Tennessee Whiskey.

19

The newspapers later reported that they had just vanished. Disappeared like Black Magic. They left the apartment not in a panic, but with purpose, moving up the avenue like shadows. Their escape wasn't a retreat, but a strategic withdrawal, a change in the battle plan. The Coyle brothers left their Erie Avenue apartment after all the police, the newspaper reporters, and the spectators went away. After men went off to work and children went off to school. After housewives locked their doors, pulled their shades and hid in their homes. They left the canvas bag with the broken milk bottle, some of their clothes, and Ralph Gallagher's wallet. About forty empty milk bottles and a floor stained by milk. They left an arsenal of weapons, boxes of ammunition, military gas masks, containers of sulfuric acid and strips of adhesive tape, nitric acid and a bottle of glycerol. They wrapped themselves in ammo belts and stuffed their pockets with guns and ammunition. They booby-trapped the front door with the sawed-off shotgun. And when they slipped down the back stairs and started down the avenue, the .38 Smith & Wesson that took Jimmy Kane's life lay open and harmless on the kitchen table.

They walked away like hunchbacks, dressed in layers of clothing and wearing the burden of their entire lives. In the hot and sultry weather, they quick-stepped up the busy avenue side-by-side for twenty-eight blocks and arrived two hours later at the Roxborough woods where they buried the spent shells and set up camp. And on the day that Jimmy Kane died on Sydenham Street, the brothers took the hill overlooking the Schuylkill River. John and William Coyle took the high ground.

June 6, 1959

THE WOODS HAD the pungent odor of rotting decaying things as John Coyle squatted on his haunches with a predatory view overlooking a large parking lot. He watched the men on the picket line pace the sidewalk in front of the manufacturing building. Will, back twenty yards and lost in the close vegetation of the woods leaned against a tree and urinated. A canteen truck entered the parking lot, blowing its horn and the men on the line broke. John could hear their general banter and one of them offered to pay for the coffee. His brother joined him and they squatted together. A two-door green Dodge entered the lot at the opposite end and it stopped, occupied by one man who exited the vehicle and began to walk away with a noticeable limp. They skidded down the hill, breaking revolvers from their trouser pockets, one brother raced to the front of the Dodge and the other placed himself behind it.

The pickets gathered around the canteen truck and spoke and joked with one another, broke out cigarettes and sipped the hot coffee, their signs upside down and leaning against the building. When the green Dodge drove past them with Will Coyle at the wheel, John beside him and the terrified owner in the rear. It turned out of the east end of the parking lot and headed toward the turnpike and New Jersey, and it disappeared from view.

Randolph, Massachusetts

FRANK MAHAN SAT on the fender of his vehicle, sipping on a bottle of grape and watched his boy hit the first single of his Little League career, a seeing-eye dribbler that died a few feet from the second baseman, a hit that was more like a well-placed bunt.

"That a way, Jack!" Frank said.

Later, they sat on stools at the Howard Johnson restaurant and ate ice cream.

"Finally, my first hit," the boy said. "I always play better when you're at the game, Dad."

"Got any games next week?"

"Tuesday, against the Indians."

"I'll be at the barracks. Sorry, Jack."

His son pushed the last of his ice cream around with a spoon. "Can't you get off one night? Some fathers are at every game."

"Don't you think I want to be there?"

"Ralph Hanabury's dad plays catch with him almost every day and that's why he's one of the best players."

He looked at the boy. "My job is different," he said. "Come on, you've got school tomorrow."

Jack picked up his glove and began to pound the pocket with a baseball.

"When I get a little more time on the job," he said. "I might get transferred closer to home and even if I was working, I could stop by the field and catch a little of the game."

"Really? When?"

"It's going to be a while. Probably not until the next class of troopers graduate."

"When's that?"

"I don't know." He placed his hand on his son's shoulder. "Don't ask so many questions, will ya'. You're starting to

159

sound like your mother, I can't be in two places at the same time."

"Is that what you two were arguing about?" the boy said. "About not being home much?"

"What were you doing, spying on us?"

"No. I just heard."

"How about we go to the beach tomorrow?"

"I thought you had to go back to the barracks."

"I do," Frank said. "But not until after supper. In the meantime, I want to see you knock one out of the park. That's what I want to see. And when you do, I'll be there."

They walked along the sidewalk, past the hardware store and the butcher market, his son tossed the ball overhead and Frank snatched it out of the air. "Can you keep a secret?"

"What is it?"

"Don't tell your mother yet because I've got to talk to the sergeant about getting a couple of days off."

"Don't tell her what?"

"I know a guy who owns a cottage in New Hampshire and he's letting us stay there for a couple of days."

"When?"

"Day after you get out of school."

"Is it near the water?"

"That's all I'm going to tell you for now."

"Is this a promise?"

"It's a promise."

When they reached the house, he pulled out the hose, sat on the front steps and sprinkled his lawn. While his son ran up the walk, tore open the front door and disappeared leaving the door hanging half open.

"Hey, shut the door," he said.

He sat there moving the water across the small patch of grass. The door remained half open and he heard the excitement in their voices, his children planning the number of swims they would take and the marshmallows that would be roasted over a fire. He heard them running around the house with shameless joy, burning the energy that a promise to children can create. And when Sheila told them to get ready for bed, they did so without the usual protest or bargaining.

He felt one of her hands on his neck and she brushed his hair with her fingers. She sat down next to him and wrapped her arms around his waist, her breasts brushing up against his arm and settling among his ribs. And when her lips touched his mouth, they spoke of things of the soul, of joy and the deep mysterious waters of womanhood. Her children delighted, she was delighted. They watched the water fall to the grass, her small patch of flowers and other living things.

20

Middleborough, Massachusetts

They bulled him into the room jacked-up with handcuffs and planted him in a chair.

"Sit down."

"Uh . . . okay. Can I call my wife?"

"We've already made a call."

"Please . . . Lord, how I prayed. I . . . I can't stop shakin'. I never thought I'd get outta there alive."

"Are you listening to me?"

"Yes . . ."

"Let's see if you can hold it together, okay pal."

"Yeah . . . sure. The handcuffs . . ." He twisted in the chair to show his wrists.

"Tell how us you came to be tied up with the Coyle brothers and maybe we'll make it a little more comfortable for you."

"Kidnapped . . . I told the . . . I told them in the woods."

"What is your full name?"

"William. Ah . . . Arthur Sedgwick."

"What is your home address?"

"Huh?"

"Where do you live?"

He looked at them wide-eyed. Back and forth as if he was reading their expressions. "Ah. 3219 Merritt Street Roxborough. Philadelphia. Oh, God . . ."

"Take it easy. When did you meet up with the Coyles?"

"Nine days ago. I think nine."

"June 6th?"

"A Saturday."

"You've been with them the entire time?"

"Yes."

"So what happened?"

"Ah . . . I went to the mill."

"What mill?" Come on, we're losing valuable time here while we're playing games."

"Frank Nelson Knitting Mill on Fountain Street in Manayunk. Near Roxborough."

"M-a-n-a-y-u-n-k?"

"Yeah."

"What time was this?"

"Two o'clock. No, it was 1:30."

"1:30 in the afternoon?"

"Yeah. Yeah, I remember the time because the canteen truck had just pulled up." He shook his head. "It's crazy . . . The truck arrived like every other day, blowing its horn. All seemed normal. Except the guys never saw me. I . . . I was invisible. My car drove right past them. Jeez, I know all those guys, they know my car."

"What were you doing there?"

"We were on strike." He watched one of them leave the room. "I went to the dye house to see the boys on the picket line. I heard we may be settling."

"Go on."

"I locked the car and began to walk away and this boy comes up to me. I don't think nothing of it. The next thing I know . . . No, he's the driver. They look alike."

"Just a moment. Hello."

"Is that my wife on the phone?"

"He's reported missing? Okay, thanks."

"Did the police talk to my wife?"

163

"Not yet. They verified your story though. Stand up so I can remove the handcuffs. Would you like a cup of coffee?"

"No, just water."

"Get him some water. Here, wipe your face."

"I don't mean to blubber. I thought I was a dead man."

"You were about to identify which brother was the driver. Turn the picture over and read the back."

"William."

"William Coyle?"

"Yes."

"What kind of driver was he?"

"Good driver. If the speed sign said 35, then he drove at 35.

"And John was the one who stuck the gun in your ribs?"

"Yes."

"So, we get this straight. John approached you while you were walking towards the dye building and put a gun in your ribs?"

"That's right. Said this is a holdup."

"Then the driver, William came up from behind you."

"Right. Stuck a gun in my back. Said, 'get in the car.'"

"How do you know it was a gun?"

"I didn't have to see it."

"Go on."

"I couldn't open the door because the lock don't work on the driver's side. So, I go around and open up the other side and the first one shoves me into the back seat."

"John."

"Yeah. He says, let me see your wallet. I hand him the wallet, but I kept my hand on it. He says, let me have it, kind of mean like. I'm not going to take it, he says. I'll give it back. So, I let go and he takes the cash. Then he gave it back."

"Here's your water."

"Thanks." He took the mug with two hands and drank it all.

"Did they threaten you?"

"Couple of times, yeah. When I started to think of my family . . ." He ran the back of his hand across his eyes. "I asked them if they would let me go home to see my wife or at least let her know I was okay. I said to them, give me a break. And this one here got snotty."

"John."

"Yeah, said you're not being a crybaby are you. My ankle is never going to be right. Don't hear me crying, do you? So, stop your bellyaching. Because I would rather kill you than leave you go home. Killing you wouldn't bother me none. None at all. From that time on, I kept my mouth shut unless they spoke to me."

"John's ankle is injured?"

"He walks with a limp."

"Did you have any idea who they were?"

"I thought they were just a couple of crazy boys."

"Did you know they murdered a Philadelphia policeman?"

"Not at first."

"What changed your mind?"

"They kept turning the radio dial to find a Philadelphia station. One broadcast mentioned the shooting and they looked at each other kinda strange, but said nothing. Sometimes, they didn't speak at all, just made a nod or something. Like they had their own kind of language."

"And you didn't talk to them?"

"No sir, not after what he said to me. I don't chew the rag much anyway."

"Do you know how you got here?"

"I was too nervous at first. Then I started looking at license plates and signs. Next thing I know, I'm in Massachusetts. That's when I started to shake. I didn't think I'd ever make it home again."

"Did they make any stops?"

"Yeah, they bought clothes because the ones they had on were pretty mussed up."

"Where did they stop?"

"I don't know, some big department store in Massachusetts. Just one went in, the driver. The other one stayed in the car. Yeah, that boy there. He did all the running around. He came back in about fifteen minutes with a big bag of clothes."

"William went into the store and John stayed in the car with you?"

"Right."

"What did they call each other?"

"You mean names?"

"Yeah."

"John and Will."

"Not Jack or Billy?"

"They didn't use their names very often."

"Did they make any other stops around here?"

"A little store, like a corner store. They got food and soda."

"And then where did they go?"

"They kept riding around until they found that desolate dirt road and we ended up in the woods."

"What time of night do you think it was?"

"I'd say close to eleven or twelve."

"Did they give you any reason for staying in the woods?"

"No. But they seemed to know what they were looking for because when they were driving around they missed a road and had to turn and go back."

"Was there any talk the first night?"

"No, nothing."

"How about later? Did they talk about anything?"

"They didn't talk much. But I do remember them mentioning the Russians a couple of times."

"The Russians?"

"That's what they talked about."

"Then they just went to sleep?"

"After they changed their clothes."

"Changed clothes?"

"They slept in one set of clothes and when they went out they changed into another set."

"And what kind of shape would you'd say they were in?"

"Good shape, they're young. They haven't eaten in a while though. And the younger one, he and I had dysentery one day. I think it was from some bad bologna."

"Did you leave the car that first night?"

"No. I hardly closed my eyes. But if I did and opened them, I'd find one of them staring at me in the dark."

"When did you first leave the car?"

"In the morning to go to the bathroom."

"Nobody around?"

"Not a soul. But we did go out that day, I think. I can't remember now."

"Sunday?"

"I think so. They got a little more nerve. It was kind of strange."

"What do you mean?"

"They seemed to be looking for something. I don't know even if they knew what."

"Where did they go?"

"They bought a newspaper at a little country store and got an address for a rental apartment. An awful long trip, maybe fifteen to twenty miles. They couldn't find it at first and then they asked a policeman for directions."

"Where?"

"I think in Fairhaven. There was a sign on a store. Drove right up to where he was directing traffic, bold as brass."

"And the cop didn't get suspicious?"

"No. They acted like a couple of lost college kids."

"Then what?"

"They sat outside an apartment for a while and then this one here said to forget it and they left."

"John said to forget it?

"Yes."

"Where is that newspaper now?"

"They used it for toilet paper."

"Where else did they go that Sunday?"

"First National store in Fairhaven. I figured they were going to rob it the way they were jumping around."

"But they didn't?"

"No."

"Was the store open for business?"

"There we're a lot of people in it. I think that's why they didn't rob it."

"You must have day wrong. It wasn't Sunday."

"Why?"

"Blue Laws. Large grocery stores aren't open on Sundays here."

"Oh, they went there a couple of times. I might have gotten the days mixed up."

"But you're pretty sure that they wanted to rob that store?"

"Yes, because each time they went there, they tied me up first."

"Where else did they go?"

"The beach."

"The beach? Where?"

"At a pond in Carver. The Myles Standish State Forest."

"How do you know it was Myles Standish?"

"I saw a sign. They went there by the back roads. Stayed away from the main ones."

"Did they go there any other time?"

"Almost every day."

"But there was no rhyme or reason to their movements?"

"Didn't appear to be. But the longer they sat, the crazier they became. Especially the older one, I think he's tormented. Had to be moving, scheming. But that day we first went to the beach, he was different. Said it was his birthday."

"John."

"That's what he said. It was the one time he seemed almost human. Let me stretch my legs."

"How long did they stay there?"

"Three or four hours."

"Did they swim?"

"They waded in the water. Took turns. Folded up their trouser bottoms. Otherwise, they just sat there in the sun at a picnic table, watching other people."

"And these people saw the Coyle brothers and you? No food, no blanket, no swim trunks?"

"They walked right by us. And this boy . . ."

"Why didn't you say something or run?"

"Because they both had guns. Made it very clear if I even thought about running."

"You started to say something about a boy?"

"Just before the thunderstorm. There was this family. And the father and his boy were playing catch."

"DON'T LET IT go in the water," he said.

He watched his older boy chase down a baseball that rolled across the sandy apron along the shore of the pond. A breeze picked up and it roughed the water in two direc-

169

tions. The tops of the trees leaned one way and then the other. "Looks like it might blow up," he said.

"Why don't you stop now and get him to eat?" Sheila said.

"He's getting better. Jack could be a pretty good little infielder if he put his mind to it."

"Coffee?"

"Yeah."

The boy ran to the blanket, pounding the baseball into his glove.

"Remember to move your feet and square yourself up with the ball," he said.

"Come on, Dad, one more. High fly."

"Time to eat."

"Just one."

He threw the ball high overhead over an open space of sand and the boy began to backpedal.

Sheila handed him a thermos cup of coffee and put a sandwich on the blanket. "I'm looking forward to our New Hampshire vacation," she said. "That was nice of that man to let us use his cabin."

"I don't think Art opens it up until summer. We're doing him a favor by getting it ready for him."

"It was still nice. How do you know him?"

"He hauls cars for the barracks . . ."

"Frank, is that man talking to Jack?"

"He has his baseball."

"Who are those men?" Sheila said.

"They've been sitting there for a couple of hours."

Sheila's mouth was moving and she was saying something when he walked away, the thermos cup overturned and the coffee spilt, the sand turning a cocoa color brown.

He saw the three men sitting in a strange tableau at the picnic table where the sand ended and the pine needles began near the entrance to the woods. One young man was shirt-less. He had pale skin and a flushed face with red-rimmed eyes. And he was staring down at his boy and holding the ball in his hand, sitting there in feigned leisure. A second in a sleeveless undershirt had a long, ugly purple scar on his forearm. He was of similar age and build as the first and sat across from him, looking toward the water disinterested. The third was older than the other two and he looked like he hadn't shaved in a while. He sat there in a chair wrinkled and disheveled, a countenance of pain and worry, his mouth agape.

JOHN COYLE SAW the man, saw him coming.

He sat on the edge of the table with his feet up on the bench, flipping the ball in the air and catching it. The wa-ter shimmered on the lake behind the man as he climbed the sandy embankment and John saw him. He was lean and strong with short burnt auburn hair.

He came to the table and John held the ball, rubbing it between his hands. The boy smiled and plead with his eyes. For a moment, John gazed off into the distance then turned to them, the father and the son and when he finally spoke, he said, "Hey, Buddy" with detachment in his voice. "I guess this here belongs to you." He tossed the ball up again and caught it in his hand. Held it out for all to see and then he measured the man in a coy way. The father nodded, but said nothing. "There you go," John said and he tossed the ball to the boy. The father and son turned and left. And as he watched them walk away, he said, "I might have been a little stubborn when I was young. I wasn't a bad boy. But they just had to poke you with their fingers, drive home some rule or other, jam them hard for no good reason."

The sky blackened with little notice as a quick-moving thunderstorm approached. Wind accompanied the rapid change and it lifted the sand in swirls. Pockets of sand dust and debris blew across the long length of the beach. The lifeguard blew her whistle, cleared the water and folded her umbrella as families gathered their belongings and ran for the shelter of their cars. Rain began to fall on the beach in a drumming and high lightning lit up the sky. Rivulets of water ran to the shore. Within seconds, the beach and the Myles Standish State Forest became a deserted miserable place.

"THEN WHAT HAPPENED, Mr. Sedgwick?"

"I think those boys are unpredictable in a crazy sort of way, capable of doing anything at any time. But that day on the beach, the older one, he seemed to forget who he was and what he had done."

"What do you mean?"

"He's a restless soul without a friend in the world, 'cept his brother. And he can blame everyone else for his problems, thought he deserved a pass on everything. But seeing that boy and his father seemed to trigger something in him. He never took his eyes off them."

"Did he say anything else?"

"No, not right away. Later in the car."

"What did he say?"

"He said to no one in particular. 'Did you see that man with the boy? Playing catch?'"

"'I saw him,' his brother said. 'Hell John, we all saw him.'"

"'Never did play ball with my father,' John said. 'Did you Mr. Sedgwick?'"

"My father worked his whole life in a mill, I said. Forty-one years, six days a week. Sundays, he rested."

"'You got a son, don't you?' he said. 'Did you ever play catch with him?'"

"Once or twice, I said. And this was when he started to talk peculiar."

"'Daddy was a card,' he said. 'Talk a dog right off a meat wagon. A charmer. Only problem was he talked away his life, especially when he was drinking. But you can give him a pass on that one because that's all they would let him do— talk, I mean. They wouldn't let him work. Would pick up a job at the union hall and everything would be fine. Had purpose. Then those bastards would let him go just before his thirty days were up when they had to make him permanent. Pay him benefits, you know, insurance and such. So, back to the hall he'd go. Talking and drinking.'"

"Then his brother said to him, 'What are you bringing this up for, John?'"

"I don't remember word for word what he said, but it was something like . . . 'That man playing ball with the boy. You can feel him as certain as you can feel rain. Yes indeed. And it comes on you in a rush and a shiver.'"

"What do you think he was talking about?"

"Beats me. It wasn't so much what he said though, it was how he said it. He spoke in a soft flat voice like the life had gone out of it longer than he could remember."

"So you think there was some kind of connection between John and this father?"

"I think he admired him in some odd way. And I think he would have shot him dead and not thought a thing about it."

"Hmm. Anything else?"

"Something happened between the two of them, him and the man. Like they recognized something in each other. When the thunderstorm came, everyone ran. But those boys walked away and entered the path like a Sunday stroll. In the forest, I looked back towards the beach. I could see the fam-

173

ily scurrying about gathering their things, the rain coming down in buckets. And the lightening. They were standing on the beach, loaded down like pack animals. But that father, he just stood there in the storm, staring at the place where we had all been sitting. His wife yelling at him to get his attention."

"Did either of the brothers see him?"

"No."

"And this was on Sunday, June 10th?"

"Yeah, John's birthday."

21

On the day that John and William Coyle and their hostage sat in the sun at the Myles Standish State Forest, over a thousand mourners passed the coffin containing Jimmy Kane. At the same time, on the hottest June 10th on record, Philadelphia cops from the 39th and other city districts rolled up Sydenham Street and Erie Avenue, tossed the Tioga neighborhood, stopped and pat frisked anybody and everybody and interviewed four hundred residents because a brother had been murdered—every son, husband, brother and boyfriend, student, mill worker and seaman. White collar and blue collar, the underemployed and the unemployed, ex-cons, ex-cops, loan sharks and every "swinging dick" fourteen years of age and older. They swept the neighborhood in a door-to-door and stopped everything that moved. They busted flophouses, whorehouses and gin joints in the Tenderloin area. And they rousted the Irish gangs in the Brickyard and the German gangs in Dogtown. Charlotte Hinkle told them about her polite and mannerly tenants, John and Gilbert Kessler. Polite boys, down-on-their-luck boys, lent-them-a-couple-of-finifs boys. Then those singular cops grew impatient and she fingered those boys as the wanted Coyle brothers in the FBI bulletin. The owner of Schmid's Tavern marked them as two stupid mugs who waved their guns in the wrong place and cleaned out the cash registers, knowing that a thousand cops would find them before a couple of stiffs with heaters. Margaret Taylor who blew her whistle and Sarah O'Brien who prayed her rosary put the killing on Will and others put it on John. The cops kicked in the door to the Coyles' apartment, sidestepped the booby trapped sawed-off shotgun and seized their arsenal of weapons, ammunition and enough volatile chemicals to level the apartment house and most of the buildings half a block away. They located an invoice for John Coyle from the Fairhaven and Buzzards Bay Gas Company and contacted the Massachusetts authorities. And on June 10th, the day John Coyle celebrated his twenty-fourth birthday, the Philadelphia Police and the District Attorney met the press. They released the indictments and arrest warrants for the brothers. A national broadcast was issued and a shoot-to-kill order given.

22

Jazz played in the hallway again. And light spilled out from under his door. But the saxophone improvisation heard from his room seemed a bit intrusive this night, demanding rather than being the usual respectful inconvenience.

He knocked on the door and opened it. "Bad time?" Frank said.

"Come on in," he said.

The dog stood stiffly and came to him and he rubbed his head and patted his shoulder. "He's slowing down," Frank said.

"His hindquarters are shot. Getting up to greet you is a three-act play."

"You never mentioned how you got him."

"A local farmer. Guess he was on the run and he developed a taste for chicken. So, he called the barracks."

"I'm surprised he didn't shoot him."

"I asked him about that and he said there was something about the dog. Seemed pretty sharp. He thought maybe we could use him like a military canine. I told him we've got the bloodhounds, but I took him anyways and old Charon became the barrack's dog." He looked at the dog and the dog lifted his head as if he understood the conversation and was about to offer an opinion. "I haven't got the heart to put him down. I know I'm being selfish, but he's all I got."

Inside the uncomfortable room, the window was shut and cigarette smoke hung in the air like a web. Cunningham sat barefoot on the bed, shirtless and dressed in khakis with his back resting against the headboard, his gun belt and service revolver hung from the post. His face was flushed and a cigarette dripped from the corner of his mouth. A half empty bottle of Four Roses bourbon rested between his legs. He sat there with the water glass in one of his hands and the distant look of a person resigned to a constant fate.

"Close the door," he said.

"No fan?" Frank said.

"I don't sleep well in a room with the sound of mechanical noise."

"Do you mind if we turn the music down a little?"

"Is it bothering you?"

"No, not at all, it's just a little loud in the hall."

"Shut it off if you want."

"That's not necessary."

"Pull up a seat." He turned down the volume and drew down on the water glass. He drank and then let his head rest against the headboard. "Where is everyone?"

"A few of the boys went to see *Some Like It Hot*."

"Marilyn Munroe. Now, there's a fine looking woman." The song ended and the needle slid back and forth at the spindle. He turned the record and the music lifted into the room again. "Bar's open," he said. "Drink?"

"Can't stay long. I've got In-service training in the morning at the academy."

"Have one."

"Got beer?"

"The cheap shit." He lifted a bottle of Carlings out of a tub of ice.

Frank balanced himself on a milk crate and drank his beer and it went down easy in the stifling room. He glanced at a dead grenade on Cunningham's bureau that propped up a photograph from his time in the Army.

"What's the word?" he said as he brushed cigarette ash off his khakis.

"I wanted to ask you . . ."

"You like this jazz?"

"Yeah."

"It reminds me of the stuff I heard in that little hole in the wall in Paris I told you about."

"Ever think of going back?"

"Maybe, some day. A little early right now, memories are too clear." He crushed the cigarette into an ashtray and swallowed the rest of his drink.

"Thought about what you said my first day. About not being in the service."

"Forget it."

"Sometimes, I wish I had signed up."

"It's not for everyone." He mixed himself another full glass so much so that he had to hold it carefully to keep it from spilling.

"I thought you believed every father's son should go into the service."

"Yeah, well." He sipped down the drink below the lip of the glass and placed it on the nightstand. "I think most guys can benefit from it."

"But you just said . . ."

He laughed. "I'm not making much sense. Must be the liquor." He checked the cigarette package, but it was empty. He crushed it and threw it into a bucket in the corner of the room. He opened the night stand and removed a carton of Lucky Strikes. Pulled the cellophane from a package and lit one. "I should have said some guys can grow up in the service and some don't need to. And some bastards ought to march into the arena whether they want to or not."

"Who's that?"

"The bomb makers. The tanks and all the toys of war. If you're going to build the toys, you should be made to play the game. Feel the burn. And the profiteers too. If you're going to get rich on someone else's misery, then you should live the misery."

An open ditty bag sat on the floor next to his bed and the bag contained loaded ammunition belts—one with rifle slugs, the other assorted shotgun shells. A shotgun lay on the floor. And next to that an M-1 rifle. Frank nodded to the bag. "Getting ready for something?"

"I was a Boy Scout." Cunningham stuck his hand into the pail of ice. "You know what they say, be prepared."

Frank finished the beer and stood. "I need to get some shuteye."

"You just got here." PK handed him another beer. "You started to ask me something."

"Oh, yeah. I was at Myles Standish in Carver . . ."

"Sit down."

He sat back down. "I don't know what I'm thinking."

"What are you talking about?"

"Did you ever read a Wanted Bulletin for a bum or hear a broadcast and start to think he's standing right in front of you when he's really still in Philadelphia?"

"Jesus, Priest. Either I've had too much of the holy water or you got in here without me knowing it and drank yourself stupid."

"No, listen." The milk crate snapped as he shifted his weight. "You know how you hear about some guy wanted for a crime somewhere else, particularly a serious crime, and you start to get the feeling that he might show up right in your own backyard. Maybe, there's some connection with New England or even Massachusetts. Like he grew up here or lived here once, but hasn't been back in years. And you start to believe he'll show up. Matter of fact, you're hoping he'll show up. Even wishing it so."

Cunningham studied him. "Why, did you see someone?"

"I don't know. Ah, it sounds stupid."

"If you mean you're always looking, that's a good thing. When you least expect it, Priest. It happens when you least expect it."

He could feel the sweat, the need of a shower. It ran down his legs and his shirt stuck to his back. Frank took a moist hand from the beer bottle and wiped his face. "Jesus, this place is as hot as Lucifer's balls."

"Open the window if it bothers you."

He unlocked the window, stood there and drank his bottle empty. "I should go."

"Don't run off, Priest. I'm celebrating." Cunningham fished another bottle from the ice. "Fifteen years ago today, we landed in Europe. Come on, sit down. Have one more for my anniversary."

"Last one." He took the beer and opened it.

"You gotta laugh. At the beginning of the war, I wanted in like every other guy and my mother wouldn't hear of it. I was an only kid, you see, and my father was dead. So, I tell her I am going to join the National Guard. Imagine her surprise when they reactivated the Rainbow Division and pooled the Guard from all over the country to form the 42nd."

"She must have been horrified."

"Yeah, God rest her soul."

"Where did you go?" he said.

"Ah, let's see. Marseille in December, 1944 and then to Alsace near Strasbourg. By March of '45, we were in Germany."

"Did you see a lot of resistance?"

"Yeah. We lost some good guys too." Cunningham took the photograph from the bureau and sat on the edge of the bed. He pointed to several soldiers. "This guy, this guy. Oh yeah, and this guy. I forgot about him. All gone."

"Were you close to any of them?"

"When you're living on top of one another, you can't help but be close. Some guys you like, some not so much. And some, you'd cut off your left nut for. Same thing as here. The loudmouth, you know the guy who uses his mouth to hide his fears. The religious guy who'll accidently drop a rosary from his pocket while looking for change. Maybe finger the beads when the artillery starts to fly. Then there's the intro-vert, the guy who won't look you in the eye when you pass him. Those guys are sleepers. They'll rise to the occasion like they were born for it. And then the ordinary Joes. One guy from Brooklyn talked about his family all the time. I felt like I knew them." He pointed to one of the soldiers in the picture. "That's him, Bernie Jacobs. Told me he wanted to introduce me to his sister after the war." He handed the pho-tograph to Frank. "I think he felt I was a good guy. There's honor in being trusted with someone's sister."

"What happened to him?"

"Land mine."

"I'm sorry." Frank held the photograph closer. "You guys look like you've been through hell. Where is this anyways? It looks like it's outside some kind of compound or some-thing."

"The main gate to the Dachau Concentration Camp."

"Jeez."

"We were chasing Germans back to Munich and got di-verted. Arrived about the same time as the 45th Infantry and the 20th Armored. Thirty thousand prisoners in that camp not counting the dead and the near dead." He paused "What came to greet us wasn't human. Thirty thousand bags of bones." He took his drink from the nightstand. Stared into the nearly empty glass. "When you think of it, the size of a small city."

"I imagine the survivors were alive by the grace of God."

"Think it might have been the power of hate."

"They must have been glad to see Americans."

"Yeah. So glad that some of them climbed the fence to get to us and were electrocuted."

Frank looked over at him. "Was there a battle for the camp?"

"No, the Germans were waiting for us with white flags."

"I remember hearing about a train full of bodies?"

"Yeah, a forty-car Death Train from Buchenwald. We found it outside the walls as we approached the camp, open box cars filled with thousands of those poor bastards. Stacked up on one another, flies and maggots feasting on them, bodies on top of the pile ended in desperation, the dead crawling over the more dead. Some died on the ground after they had escaped the box cars." He crushed his cigarette into an ashtray. "A lot of them had bullet holes in the backs of their heads. We figured there were about five thousand in all. The Nazis had dumped thousands of bodies before we got there and there were still over two thousand inside the cars."

"Did any survive?"

"About eight hundred. And some of them just long enough so we could bury them."

"Jesus that must have . . ."

"It was. Guys puked. Some got pissed. I remember leaving with my fists clenched. A lot of guys swore after that they would never take another German prisoner."

"When was your friend killed?"

"Day that picture was taken."

Frank shifted and the milk crate cracked again.

"They gave us roving guard duty around the outside perimeter. Me and Bernie were on a demolition team sent to sweep the area first. The German tower guards told us that there weren't any mines there. He was outside one tower and I was by another. I heard an explosion and I knew right away. He stepped on an old land mine and it shredded him. Sat there in a pool of his blood, staring confused at a place where his legs should have been." He paused. "I don't know what they could have done for him."

"How old was he?"

"A kid, eighteen, nineteen maybe, one of the younger guys in our unit. A smart son-of-a-bitch. He was the last guy I figured would set off one of those explosives. But we had been in some fierce fighting days before we got there. I think he was wasted. Hell, we were all wasted. Just lost his concentration."

"That would have pissed me off."

"Bet your ass." He wiped his mouth with the back of his hand.

The curtain on the window lifted briefly as a small rush of warm air entered from the night. The music began to repeat itself while the needle on the '78' slid back and forth across a scratch in the vinyl. Cunningham stared at the player while a piano solo began again and again.

"Do you want me to fix it?" Frank said.

"I got it." Cunningham leaned over and lifted the needle and put it down on a different place on the record.

"I'm sorry about your friend, PK."

"Yessir."

Frank put his empty bottle into the waste basket. "I've got to go, the first class is at 0700."

"And you don't want to be late for that first class."

Frank ignored the sarcasm. He laid the photograph on PK's bureau. "The Germans, they told you there were no explosives, right?"

"Yeah, that's right."

"The tower guards?"

"Yeah." Cunningham looked up at him. "We pulled them out and lined them up."

He stood by the door and he stared into the uncomfortable room. Cunningham sat on the edge of the bed with his forearms resting on his thighs and his hands clasped. "We heard shooting coming from the coal yard behind the interior wall, a machine gun. This lieutenant from the 45th comes running out of there and he's screaming at us, 'Shoot them bastards. Shoot them all.'"

"Kill them?"

"At the base of the tower? Yeah, we lined up the sons of bitches and shot them all."

Frank looked at him. "But they lied about the land mines, right?"

"They didn't know."

"Why wouldn't they have known?"

"We found out later that the camp guards and the camp commandant screwed the night before we got there. These guys were regular Army sent there the day before the surrender. They had nothing to do with the camp." He reached up and pressed his fingers into his forehead. "There was an investigation."

"What happened?"

"Nothing."

Frank blew out his breath.

"Times I think, who gives a shit. But it gets to you, you know. Some particularly bad nights, it comes in odors."

"Ever talk to anyone?"

"Like who?"

"Some of the guys who were there."

"What's to say?"

"What about a priest?"

Cunningham looked over at him.

"They hear terrible stories all the time."

185

"Yeah, I just did."

"I'm not a priest, PK."

"You'll do."

"I don't think anyone would blame you."

"I think at times it's just a bad dream, or a lie someone told me."

"Maybe if you . . . Did you ever go see them?"

"Who's that?"

"Bernie's family."

"No. No, I never did. I suppose I should have."

Frank opened the door. He stood there holding it open. "Do you want me to douse the light?"

"Nah, it's okay."

Frank stood there.

Cunningham looked up. "Priest?"

"Yeah?"

"You're the first person I ever told about that."

Frank nodded. He closed the door slowly. The catch snapped shut and the metallic click echoed in the hall. Cunningham collected his drink and he sat there with the light jazz playing. The dog struggled to stand and he came and rested his head on his leg. PK stroked his head and when he stopped, the dog nuzzled his nose into his open hand. He resumed the massage and rubbed behind his ears, his neck and the length of his back. When he stopped, the dog puffed out a breath and then turned in circles until he found his place and lay down, his head resting on his front paws. After a few minutes, Cunningham drank down the bourbon and water and then stood and locked the window. He lay back down with one hand and arm behind his head, the other wrapped around the M-1 rifle. Listening to the jazz, listening to the bass and the wire brushes dusting the skin of a snare. Dressed in his khakis and sleeping the broken dreams of the tormented. And all of this in a well-lit room.

23

Middleborough, Massachusetts
Monday, June 15, 1959

They drove out of the woods again in the two-door green Dodge, down the trail of pine needles and sand, chased by a cloud of yellow-gray dust. Out of the woods where they had hunted with Charles Harnett, close to the intersection of Route 28 and Pine Street and Lindstrom's Gulf station. Where they had hidden away with their hostage, William Sedgwick, for nine days. From where they had traveled back country roads with him tied in the back seat while they conducted another reconnaissance of the First National store in Fairhaven. From where they had driven to the state park in Carver to sun bathe and wade knee deep in the cool June water. Where they watched ordinary people enjoy a day at the beach.

They had sat for days through periods of curious introspection at Myles Standish, through long silent rides along the Massachusetts coastline, through old whaling towns and towns with ghostly mills that once hummed with the promise of immigrants and American manufacturing. They broke down their five pistols after a day of rain and humidity, cleaned and lubricated them with penetrating oil found in Sedgwick's car. And when night came, they covered the back window sill with newspaper and laid the guns under the glass to complete the drying.

Sometimes at night, they just sat on the fenders of the Dodge speaking in short clipped sentences with meaning that Sedgwick failed to portend, acting like ordinary American boys hanging out at a local hamburger joint, sitting on the fenders of their souped-up jalopies and listening to Fats Domino or Ricky Nelson on the radio. Or they sat in silence bathed in Citronella with newspaper hats to protect their heads from the mosquitoes, wearing long sleeve shirts buttoned at the neck and wrists, the night air ripe with pine resin, listening to the wind break through the trees, the insects, the birds and the breath of nature. They sat there and heard things that most people will never hear, seen things right in the sight of every man, only submerged beneath the clamor of civilization.

The mission that John and his brother had selected hadn't been realized, at least their expectations of it. It faded somewhere on the highways between Pennsylvania and Massachusetts. They hid in the woods, their sustenance at first cheese and baloney sandwiches and Hostess cupcakes, which they shared with their hostage while they decided upon a course of action. As the money dwindled, so did the groceries—the cheese and baloney sandwiches replaced by small stale cake shells that tasted like sawdust and ice cream cones dropped by children and recovered in the trash. They stripped spent cigarettes, scavenged the tobacco and rolled their own. During the day, they aimlessly drove the countryside until they no longer had money for gas. And on the days leading to John's epiphany, the brothers and Sedgwick subsisted on crusts of bread and the slow purposeful consumption of two stale marshmallows.

On their ending Friday, the three men began an involuntary biblical fast. It was about this time that Sedgwick for some unknown reason found solace in the car's dashboard clock. After nine days of confinement in the Dodge with the two youthful murderers and put out of his mind, the non-threatening round face gave him comfort. Like the innocence of a child's expression. He was gaunt, dehydrated and foul smelling. Something the brothers didn't seem to mind, since they were only a tad bit better themselves.

The Coyles longed for freedom and the excitement of confrontation. They argued as to their next course of action, out of Sedgwick's listening distance. He could see them through the windshield across the clearing and assumed by their postures that Will was restless and John was calculating. Then on Sunday, John came upon some idea that Will acknowledged and the hostage knew by their preparations that they were about to become active and dangerous. The energized brothers discovered a vigor that had escaped them and their movements became purposeful. They wiped down their revolvers with oil once again and loaded them. Filled up three cartridge belts and fitted them to their lean feral bodies.

John thought on it some and submitted that the lack of food had been a good thing and he took to his preparations with a newly found focus of mind. He said that he envisioned a new beginning for them. That people would remember them years to come. Through Friday, Saturday and a quiet Sunday evening, the weather remained warm and uncomfortably humid while the brothers committed to a disciplined, centered existence. And it was during a quiet moment the last night with the clearing bright in the harsh light of a full moon that John sat on one of the car's fenders looking into the star scattered black sky. And Sedgwick sitting in front of him cross-legged on the forest floor.

"The spectra of all this allows you to make some considerations," John said.

Sedgwick looked back at him.

"What are your considerations?"

"In what way?"

John leaned back and stretched out his arms, indicating the whole of what surrounded them. "This, nature, the universe."

He followed Coyle's gaze to the sky. "It is God's handiwork."

"That's your first mistake."

"Why?"

"By placing someone even a god in charge of this natural place, a hierarchy is implied. If God first, then whom?"

"The Creator decides all things."

"But by empowering someone with the right to decide whether others may benefit from the natural order, you create anarchy."

"I don't know about that, but I believe that every gift of God in this universe is a blessing on all men."

"And I believe by creating the mythology of God, certain powerful men assume the right to grant access to all things including nature."

"There has to be order. Someone must make the rules."

John looked at him and then returned his gaze to the night sky. "The rule makers justify themselves by invoking God's name."

"He is the source of all things."

"The problem with your argument is that when the thought of God is established and the ladder of hierarchy created, someone is always designated the slave. All civilizations declare ownership of slaves."

"Slaves?"

"All of us who do the bidding for someone other."

Sedgwick looked up at him. "God will judge every man someday, including the rule makers."

"I have one more for you," John said. "What is our purpose here anyways?"

"Here?"

"This place. Our existence. What is our purpose?"

Sedgwick thought, here is an advantage. "God has a plan for all of us and He speaks to us in so many ways."

John looked down at him with a bemused expression.

"Really," Sedgwick said. "He does."

"And you believe that?"

"We have to."

John smiled. "It's a trick question," he said. "There is no answer to that inquiry. None at all."

Will joined John and they sat on the fenders looking at the sky. They appeared to assume the posture of a crude meditation and when completed, they bedded down for the night. In the morning, they changed into their public clothes, tied up Sedgwick once more and secured him in the back seat of the Dodge, promising to keep him safe. They drove onto Route 28, along the Cranberry Highway. They had found their life's fulfillment.

A HALF MILE away, Mrs. Kennedy tried to remember everything her son had told her about opening up the package store. But Mary had already broken the first rule— never open the store alone. Well, that couldn't be avoided, she thought as she closed the front door. The reason she was here in the first place was because her son couldn't get out of bed. Darn influenza. Her small brown Spaniel almost tripped her as it circled her feet while she searched the wall for the light switch. She walked the aisles as she had been instructed and inspected the shelves for cleanliness and product display. The safe was locked and she was glad that she didn't know the combination. The receipts and the cash that Billy had given her from Saturday's business, she placed into the register. The front door bell rang and she realized that she had broken her son's second rule— never leave the front door unlocked before the store is open. "Golly, I'm of a less suspicious nature than him. And God knows, I only have two hands."

"Hello Billy, you here? Sam Baker, the Miller salesman," a voice called from the front of the store. "Hello?"

"I'll be right there," she said.

The Miller salesman took a count, wrote an order for sixteen cases and left. She wiped down the counter and straightened the plastic Calvert Whiskey sign that hung on the wall above it. "This place could use a little brightening," she said and drew the blinds on the picture windows, the morning sunlight falling across the old wooden floor in wedges. Then she lifted the shade on the front door and turned the sign to read 'open'. The telephone rang and she went behind the counter to answer it.

"Checking in on me so soon?" she said. She wrapped the cord around her finger as she spoke. "Did your brother tell you to call me to make sure I hadn't burned the place down yet?" She laughed at her own expense. "Everything is fine. No, no problems."

The Coyle brothers entered the store and similar to the manager of the Buzzards Bay First National, Mary's first impression was that these clean shaven baby-faced boys were a couple of pranksters. Even though one held a black pistol in his hand and the other, the boy with the long thin face, held a silver plated one.

"This is a holdup," John said. "Mam, put that telephone down."

"Now, you listen boys. I know you're both underage, so don't be expecting to get any liquor here. My Billy would kill me."

John went directly to the cash register and began to clean it out.

"What are you doing?" she said. "Close that right now."

"Put the phone down," Will said. He jumped behind the counter and attempted to take the telephone from her hands. She pulled the receiver to her breast and turned her shoulder away while he wrestled with her to gain control. The Spaniel growled and pulled at Will's trouser cuff with his teeth. She stumbled and the two of them fell against the wall. "Call the police," she screamed. She heard her daughter say, "What did you say, Ma? I can't hear you." Will pinned her there and they hand fought over control of the receiver.

John jacked a round from his revolver. The bullet ricocheted off the counter, passed through the small measureable space between his brother and Mrs. Kennedy, struck a bottle display and penetrated the Calvert Whiskey sign behind them. It fell harmlessly to the floor.

"You damn fool, you almost hit me," Will said. He took control of the receiver and placed it into the cradle. Then he shoved Mary to the register where John stood with two lengths of rope.

"Get on the floor," John said.

"I'm not getting on the floor," she said.

Across the highway, Sedgwick thought he heard a shot and he wiggled himself up high enough to look out the car's window. Just arriving outside the liquor store, a young boy stood with a bicycle, neither looking in the store's window nor moving towards the door, just waiting. Somehow or other placed there like the subject of a period piece with his foot resting on the step. A chill passed through him and he became distressed. The possibility of tragedy seemed very real to him. He lived the hunger and the stress of the past nine days with the Coyles. And he had lived with them in such a relationship that a change of mood could be measured by an inflection in their voices or in the manner in which they held their heads. They were hungry like him and angry about something that no one could satisfy. He believed they could be polite and mannerly and then shoot without a change of facial expression. He believed that they had reached their civilized ending and he believed that the boy could be harmed by those two crazed brothers. He pulled at the rope, but the knots were turned from his fingers and each time he moved, the knots became smaller and tighter. A car passed on the highway and blocked his vision. He stretched himself tall, put his mouth near the open window and took a breath to yell. The car passed and he had a clear view of the storefront. The boy was gone. He collapsed back and slumped into the seat. And he prayed to the dashboard deity in thanksgiving for the bountiful gift of grace.

The brothers gained control of the woman and John tied her at the wrists and the ankles. He pulled her down onto the floor when the telephone rang again.

"Do you hear that?" she said. "The phone? That's the burglar alarm. The police will be here any minute."

"Let's get out of here," John said. He ran to the front window and looked out onto the highway.

"Wait," Will said. He rummaged through a box under the counter, removing a couple of magazines and then continued his search.

"What are you looking for?" John opened the door and looked up the road.

Will found a grocery bag and jitter-bugged between the counter and the cooler, filling the bag with beer and cartons of cigarettes. "Here, take this." He handed John another quart bottle of liquor. He grabbed one of the discarded magazines next to the box, but never saw the four hundred dollars hidden at the bottom of the box that Mary Kennedy's son had put there for safe keeping until he could get to the bank.

The brothers ran for the car on the other side of the highway, carrying the bag. They stopped in the middle of the road to let a pickup truck pass. They watched it continue up the highway until it went out of view.

"Let's go," John said.

The motor shuttered, Will pumped the gas pedal and the Dodge stalled. He tried several more times and each time, it sputtered and then stopped. On the fourth attempt, the Dodge roared to life and they pulled out onto the highway, leaving a short strip of burnt rubber. A couple of hundred yards up the road, they passed the pickup that was now parked along the shoulder. John looked into the truck as they came abreast of it.

"Two negroes," he said.

Will looked into his rear view mirror. "They're coming out." He sped up the Dodge and it skidded in the dirt as it turned onto Pine Street, gravel peppering the undercarriage and spitting up stones with the car's tires. "They're following us."

"Following us?" John turned in his seat.

"Should I try and shake them?"

"Pull into the trail. If they're following us, I'll take care of them." John opened the door and stood looking back. Within moments, the truck passed the trail and continued down the road. "They're gone," he said. Will drove into the woods until they found the clearing and parked. They sat there in silence, breathing heavily, still high from the rush of the robbery.

"How much did we get," Will said.

"About a hundred," John said. "The fast is done. We can eat." Will climbed into the rear seat and undid the rope knots on Sedgwick's wrists. Sedgwick held onto the rope, fingering the frayed fibers on the end. John broke out two bottles of beer, handed one back to Will and stretched his legs. Will guzzled a third of the bottle on the first breath. Then he drank more slowly with his eyes closed, savoring the cold liquid. Sedgwick took the end of the rope where it had come undone and began to back-braid the loose strands, staring at the dashboard clock face and the exact time of his life. John looked back at him. "I got whiskey here." The hostage remained glazed and fixed on the clock. The older brother studied the man he had held for near on ten days. And then he turned back to the front and looked out through windshield. "Let's find some food and go to the beach," he said.

24

The two cruisers raced down Route 28 and passed the truck, one tailgating off of the other, their tiny dome lights, spitting out blue light like oscillating lawn sprinklers.

"I knew it," the older one said. "I'll bet you those two boys on the highway robbed that liquor store. Robert, you got that piece of paper with the number there?"

"Yeah, right here. Whoa . . ."

Rudy u-turned the pickup truck. "I doubt the boss will mind."

"You sure this is a good idea?" Robert said.

"Mister Bullock knows the owner of that store. Say they're good people. I ain't doin' it for the police. It's just the right thing to do."

"We could just call the station and give them the number. Leave us outta it."

"But they might get away. We know where they are."

"Man, I hope you know what you're doing."

At the package store, the two men entered within minutes of the police. They found a trooper and a local officer, speaking to the owner.

"What do you two want?" the local officer said when he saw them.

Robert glanced at Rudy.

"I think we know who robbed the store," Rudy said.

"How's that?" the officer said.

"Did you see something?" the trooper said.

"Yes, sir." Rudy handed over the paper with the Pennsylvania registration on it. He provided most of the details of what they had observed and Robert supported his friend's observations with hesitant nods or other affirmation. Said they worked for the L.B. Handy Company in its cranberry bog and were on the way to check the flumes. They were shown wanted posters of the Coyle brothers and Rudy said, "Hmm, hmm. It looks like them. But I don't think I could identify them, I was more interested in their actions." Robert added, "One was taller than the other and he had lighter hair, I think. I was paying attention to the license number."

The trooper asked them if they could recite the registration number of the car without the benefit of the piece of paper and Robert answered, "Pennsylvania 184-108."

"A 1951 Dodge, you say, color green, trunk lighter?"

"Yes, sir."

"And you think there are three people in the car and that it turned into a trail off Pine street?"

"Two or three. I ain't exactly sure. But definitely more than one."

"It turned off Pine street?"

"Whatever that street is right before the Gulf station," Rudy said. It don't have no tar on it, just dirt. Real quiet place. At the beginning of the trail, there's an old ramshackle of a house. Don't look like anyone's been living in it for years."

"How long ago did you see them?" the town officer asked.

"'Bout ten minutes ago," Rudy said.

"Leave your names and addresses here at the store," the trooper said. "We'll pick them up later." He and the Middleborough officer turned to the door. "Oh, and write down where you work."

They rode together, Trooper Danny Sullivan of the Middleborough barracks and Officer DR Guertin of the Middleborough police. An unlikely pair, Sullivan an old salt and Troop supply clerk and Guertin, his uniform and equipment still bright, shiny and new. The state police cruiser hit the corner of Pine Street in a slide. They slowed at the skid marks on the road and followed the tire impressions in the trail, rolling on easy into the woods.

JOHN HAD HIS head back, sitting behind the wheel in the front seat, staring out through the windshield. "On the way to the beach, we'll stop and get some food," he said. "Hamburgers and milk. Yes indeed, real American food." Will sat behind his brother, drinking the last of his beer. And Sedgwick next to him, humming and shuckling in the old tradition and barely audible in quiet supplication to God for His infinite mercy, the weight of the nine days pressing down on him hard and the hope of returning to his family slowly leaking away. *And when I think that God, His Son not sparing, sent Him to die, I scarce can take it in.* Was when John lazily looked into the rear view mirror and sat up.

"Someone's out there," he said.

"Come out with your hands up!"

John heard the command, heard it plain. And complied in the only way acceptable to him now. He rolled out the door, gun in each hand and shot with both weapons at the state trooper who was now prone and returning fire from the underbrush. Will followed him out of the car and jerked off a round before he was standing. The brothers stood side-by-side firing, John in a helter-skelter beat-'em by numbers barrage and Will more exact and deliberate, moving and backing up and firing defensive containment rounds. The two brothers stood no more than twenty paces from Sullivan, firing until one of John's guns emptied. Sullivan shot purposefully, some in a single action delivery that kept the brothers from advancing and pinned them down behind the Dodge.

The first few pistol shots that broke the peace now came in clusters and echoed loudly through the woods until the exchange dominated the natural state. The gunfight traveled for miles, Will's .38 and the police service revolvers reporting in a greater expression than John's .32 caliber. A round passed through John's pants, raising the hairs on his leg and several rounds struck the rear of the Dodge and entered the trunk. And some rounds scorched the door along the driver's side or skidded across the roof. The brothers shot wildly in response to the trooper's bullets that passed so close to them they could hear the lead, buzzing like summer insects in the hot humid air. The bullets ripped the ground and kicked up the dirt near their feet as Sullivan now shot at their legs, the brothers jitterbugging in place to avoid being hit. Other bullets whistled over their heads from their flank and they realized that they were taking fire from two directions. Rapid thuds struck the passenger side of the car. Will located the Middleborough officer just off the clearing to their left, down on one knee, and he began to fire on him.

"There's only two of them," the younger brother yelled. "Try and get them both."

When the first shots sounded, Sedgwick, still tied at the ankles, clawed and wiggled himself to the storage space between the back seat and the trunk and curled himself small. Bullets slammed against the car, some penetrating and others falling away. And some so close Sedgwick could smell the putrid breath of death. He pleaded for mercy and God's sustaining love. He thought of his family. Prayed for strength and begged for resolution. And he prayed like he had never prayed before because this was a terrible way to die.

John left the protection of the Dodge and slipped away into the scrub, moving in a westerly direction and reloading as he ran. He came out of the southern sun as a black silhouette upon Guertin's blind side, firing on him with both guns while his brother pinned him down on his front. Seeing that he was encircled and now taking fire from two directions, Sullivan moved to support him. "Back up towards me!" he yelled. "And concentrate on the guy in the woods." He followed with a volley of his own in rapid succession at the younger brother and kept him occupied, the bullets peppering the Dodge, one hitting the front tire and the tire deflating into the soil.

"I'm hit," Will yelled.

Guertin turned and ran to the trooper's position, zigzagging his way back to Sullivan. "Did you hear that?" he said. He fumbled with his revolver and dropped several .38 rounds onto the ground. "Damn it."

"Forget it." Sullivan watched the brothers run into the brush.

"One said he was hit."

"I heard it," Sullivan said. "I don't believe him." He dumped his empty casings and reloaded quickly.

"I need more ammunition," Guertin said.

"Come on." Sullivan began to back away.

"One of those rounds damn near parted my scalp," Guertin said. "How many you figure?"

"Shots?"

"Yeah."

"Twenty-five or thirty, I'd guess."

"And no one hit?" Guertin said.

"Doesn't speak well of the shooting, does it?"

The two officers fell back to the cruiser to reload their weapons and call for support and as they did, the brothers returned to the Dodge, seized a loaded bandoleer, another loaded revolver, a sack with a few essentials and the money they had left on the front seat. Inside the crawl space, Sedgwick lay curled up on one side, trembling no longer because of the bullets that had come so close to taking his life, but because he thought he had finally been freed of the Coyle brothers. But there they stood just outside the window. He held onto his legs and pulled them to his chest, moaning something incoherently. John grabbed the money and looked back at him in disgust. "You'd like to be rid of us?" he said. "But we're bonded forever." He stepped back from the Dodge and fired two rounds into the car.

They ran through the underbrush, Will vaulting the scrub, hurdling it in single bounds and John, limping noticeably, lumbering and plowing the tangled mass like a fullback, them moving through the thickets, the wild roses and the high bush blueberry, the briars and the thorns tearing at their skin, slapping at black flies and mosquitoes in cluster. The heat, the humidity so extreme that within minutes their clothing clung to them like wallpaper. They ran a diversionary route, fish hooking and changing direction often, and in two minutes time they reached the power lines and for two more they rode the rim, running in their own shadows. And in ten minutes time after they had fled the Dodge, before Sullivan and Guertin reentered the woods, before a cavalry of troopers arrived at Pine Street, before the hounds began to track, before helicopters from Otis Air Force Base and civilian fixed wings flew above them, the Coyle brothers crossed over and immersed themselves into the mire of the marsh, first amongst the tall grasses and across the solid bog. Then the land of prickly briars, muddy land, swampy with thick vegetation, forty foot pin oaks, red maples and the deep brown gravy waters where a blanket of yellow pine pollen grew out from the shore. Where a green living canopy hung high above their heads and cones of filtered light shone down through the top, the light reflecting off the water's surface like a mirror. There, they hid their guns and ammuni-

202

tion in the crooks of trees, hung the sack over a low-hanging branch, stripped themselves naked, hid their clothes and settled amongst the skeeters, submerging themselves into the swamp with their eyes like periscopes just above the water line while they scanned it for predators and the S pattern of snakes.

SULLIVAN AND GUERTIN, reloaded and, carrying more ammunition than when they first encountered the brothers, made their way back on either side of the trail. The trooper now carrying a Remington shotgun. As they began their approach to the Dodge, he glanced at the sky. A large bird soared among the tops of the trees, insects whined and he noticed for the first time that rainwater shone on the vegetation. He saw sand and pine needles attached to his uniform and prickly burrs clinging to the front of his shirt. He sensed that he now was in time and rhythm to this place and felt acutely aware of its natural state. And he listened for any unfamiliar disturbance.

When they came within twenty-five feet of the car, he stopped and knelt on one knee, surveying the area and listening for that one thing. Guertin did the same. Sullivan scanned the wood line and he could see where the brush had been trampled. He turned his ear to capture a sound. A strange declaration like the whine of a small animal came from the Dodge and it repeated itself until he determined that it was of human origin. He signaled Guertin that he was going to approach the car. He closed the distance, sweeping the area with the shotgun and when within feet of the passenger door, he saw the top of a head.

"Come out with your hands up," he said.

Sedgwick struggled with the rope that still bound his ankles, his hands shaking uncontrollably. So much so that he couldn't untie the knot.

"Get out here or I start shooting."

"Don't shoot. Don't shoot. Please . . . don't shoot." He pulled his shoes off, tore at the rope until it cleared his feet and stepped out of the car with one foot on the ground and hesitated when he saw the trooper and the shotgun pointed at his chest. He let out a soulful cry and fell back into the car. Sullivan lunged at him and yanked him out and pushed him down on the ground, holding him by the shirt.

"Where are the others?" he said.

"Oh, my God." Sedgwick said in a high-pitched keening.

The trooper shook him. "Where are they?"

He began to wail hysterically. He cowered under the larger man and he spoke random words of nonsense. He looked up wild-eyed, licked his lips with his tongue and began to shake his head in a negative tremor.

"Where are the other two, I said?"

He flinched and continued to speak in a kind of rapid gibberish.

Guertin came to the car. "What's your name?" he said.

"Kidnapped . . ."

"Get the hell back there," Sullivan snapped at Guertin, "And cover my ass."

Sedgwick continued to lick his mouth. "Kidnapped."

"On your feet." Sullivan pulled him up. "Quiet." He listened for a few moments and then looked over at Guertin. "I didn't want those two bastards to sneak up on us."

"Right," Guertin said. "What's your name?" he said to Sedgwick.

Sedgwick responded, "Gone?"

"I don't know," Sullivan said. "They could be lying right back there in the weeds."

"Are they the Coyle brothers?" Guertin said.

Sedgwick nodded his head. He jerked it towards the woods.

"I hear other cruisers on the road," Sullivan said. "Let's bring this guy out and find out who the hell he is."

25

He leaned against the wall of the telephone booth and looked down the company street.

"Did you start packing?" he said.

"I've laid out clothes for everyone," Sheila said. "I just have to get the suitcases out of the attic and fill them."

"Great."

"Now if I can just separate you from that job for a few days."

"Believe me. I'm looking forward to it. Going to take the boys fishing."

"Do they have a boat?"

"A rowboat."

"When do you think you'll be home?"

"I have one class Wednesday morning and I'm done. One of the guys is going to drop me off."

"What time will that be?"

"Twelve, twelve-thirty."

"And when will we get to New Hampshire?" she said.

"You sound like one of the kids."

"They're excited."

"You mean, you're excited."

"We're all excited, Frank."

"If we can leave by one thirty, we should be there by five."

One of his classmates passed and pointed to his watch. "I've got to go. I'll see you on Wednesday. Love you."

"Love you."

He hung up the telephone and he began to run.

HE RAN BETWEEN two rows of Quonset huts, the heat, the humidity hanging heavy on the academy compound and caught the other In-service members as they entered the classroom. A sergeant held the door. "Anyone else behind you, Mahan?"

"I think I'm the last one."

"Grab a seat."

As soon as he entered, the sergeant called the class to attention. Captain Martin Munroe entered and took the podium.

"This morning, one of the Middleborough troopers, Daniel Sullivan and a local police officer responded to an armed robbery at a liquor store," he said. "As a result of a tip, they followed a car into the woods where they became engaged in a firefight with two men and approximately thirty rounds expended. Fortunately neither of them was injured. But the two robbers escaped into the woods. Some of you were from Troop D are familiar with these guys because they're the same two who robbed the First National in Buzzards Bay and shot two of the employees day after Christmas last year. The fugitives are John and William Coyle from Pennsylvania. On June 5th while stealing milk, they shot and killed a young Philadelphia patrolman, who had just returned to work after an illness to his five year old son. In addition to these crimes, they have been implicated in two kidnappings and several other armed robberies."

Munroe looked over to the sergeant. "Are we all blue here?"

"Yes, Captain."

"This isn't catch 'n release. The Coyles executed Officer James Kane in cold blood, stalked him like an animal after they wounded him. Hounded him when he tried to retreat. And shot him five times until they were sure he was dead. Then they left him in the gutter." The captain paused. "We want these bastards, one way or the other. Philadelphia Police are on their way and they don't give a damn what we give them, a body or a body in a bag. But the conditions are difficult and not advantageous to us. It's a challenging place, a mosquito infested land with snakes, cranberry bogs, dense woods and a swamp with a bottom that can disappear in a moment. And plenty of places to hide. We have almost one hundred troopers, local officers, Fish & Game wardens, and air support from Otis and the Civil Air Patrol on the scene. And as of the last few minutes, we have hounds in the hunt. We have them contained and we will get them. And the way they come out is up to them."

He glanced at a message handed him. "I wanted to give you an up-to-date because every resource of the department is dedicated to the capture of these two. Check your gear and if you need something, hit the supply depot before the end of the day. Everyone is on deck. The chances of you going to Middleborough are slim. But I want you ready. For the present, you will continue your In-service training. And as soon as we have more information, we'll pass it along."

The captain left the room and the sergeant took the podium. "Now that the captain has you all pumped up, we'll be discussing recent amendments to the motor vehicle and criminal laws."

THE BLADES BEAT the afternoon air above them. Military birds canvassed the bog, the marsh and the swamp and the petrified woods, at times hovering so close that they created a surf in the water, parted and laid down vegetation and swept aside the tops of the black swamp oaks while spotters peered down onto the rotting forest floor. And under the power lines, they raised up cones of granular powder, thirty-foot dust devils spinning and dancing in the afternoon heat. Over the choppers, fixed wing aircraft patrolled with a quieter presence, covering a greater portion of sky and capturing photographic imagery for the ground patrols. The brothers remained embedded in the swamp all through the late morning and early afternoon while the sun seared their faces and their pale unprotected skin. Every few minutes or so, they submerged themselves in the water to cool their heads and rid themselves of the relentless attack of mosquitoes that feasted on their blood and left large red welts. And when they broke the surface, they coughed and cleared their throats, but did so with the sound of the choppers overpowering all other sounds.

They remained there through the heat of the afternoon until the helicopters throttled up and turned to the sky and the fixed wing plane took its constant whine on a southerly course. Then John came to move. He calculated the approximate time of day from the position of the sun and floated toward his brother, barely touching bottom and drifting through the vegetation with the lazy natural rhythm of the pool. He came within feet of Will when his brother waved him off. He stopped and quietly re-submerged himself, slipping below the water level, his chin coming to rest on the surface. A dragonfly flew past and then returned and perched itself on the top of his head. On the bank of the marsh less than fifteen feet away, a state trooper stood straddled on the spongy moss apron, a shotgun balanced with one hand, the butt resting on his thigh. He looked across the water beyond where the brothers were submerged and directed a stream of urine into the pool. Other troopers moved past him, their profiles fragmented by low hanging scrub branches and indigenous plants that grew about the embankment. They spoke in whispers or with hand signals as they inspected the pool and its tangled green garden.

They moved past in columns, strung out on either side of the apron for as far as John could see. Grim-faced men with shotguns at port or resting on one of their shoulders with their trigger fingers against the guard, heavy movement, the chafing of leather, measured breathing and wet field boots slathered in mud, their uniform shirts stained with perspiration. The detail stopped. So close that the brothers could see the sweat on their faces and smell the odor of insect repellant from their clothing. Off in the distance and to the South, the hounds bayed, a hand signal given and the troopers quick stepped to the call.

The brothers remained submerged for another fifteen minutes while they assessed their condition. They kept close watch on the embankment, the apron and their protective environs. And when John decided that they now must be behind the state police ground patrols, they climbed out of the water and dressed, retrieved their weapons, ammunition belts and Will's sack and left the security of the swamp. They negotiated the uneven tracks, passed a cranberry bog, running in a zigzag easterly pattern and completed the approach to France Street on their bellies. A half mile distant, North and South, cruisers blocked the road at the intersections with troopers beside them. At the southern roadblock, additional details of troopers stood in waves of road heat. And they moved in heavy procession down the road. John and Will ran across the street and settled into the confines of yet another marsh and cranberry bog, turned North and sprinted the tracks, pausing every few minutes to assess and listen for aircraft, each occasion dropping down and enveloping themselves in the green vegetation. They ran parallel to France Street and once clear of the northern roadblock, crossed back over, entering the forest and the three thousand acre wooded maze where they had hunted—its swampland, its closed green canopy and its labyrinth of old logging trails. Fresh spring water ran through the forest and it provided them sustenance. Time passed and the day lengthened. The Earth turned away from the sun and it came to grace but one edge of the trees. The aircraft turned. The sun set. And in the waning hours of light, the Coyle brothers were left to run free.

THEY HIKED IN silence and pushed through the forest, circumventing pools of opaque water and aprons of mud, covering as much ground as the nocturnal terrain would allow. And in time they found their true North, the ground firm and cold and the trail awash in moonlight, the woods a strange carnival of mysterious shapes and several degrees of darkness. They heard the rush of things in the brush and along the forest floor or above them, the briefest rustle at the tops of the trees like the crumbling of newspaper. On and on they marched until they reached the forest's northern boundary, five miles distance. There, they made their way to the road and not a soul beyond or around it. Across the road, they found the shelter of an empty cabin. And thirteen and one-half hours after their standoff with Sullivan and Guertin, they pushed in the front door, exhausted but free. There were provisions, bacon, eggs and milk in the refrigerator, dry clothing, running water and the light of a kerosene lamp. They ate egg sandwiches while they watched cruisers pass on the road outside. Then they bedded down together, sleeping in three hour shifts. Just as the rain began to fall.

WHEN NIGHTFALL CAME, residents either abandoned their homes or if they'd chosen to stay, shuttered their families in buttoned-down houses, listening for the bark of the dog. And never a child seen in that eleven mile area. They locked their doors and sat in well-lit rooms with hunting rifles, shotguns and pistols across their laps. Josiah Holmes, who was born and raised in his modest farm house, sat with two guns on his living room couch. "I've done my share of hunting," he said. "I'm not worried." His boys, nineteen and fifteen years old, held their own positions in different corners of the house. And the diner across the street and the tavern further down remained open for business long after their permitted times, some of the town's residents standing or sitting at the bars, idling with pistols fixed in their belts. Retired Chief of Police Elmer T. Townes said he was born on this land. He told them about the loggers who drove a team of horses into that godforsaken swamp where the fugitives were held up. "They 'came mired in the mud hauling a load of timber," he said. "And they just never did come out."

26

A Roman camp and a village of tents brought a carnival atmosphere to the Town of Middleborough. Not since the traveling sideshow set up business in an open field the previous summer had the town been injected with so much life. There was light and noise and the kind of human activity that can affect the natural order of things—a Command Post, a resting station with cots and tables, a trailer for the Civil Defense volunteers, an American Red Cross station offering first aid, hot food and coffee, a semi-trailer that acted as a supply depot, and a large camping tent where six newspaper reporters sat at typewriters—all rose up overnight and occupied the land near the intersection of Route 28 and Pine Street. And there were vehicles of every design: state police cruisers, county sheriffs' vehicles and cruisers from every local jurisdiction. Some were identified as cruisers in name only, and others by the signage on their doors. And boats sitting on trailers and black nondescript FBI vehicles, a state police bus, military trucks and off road vehicles, a Forestry water buffalo and an ambulance. And behind the tents, a hearse idled conspicuously like the angel of death waiting for its appointed soul. Civil Defense lighting plants that turned the camp from night to day, and flood lamps running on generators, stood every half mile along the search perimeter — the natural place now a war zone bathed in light.

Crowds grew with each passing hour, the curious came, some from across the country. The regulars who arrived early each day were mostly old vets from one of the world wars and retired farmers if there ever were such a thing. They stood in groups in bib overalls and long sleeve shirts. And in thermal underwear tops with their arms folded, smoking their pipes and assessing the cops' strategy. A few local rednecks offered to hunt the Coyles down for a cash bounty. While others petitioned and prayed to the Almighty for the brothers' deliverance, claiming that they were just misguided boys, and quietly hoped that the brothers had gone like dust. They all took their places behind the barricades as witnesses to the spectacle and they stood patient and resolved in their particular positions. The residents who chose to remain in their homes took pleasure in the circus that had come to their sleepy agricultural town. Some set up tables near the camp with homegrown fruits and vegetables, preserves, home-made breads and Kool-Aid. They sold clean dry socks and slightly used gardening gloves, Gold Bond antifungal foot powder and insect repellent.

Nearly four hundred police officers from various departments armed with weapons of all types, and looking like a guerilla army, now patrolled an eleven-mile perimeter and searched every vehicle that entered it. They stood at posts along Route 28 from Middleborough to Plymouth like an occupying force and created an unlikely traffic jam that lasted for miles. On Pilgrims Highway and Route 3A as far south as the bridges, the gateways to Cape Cod, roadblocks were installed that shut down easy access to the beaches and cottages.

In Cushman's swamp, sixty troopers wrapped in olive drab raincoats waited patiently in the miserable, dank-infested place where mosquitoes flew in swarms and blue-gray and brown water snakes foraged among the submerged vegetation. Muddy water leaked into their boots. The thick underbrush surrounded them and it tore at them like barbwire. There they laid in wait not ten feet apart yet invisible to each other, close to the power lines and the place where the brothers had last been seen, where Bunny the bloodhound had tracked their scent. The morning arrived gray and soggy and the troopers remained still in that terrible place, waiting for that one good shot.

CAPTAIN MUNROE STOOD bent over a table in the Command Post and traced a path on the map with his finger. He paused and reflected on the suspected route of travel taken by the Coyles and sipped his tea. Drizzle continued to fall onto the canvas above him, the rain water rolling off the edge of the tent in a steady monotonous drip. He looked up from the map and tapped his finger where it lay.

"I think this son-of-a-bitch is going to be one brutal campaign," he said. He puffed out a long resigned breath of air. "We don't know whether they're gone or not. And whether we're just chasing our tails."

The corporal suspended his log entry and turned away from the typewriter. "They were seen on the high tension lines yesterday by the ground patrols and observed entering that swamp from the air. Right about where you've got your finger. It's just a matter of time."

"Could be, but from a half mile distance?" the captain said. "Might have been the Coyles and it might have been one of the volunteers or members of one of the other agencies. And if I hear again about another one of those idiots, discharging a weapon." He sipped his tea again. "The Coyles know every road, every turn, every ramshackle house and every barn and whether it holds farm animals or swamp rats."

The corporal looked at him. "Did you get any shuteye, Captain?"

"A couple of winks after we returned from the Federated Church. Another waste of time. Either they got out of there before we arrived or they never were there."

"Where did that tip come from?"

"One of the parishioners driving by." Munroe stood with a boot up on a folding chair and balanced the mug on his knee. "If it was them, then they had the better part of the night to escape."

The telephone rang and the corporal answered it. "Yes, sir. I'll tell him." He hung up the phone and looked up. "The Colonel. He and the commissioner will be here within the hour. They want to give an update to the newspaper people and some local politicians."

Munroe looked out at the camp. Volunteers moved in and out of his view. The morning air had the unpleasant musty odor of skunk cabbage, pungent as the earth he stood on. "These two are making monkeys out of us. Almost four hundred to two. The goddam reporters are writing about them like they're cult heroes." He shook his head as if he agreed on something. "When you think about it, I guess they've got to write about something. They sure as hell aren't getting a story from us."

"Heroes?" the corporal said. "That little old lady at the liquor store working for her sick son wouldn't call them heroes. Knocking off a grocery store and ambushing a young Philly cop for a bottle of milk. Yeah, they're regular Horatio Alger characters."

"Our guys are worn down," the captain said. He looked out into the camp again. "When this rain ends, it's going to be hotter than hell." He nodded. "If we're still here at the end of the day, I'm calling for fresh troops. I'm not letting these bastards beat us."

216

The corporal picked up the day's newspaper. "Jesus, would you look at that."

"What are you talking about?"

"Superman, George Reeves."

"What about him?'

"He's dead."

"Dead?"

"Yeah, supposedly killed himself."

"Son of a bitch."

27

Water dripped from the leaky faucet and it fell in clock rhythm.

John Coyle leaned against the sink and looked out the window onto France Street where it intersected with Rocky Gutter Road. Will sat at the small kitchen table. "Let's continue North," he said.

"Where did you put our clothes?"

"In the attic."

John held away the end of the sport shirt he was wearing. "The guy who lives here must be about our size," he said. "These fit pretty well."

"John, did you hear me? I want to go North."

"I heard you. Here comes one now."

"I'd like to know what their plan is," Will said.

"Bet it's in the newspaper." The elder Coyle picked up his coffee and watched the headlamps approach and then the cruiser turned the corner. "They must know who we are by now. Yes indeed, got our pictures in the paper." He looked up at the clock on the kitchen wall and timed it with the passing cruiser. "They're predictable, almost to the minute." He returned to the table and continued to make sandwiches with the cheese he found in the refrigerator. "First, the state police, then a town cruiser. They're following a schedule."

"Time to move." Will said.

"I'm guessing they already checked this place," John said. "But once the rain lets up, they'll be back. We better get out of here."

"I want to continue North!"

"All right! I heard you the first time."

"We've got a step on them right now. Let's go before we lose it."

"How many police do you think are out there? Choppers and fixed wings all day yesterday. The search party's got to be huge. So, we've got plenty of company here." John wrapped the sandwiches in wax paper and slipped them into the sack with the other provisions he found in the cabin. "The next cruiser should be coming by in about fifteen minutes. Soon as it passes, we'll move back into the swamp and the woods."

"And get eaten by mosquitoes again?" Will said.

"Here, wear these." John tossed him a pair of nylon stockings he found in the cabin.

"I want to move North. I think their perimeter ends right here. That's why we're just seeing cruisers. We can make some good distance between them and us."

"We don't want to outrun our protection. If the patrols remain the same, we'll go North."

"Let's go."

"Give it a little time, Will. Let's sit and watch them for a while. We've got a good view of both streets and should know pretty soon what they're up to. Then we move."

A FEW MINUTES of laying up in the swamp, the brothers watched the cabin's owner return. He approached the kitchen door and when almost at the stairs, he stopped short and looked around. He lifted one foot onto the first step and leaned closer to the cabin, listening. Stayed in that position for near on a minute, then he moved up the stairs, appearing to the brothers to be walking tiptoed. They saw him slowly open the door and lean into the confines of the cottage. After a few moments, he backed down the stairs quickly and ran until he disappeared from view. Within minutes, the area became thick with cruisers and police on foot. Troopers stormed the cottage. Loud angry voices and commands resonated from within and without the house. A voice yelled out to the others. "They're gone."

Will took his thirty-eight and drew down on a cluster of police just yards away. John placed his hand on the barrel and shook his head. The younger brother backslapped his hand away from the top of the gun and a trooper looked up into the place where they were hiding. He squinted and stared, looked one way and then the other. A cruiser stopped where he stood and he turned away. They could hear him talking and then he moved toward the intersection of the two roads. The brothers watched the searchers take up positions along both roads and they set up a roadblock there.

"We had our chance," Will hissed. "We're trapped."

John continued to watch the police. "No, we're not. They don't want to come in here." He leaned against a swamp oak and took the cover off of a thermos bottle and poured.

They remained there surrounded in the swamp, eating sandwiches and drinking lukewarm coffee and observed the comings and goings of the police while the mosquitoes continued to gorge themselves on their unprotected skin. The brothers waited out the hours and the light of day, the slow change at the horizon. And they anticipated the coming of darkness.

State Police AcademyFiring Range
Framingham, Massachusetts
"HOLSTER AN EMPTY weapon. Look to the right. Look to the left. If the line is safe, proceed to the butts and check your target."

Frank shielded his eyes from the glare and walked down-range. The night's rain wetted the leaves of the trees and surrounding vegetation and all glistened in the sparkle of morning sunlight.

"First shot?" the range master said to him as he pushed the tip of a pencil through a hole outside the ten-ring.

"Yes, sir. I think so."

"But the rest of them are in a nice cluster. That's good shooting, Mahan."

"Thank you, sir."

"Strike your target and bring it to the table for scoring."

"Sir, can I ask you a question about the ammunition?"

"What is it?"

They walked together to the scorer's table.

"How come we practice with wadcutters, but carry a different round?" Frank said.

"The wadcutter has a flat nose. Gives a clean well-defined hole for scoring."

"I notice that I shoot a lot better with them."

"That sounds right. Less recoil than the full metal jacket round and better accuracy in shorter distances."

"How far would you say?"

"For an accurate shooter, I'd say about fifty yards.

"So, why don't we carry them?"

"For one thing, they're more difficult to load because of their shape." He wrote the score at the top of Frank's target.

"And the other?" Frank said.

"Our Rules & Regs."

"Do you think we'll ever change over?"

"If we do, it'll be to a hollow point, semi-wadcutter. But a difficult sell to politicians who don't hear that a soft lead bullet is safer because it doesn't pass through a body and injure an innocent person. They only hear that it creates more internal damage after it enters human flesh."

Frank had his score recorded, rolled the target and put it into his bag.

"Load your issue rounds, holster a safe weapon," the range master called out. "Police your brass and dump your unexpended rounds in the buckets. As soon as you're finished, mount up."

He loaded his weapon with the department issue and took a seat on the bus. He sat by a window and watched the range master place buckets of the used brass and unexpended practice ammunition into the trunk of his cruiser. He took out a handkerchief and wiped the sweat from his face and arms. He reached into his pocket for his watch and placed it on his wrist.

"They still haven't got them." One of his classmates said as he sat down next to him.

"What do you hear," he said.

"I heard our guys closed in on a cabin and found that they had been there. But they're still running. Lots of places to hide." An unlit cigarette hung from his mouth and he fished around in his pockets. "Got a light?"

Frank pulled out a book of matches and a half dozen wadcutter rounds and held them in his palm. He picked out the matches and handed them to his classmate.

"Extra practice?" the classmate said, nodding to the bullets.

"Yeah."

He lit the cigarette. "Are the kids excited about their vacation?"

"I don't know who's more excited, my wife or the kids."

"When are you leaving?"

"Tomorrow, as soon as I get home."

"We should be released by eleven, eleven-thirty. If we don't get called out to Middleborough."

"They've got four hundred cops there."

"Yeah, I know," the classmate said. "But you never know."

"I wish they had called for volunteers," Frank said.

"Let's see, stomping around in a mosquito-infested swamp or fishing on a lake in New Hampshire? Are you nuts, Mahan? Your wife will kill you."

"I think she understands."

The classmate flicked his ashes onto the floor. "They thought they had them pinned down. Then they show up five miles from where they'd been searching."

"They have the advantage," Frank said.

"Still takes a man to enter that hell hole to get them out. When all is said and done, it'll take a man on man."

"Yeah," Frank said.

28

Come midnight, the Coyles rose up and out of the rotting decay like swamp zombies wandering amongst the graves of the dead. And they began a southerly march. They wore gray woolen blankets over their heads that they took from the cottage and painted themselves into the shadows and the natural environment. John convinced his brother that the advantage of moving during the night was free passage and surprise. They needed a car. Preferably one with an owner who couldn't report it stolen. It had worked with Gallagher and it had worked with Sedgwick. So, why shouldn't it work again? He convinced Will that the concentration of police told him that the perimeter had been moved and if they had run North, they would have been discovered. But going South, where it had all begun, they would outfox their nemesis. He had studied the police and their movements, observed tired men, less guarded men. He watched them at the roadblock, once standing vigilant, now talking unguarded in groups of threes and fours. Or sitting in their cruisers, the windows diffusely lit and opaque with steam.

The brothers left the woods and set out on France Street passing within feet of a running cruiser. They walked on the black invisible road, the articulate sound of thunder rolling up in fitful bursts shaking the night sky, the drizzle of rain along the macadam and the myriad of strange shapes

224

created by sparks of heat lightning. They marched on, silhouetted against the electric sky and retraced their steps to outsmart the scheme of the police. All night, the two of them on foot unchallenged and free, slipping off the road at times to follow the Weweantic River. Ghostly mirages in the night wrapped in ammunition belts, running the darkness.

"DID YOU CALL your wife?" his classmate said.

"I didn't want to upset her," Frank said.

They left in an uneasy silence in the predawn night, the bus turning off the academy road and onto Route 9 with cruisers running escort fore and aft. The convoy traveled single file in the passing lane at a speed close to the limit of the bus, moving stiffly and clumsily on the road, rolling side to side, the wipers drumming across a wet-dry windshield. Frank put his head against the window and closed his eyes. But each time the bus hit a bump or made a turn, he opened them and looked about like he had been disturbed in the middle of a dream. In the dark, he identified his classmates by profile, shape or size; most of them rode with their heads down, their garrison caps pulled over their eyes, their leather grinding when they moved in their seats. He heard the stalk of a shotgun rap against the floor. In the back, a trooper cleared his throat and one coughed. Streaks of white light and colored neon flashed into the windows and he watched the telephone poles pass by in tics. The radio hissed. The dispatcher at headquarters called code 6s and he heard the cruisers give their locations, sounding like space travelers thousands of miles from Earth. The sergeant in charge of the detail rode in the stairwell. He stepped up and stood next to the driver.

"It'll be about an hour's drive," he said. "In case you shit yourselves, there's toilet paper in thc back."

Restrained hard laughter broke the silence. They traveled East then South and the men aboard became quietly grim again.

AS THE BUS turned off Route 28 and came to a stop, Frank peered out the window at a black-over-blue sky and the first gray light of the new day at the horizon. The sergeant told them to stay put and he climbed down from the bus and walked to one of several tents. Outside the bus, a spectacle lay before them. Men of many shapes and designs, some in regulation uniform and some in a variation thereof, some in hunter's or military attire and others clothed in the business suits of detectives and administrators, moved about the camp, busy with one thing or the other. Preparing to get on with it for another day. And there were dogs sitting with their handlers, military dogs and dogs that hunt the woods, dogs that hunt a man. The smell of bacon and coffee drifted through the camp and made its way onto the bus. Rows of cruisers parked eight deep were laid out in the adjacent field, the idle cruisers creating a rolling metallic wave wed to the contour of the land. A military helicopter stood behind the cruisers on a high clearing with two standing uniformed guards.

The sergeant returned and was accompanied by Captain Munroe and two other men in civilian attire. Munroe appeared tired and weary of the three-day hunt. He hadn't slept for days and the stress and frustration of the operation wore on him visibly. He told them that he had requested their deployment because the operation required a different strategy. He wanted to run "these bastards" down, use a disruptive blitzkrieg approach with military equipment, off road vehicles, dogs and fast young troopers, members of the last two recruit classes. A sweep, he called it, a quick-paced assault in the forest to roust the Coyle brothers from where he believed

226

they were hiding. And he intended to use lots of noise. "We want to disrupt them, shock them and bully them right out of those goddam woods."

Munroe introduced two Philadelphia Police officers who described their loss and anger over the killing of Jimmy Kane. They offered a $5000 reward to anyone responsible for the capture or killing of John and William Coyle. "We don't care how you bring them out," they said. "Dead or alive." Then they thought on it a moment and said, "Preferably dead." And by the time the men finished speaking, the morning broke dank and the swamp and the woods were wet and unaired and at the earth's edge, a pale smoky mauve.

29

They just flat out ran.

Right across route 28, past the armed camp and all the cruisers, helicopters and planes, past the four hundred armed police. Ran within a few hundred yards of the command post. A car even stopped to let them cross. So, while the police concentrated on the northern end of their perimeter five miles away and Captain Munroe readied his plan for a running assault in the dense forest, John and William Coyle backtracked. All night, all the way back to the starting place, crossed the state highway on the other side of the road from Lindstrom's Gulf station and the woods where they had camped with William Sedgwick. The gambler, John Coyle, double-downed, double-tracked and played his hand. The brothers crept near a farmhouse that abutted more woods, a marsh and a bog and approached a car.

"WOULD YOU LOOK at that?" he said. "There's someone crawling around in the vegetable garden." Walter Schmidt sat at a table near one of two windows that overlooked the marsh and the cranberry bog.

Betty Schmidt walked into the kitchen in her nightgown and stood next to her husband. "Where?" she said.

He pointed with a butter knife. "There."

She stood in full view of the windows. She modestly stepped back and pulled her robe around her. "Oh, I see where you mean. That might be the older boy upstairs."

"He looks bigger than that boy."

Betty walked closer to the window. "Can't imagine what he's looking for."

"I think he was near our car."

"Do you think he's one of those fugitives?"

"Not sure."

"Under the circumstances what's going on around here." She picked up the telephone.

He leaned across the table for a closer look. "We've been here only a week and we've got an army of police surrounding us. Thought you said it was quiet in Middleborough."

"It is, just farms and nice people." Betty dialed the telephone.

Her husband stood to take a closer look.

"Hello operator. Would you give me the Middleborough Police Department?"

The butter knife dropped and it fell to the floor. Betty looked over at her husband. "He saw me," he said.

"Saw you?"

"He looked right at me."

"Are you sure?" she said. "Hello, officer . . ."

"Right at me."

"There's a man. He's crawling near our garden by the wood line. We can see him from our window." She walked as far as the telephone cord would allow. "He keeps sticking his head out and looking back at our house. Yes, sir." Betty hung up the phone.

"What did he say?"

"He said they're on their way and to lock the doors. And stay away from the windows."

Walter stood back. "There's a Judgment coming here to-day. Hell to be paid."

"MOVE." THE SERGEANT ran in company with the detail to the Command Post.

Frank bumped against his classmate in line and dropped his ditty bag to the ground. Stood at attention and waited for the captain to speak.

"Stand at ease," he said. "We have a sighting of a man or men crawling around at the back of a house across the road. It's probably not the Coyles. We think they're in the northern end of the woods about four to five miles from here. But these boys are clever and they know this ground better than we do. So before we run the woods, we're going to sweep the marsh and the bog behind that house." He removed his blouse and cross strap. "Strip down to your shirts. Raincoats if you want. But otherwise, take off your badges, nametags and any other metal. As soon as we break formation, safely check your weapons and your cartridge cases. Shotguns if you're carrying one and make sure they're loaded."

Within minutes, the eighteen-man detail crossed the highway. They passed through yards and in one, a boy about seven years stood watching them from a lip of land at the back of his house. He wore a holster tied to his leg with a white-handled cap gun. They passed on. A woman scolded them for crossing her land while carrying guns in the open, cursing and using the Lord's name in vain. The captain and the sergeant went to the Schmidt home and spoke to Betty and Walter. The detail swept all of the property to where it ended at the adjacent woods. They searched the backyard, the bushes, the vegetable garden, the barn and all of its stalls. They opened up a root cellar and crawled under the porch. And when the point man was ordered into the tall grass, the sergeant and the others followed. Into the wetlands and into the quagmire, some closely tangled underbrush with stunted woody reeds like hardwood knives that cut into their leather. Prickly greenbriers tearing at their uniforms and their exposed skin, some were smeared in their own blood. They tripped and fought to keep their weapons from jarring free. Some disappeared for a moment lost in the brush and then rose again. One of the troopers, his pistol they never recovered. Some came out of the mud and took to the woods and ran a high flank to the others, running the western side of the marsh.

The point man pressed on barely visible in the high grass, moving toward the bog in an apish stooping gait. God's beauty in radiant splendor, the mist now levitating over the marsh and the land sunlit with grace. The trees in the adjacent woods brilliantly adorned.

And then, "Is that you Coyle?"

The point man called out. His voice rose up and out of the grass near the bank of the bog. It rose in an echo and entered the farmhouse at the top of the knoll. His words carried for miles. Walter and Betty Schmidt heard it, looked out from the window and gave witness to it all.

"Do you hear that Walter?" his wife said.

"They're calling them, Betty."

"Get away from the window."

"It's the reckoning." He moved closer to the door, cracked it open and he placed his eye between the edge and the frame.

"Shut that!" she said. "Do you want to be shot?"

"Is that you, Coyle brothers?" the voice repeated.

He slipped out the door and crawled to a wood pile, stood in a place with a high ground advantage.

"Walter!" his wife called to him.

"Coyle brothers!" the voice commanded. "Give up."

A pistol reported. A single shot. It carried the answer and it disturbed the tranquility of the bog. Birds rushed up. The sound traveling in waves, a chattering and then the sky ripe with birds.

"Get down, Len!" someone yelled.

"They're here!" the point man answered.

Walter could see it all now. A trooper near the bank of the bog stood to the left of two men hunkered down small in the sun-drenched grass. The point man so close that he thought that he must have lost his way in the denseness. Other troopers behind the first, breaking their way through the underbrush.

"I see you, Coyles! Drop your guns!" the point man said.

Two men jumped up and they rose as phantoms, standing in the grass, open and unafraid as if they welcomed the test, the challenge to their mortality. They shot in clusters and fought as if some long ago hatred had been evoked in them. There was fire and muzzle blast and multiple shots that roared through the reeds and tore at the peace of the bog. The point man dropped down and disappeared as worms of white smoke lifted up and drifted over the bog like lace. More troopers now in the grass closed the distance to their man.

A crossfire shot roared from out of the shadows of the woods that the fugitives turned to and responded in fury. Walter saw the specter of a man standing near a tree and the fire from his pistol as he answered in multiple rounds, shot into the sundrenched grass. White smoke rose again.

One of the fugitives stood, turned to the wood line and fired his pistol several times. He remained there fixed in a juxtaposed position as if he had a sudden thought. Walter saw him. He was just a boy. And for a moment, the place was still.

Then a single crossfire round broke from the trees. The clap echoed throughout. It shivered in the heavy morning air. And the bog became quiet again.

"I'm shot, you got me!" the boy yelled. Walter heard his exclamation, his punishment, rising up with great suffering. "Jesus," he said. "John?" Then he fell back weightless into the bed of grass and disappeared like he had fallen through Earth's trap door.

Betty ran from the house and joined Walter behind the wood pile. They saw the point man stand with his pistol out straight, deliberately moving toward the fugitives.

"John Coyle!" he said. "Come out with your hands up!"

Coyle stood with his arms raised, guns in each hand and pale as death. He turned back to where his brother lay. "Will?" he said as if he didn't want to disturb him. His brother's expression fixed like he had seen something wonderful and terrible too. John stood there for a moment and then turned to the darkened tree line. "You shot him!" he said. "You killed my brother!"

"Drop those guns!" the point man said. "And jump across the ditch to me."

Troopers ran to John Coyle, took hold of him, stripped him bare and carried him away. Other troopers stumbled with a stretcher and his lifeless brother and they ran with him to a waiting cruiser.

Betty clutched Walter's arm. "Is it finished?" she said.

"Yes."

They stood up from the protection of the wood pile and saw the shooter emerge from the darkened tree line. He stepped into the sunshine. A trooper, he looked to be not much older than the brothers, stood there alone. Stared into the marsh and the moist spring grass, into the blood-drenched grass. A pistol hung away from his body. He holstered the weapon, blessed himself, turned and departed, his raincoat lifting away at the sides like a vestment.

"An eye for an eye," Walter said.

Betty held her hand to her face. "There's no pleasure in killing," she said.

"No," Walter said. "No pleasure at all."

The cruisers left and they could hear the sirens growing distant. And the bog became still and quiet again, like nothing had happened there at all.

30

John Coyle faced the door and the hallway. Above him, a ceiling fan warbled in an uneven rotation. He sat on a stool in the middle of a moderate room at the Middleborough barracks with the wool blanket wrapped around him. Other than the blanket, he was naked.

"How about now, are you hungry?"

"I don't want anything to eat," he said.

"Okay, if you change your mind, you let me know."

Detective Lieutenant Michael Cullinane faced him in a swivel chair with his back to the door. He sat close to the edge of the seat and turned a pencil in his fingers like a baton. A woman stenographer sat to the left of the lieutenant recording the interrogation. At the rear of the room and behind Coyle were six to ten other officers and agents from several jurisdictions, a fluctuating number that was dependent on the participants' interest at the time and the degree to which they could tolerate the uncomfortable conditions. And during the course of the eight-hour interview, a continual parade of police officers, witnesses and dignitaries entered and exited the room. Coyle did not wither during the examination and seemed to delight in the theater that surrounded him. Each time the door to the hallway opened, other police officers and civilians paused as they paraded past his door that they might catch a glimpse of the notorious criminal. And he in return, shifted to one side of the stool or the other to accommodate them with a better view. Rather than a distraction or an intimidation, they contributed to his want for attention.

Cullinane nodded to his arms. "Those briars and burrs tore you up pretty good."

"Nothing I couldn't handle."

"Well if there is anything that we can do to help, you let us know. We can get a nurse or a doctor in here to take a look at you."

"I'm fine," he said.

"Okay." Cullinane leaned back in his chair. "So, we were talking about your activities from September 1958 to December 1958. Did you or your brother commit any acts that could result in your arrest during that time?"

"We robbed the First National store in Buzzards Bay," John said.

"The First National grocery store?"

"Yes, day after Christmas."

"And when you say *we*, you're referring to just yourself and your brother?"

"Yes."

"Was it always just you and your brother, John? I mean, no women or close friends?"

"Why would we want women in our lives? Did you see what happened to Dillinger because of that woman?

"So, no one else?"

"Just me and my brother."

"How did you happen to decide on the First National?"

"We bought groceries there."

"So, you were familiar with the store?"

"Yes."

"And this was your first robbery?"

"Yes. We needed money and we decided we might as well try it."

"Who suggested that?"

"I did. I said, we can try it anyway. See what happens."

"What did your brother say?"

"He said, 'All right.'"

A uniformed trooper entered the room, approached the lieutenant and whispered in his ear. Cullinane held the pencil still and stared at the floor. He nodded. The trooper left the room and the lieutenant swiveled back to Coyle.

"From what you have told me, it appears that you made the plans and your brother went along with them."

"We both talked it over."

"Let's be honest here. You were the leader."

"I guess so."

"You were the more forceful brother."

"I wouldn't say that."

"You wouldn't? Whatever you suggested doing, your brother went along."

"Not always."

"You suggested the first robbery."

"Yes."

"And it was your idea to steal a car and take the owner."

"Yes, but . . ."

"And your brother agreed."

"I guess so."

"And everything else. The bar holdup, the liquor store, the two kidnappings. You were the brains."

"We both decided."

"You mean, you decided and he went along." Cullinane looked down at his notes. "At the beginning of June . . ."

"I always took care of him."

"At the beginning of June, you were living in Philadelphia . . ."

"We were running out of money."

"What did you do?"

"We planned to rob a Savings & Loan."

237

"Did you?"

"No. We went by it a few times, but we didn't do it."

"Why's that?"

"Because we shot a policeman."

"When did you shoot him?"

"When did I shoot him? I didn't shoot him. My brother shot him."

"Your brother shot him?"

"He shot him."

"Why?"

"Why?"

"Yeah."

"Because the policeman caught him, that's all."

"And where were you?"

"I was down the street in an alley."

"What was your brother doing?"

"He was clipping milk from the porches, just around the corner from Erie Avenue where we lived."

"And this was . . . ?"

"About two weeks ago."

"And the time of day?"

"Five o'clock in the morning."

"So what happened?"

"They were going round 'n round a car and the policeman told him to halt or he would shoot. But my brother fired first. Five times—bang, bang, bang—like that."

"How did you know he was shot five times? Did you count the shots?"

"I read it in the newspaper."

"Did you see a gun in the policeman's hand?"

"There was a flashlight in his hand. That's all I could see. It was dark."

"And you were in the alley?"

"Down the street."

"How many times did you fire?"

"I didn't fire. I had my gun pointed up the street. I couldn't see, there were cars in the way. Then my brother ran right past me."

"And if it had been the policeman who ran towards you?"

He looked at Cullinane with an expression like he had been waiting for that question his whole life. "I would have shot him."

"What did he ever do to you?" Cullinane said.

"Nothin'," Coyle said. "He never did nothin' to me. But my brother was the only person I had in this world. And I always took care of him."

"Yeah, you mentioned that," Cullinane said. "Except for today."

"What?"

"Except for today, I said. You didn't take care of him today."

Coyle looked about the room and then stared at his hands.

"And there isn't any doubt if that policeman had run towards you, you would have shot him?"

"I would have shot him."

"Why?"

"Why?"

"Yes, why?"

"Because wc had a lot in front of us."

"So, you would have shot the policeman or anyone else?"

"Yes."

"If anyone got in your way."

"Anyone."

"And you have been truthful?"

"Yes. I would have told you if I had shot him."

Cullinane put his notes down. "Even though I tell you now that your brother died this morning?"

"That's true?" He pulled the blanket closer. "He did die?"

"Yes, he did."

"Did that trooper tell you?

"What trooper?"

"The one who whispered in your ear."

"Yes."

"Okay. You want me to say I shot the policeman. I didn't shoot him, but I don't care. I didn't shoot him, but I was there. It's the same damn thing isn't it?"

"Of course it is. I only want the truth."

"Will is dead?"

"Yes."

"You want me to tell the truth. Well, you got the truth. What else have I got to lose?"

"Your life," Cullinane said.

John shifted his feet on the rungs of the stool. He watched more officers enter and leave the room. "I get uneasy around police," he said. But I'm telling the truth."

"A lot of people get nervous when talking to the police. But some don't."

"Who?"

"Lifetime liars." Cullinane stood. "Let's get something to eat. Give you a chance to stretch your legs. Stand up. What do you want to eat?"

"I don't need to walk around. And I don't want nothing to eat. I can stay right here."

Cullinane went to the door and spoke to someone in the hall. "Can I have those clothes, please?" He looked back at Coyle. "You don't look tired at all, John. Other than a few marks on your body and a little sunburn . . ."

"I can take it pretty well. My ankle's going though. That swamp tore it up and the mosquitoes ate us alive. If it wasn't for that I'd be pretty good."

"I have some clothes for you. The stenographer is going to step out and you can put them on."

While Coyle dressed, Cullinane looked at his notes deciding where to begin again. He picked up his mug of coffee, sipped it while Coyle buttoned the shirt. He placed the mug on the desk next to him. "I would have expected you to have a five o'clock shadow," he said.

"We shaved while we waited in the swamp. Wanted to look presentable if we approached someone with a car."

"You've got good manners, John," he said. "Most of the people you came in contact with said you were polite. I mean most of the stiffs we do business with talk in 'shits and fucks' or they grunt because they don't know any better. Did your parents teach you those manners?

"My mother."

"Where did you go to school?"

"St. Vincent's Grammar in Philadelphia and Northeast Catholic in Germantown."

"What year did you graduate?"

"I didn't. Tenth grade."

"Then the service?"

Coyle pointed to some papers on the desk near Cullinane's coffee. "Are those warrants for me? Isn't it about time I got to read them?"

The lieutenant stood as several men entered the room. "Commissioner." He nodded. "Colonel." He turned to Coyle. "There are newspaper men and TV men looking to get a few pictures. We would like to get that over with quickly."

"What are the newspaper men going to ask?" he said.

"Only pictures, no questions," Cullinane said. "And while we're at it, you haven't said anything about an attorney. Anything in mind as far as that is concerned?"

"No."

"Can the local District Attorney get you one?"

"I guess so."

"You realize that there are crimes in Massachusetts, Pennsylvania and federal crimes?"

"Yes."

"Do you know what the crimes in Pennsylvania are?"

"Murder and armed robbery, I guess," Coyle said.

"Suppose in court in the morning, the District Attorney from Philadelphia is present, how would you feel about going back to face a murder charge?"

He held his hands on top of his knees. "I guess I have to face the serious charge. And murder is it."

"So, you're agreeable to going back right away?"

"It's all right with me."

"Voluntarily?"

"Yes."

Cullinane took Coyle by the arm. They stood about the same height and when the lieutenant spoke to him, he looked at him closely. "So, it don't bother you at all to go back?"

He shrugged his shoulders. "You can't win 'em all."

Coyle walked into the adjoining room with the lieutenant and the other men. A few minutes later, he and Cullinane returned. The lieutenant poured himself a glass of water. He held up another glass to Coyle and Coyle shook his head. Two men appeared at the door and Cullinane waved them in. "John, these guys have been waiting a long time and I'm going to bring them in now for identification purposes." Coyle watched them enter and nodded.

"State your names, please," Cullinane said.

"Rudy Silva."

"I remember you," Coyle said. "You were in the truck that followed us to the woods."

"Robert Mott."

"That's right," Rudy said. "I told him to stop."

"And I said, hell no." Robert said. "We saw you coming out of the liquor store and I told him they're up to something.

Then I saw the car go into the picnic grove there. The two-door green Dodge."

Coyle nodded. "I told him, 'Watch that truck.'"

"Was that your brother, driving?" Robert said.

"Yes."

"I used to be a Special cop," Rudy said.

"Now, there you go." Coyle pointed at Silva. "I'd hate to have this fellow checking up on me. If it wasn't for him . . ." He turned to Cullinane. "Well, they made me. Might as well let 'em go."

The lieutenant walked the two men to the door and they left. At the same time, Captain Munroe and his eighteen-man detail entered and stood in a group at the front of the room.

Cullinane leaned against the desk between the troopers and Coyle. "John, do you recognize any of these officers?"

He studied the troopers and the one sergeant. "That one standing there," he said.

"Which one?"

He pointed to a trooper on the far left.

"Step up," Cullinane said. "State your name, please."

"Trooper Leonard Von Fursten."

"I remember you," Coyle said. "Had you in my sights, drew a bead down on you. I tried to get you, but you crouched down in the grass."

"How many times did you fire?" Cullinane said.

"Four or five times I would say."

"And you meant to hit him."

"Yes."

"And you would have killed him if you could have?"

"If I had to."

The lieutenant clasped his hands in front of him. "John, you seem to have an obsession with policemen."

"I just wanted to get away. And that was the easiest way."

"To shoot him?"

243

"Yes."

"Why?"

"It was me or him."

"Just like the policeman in Philadelphia. If he was the one who ran by you instead of your brother, you would have shot him down."

"Yes."

"So, today in the bog when you saw your brother shot . . ."

"I was firing away."

"Where was he shot?"

"In the head."

"In the head?"

"Yes."

"Did you think he had a chance?"

"I saw his eyelids flutter. That's all."

"Now you know your brother is dead."

"I guess so. If you say he is."

"And that was when you surrendered. When your brother was shot?"

"No. I thought I had a chance. I only saw three policemen. Then I saw many more."

"These men here."

"Yes."

"And then you surrendered."

He folded his hands in front of him and he looked down at the floor. "We should have stayed in the woods. Never would have surrendered."

"What did you say?" Cullinane said.

"We should have stayed where we belonged."

"What do you mean by that?"

Coyle continued to look at the floor. "We had you."

"But you did surrender, didn't you?" the lieutenant said.

John lifted his head with a fixed expression.

Cullinane stood up. "Before these men are dismissed. Is there anyone else here you remember?"

He singled out three other troopers and the sergeant and they stepped forward.

"What do you remember about these officers?"

"They shot at me and my brother."

"And you shot at them."

"Yes."

"Okay, I guess that's . . .,"

"I know him." Coyle leaned forward slightly from the stool. He pointed at one of the three troopers.

"Step forward and state your name, please," the lieutenant said.

"Trooper Francis Mahan."

"What do you remember about this officer?" the lieutenant said.

He stared at Frank for a long moment. Laughter could be heard in the hallway outside. "I've seen him before," he said.

"In the bog?"

Coyle turned to the lieutenant. Then he faced Frank again. "I remember him, that's all."

"Alright, that should do it." Cullinane walked to the door with the detail of men and they left. He looked at his wrist watch. "It's now 6:40 John, how about that food."

"I don't want anything to eat," he said.

"That's your third refusal. You haven't had anything all day."

"I'm not hungry."

"Is there anything else we can do for you?"

"No, nothing."

"Well, is there anything we can do for your brother? Notify someone?"

"There's nobody but me."

"No one?"

245

"Just my brother and me."

"No one in Philadelphia?"

"Not a soul."

"How about relatives?"

"We haven't seen them in years."

"Well, someone called. A sister or an aunt?"

"Maybe, an aunt."

"We lost the connection. Hopefully, she'll call back."

"What can she do?"

"She could arrange for the funeral."

"Why bother with that?"

"There must be someone we can call to help out with the arrangements."

"Don't bother. It's just my brother and me."

AFTER JOHN COYLE left the room, Cullinane spoke briefly with the stenographer about the transcription and she also left. He dropped his notes on the desk and collapsed down into the chair. Someone brought him a fresh cup of coffee and he was sitting there alone when Captain Munroe entered.

"He's a pip isn't he?" the captain said. "Sure can talk a blue streak."

"Couldn't get it out fast enough," the lieutenant said. He drank his coffee. "I think he's at war with life, thrived on it. Consumed by it. And finally, devoured by it."

"Well, you've got a knack, Mike. They picked the right man for this."

"It took me years to realize something."

"What's that?"

"You don't have to beat them over the head with a stick."

"You mean talk to them?" the captain said.

"Why go through all the bullshit. No need to be screaming, threatening, wasting all that energy. Put the spotlight
right on them. Not you, not the victim. It's their story."

"Sell them."

"That's right, sell them on themselves. Because that's
what it's all about. When Coyle was robbing that liquor
store, he was screaming at the top of his lungs, here I am,
you cocksuckers."

"And he told you."

"He's been waiting to tell me his whole miserable life.
Couldn't get it out fast enough."

"Well, it doesn't seem to bother him one bit," Munroe
said.

"No. You'd think he was in church. He sat on that stool
and told me he would have shot the Philadelphia cop and not
thought a blessed thing about it."

"Makes you wonder."

"Their buddy in the Air Force, the guy who hunted with
them in the woods, said the younger brother was one of the
nicest guys in the world. Never looked for trouble. But when
John came around, he changed. William told this guy 'I'm
taking off, going to be a juvenile delinquent'. Said they were
sick of taking orders, sick of being suckers. Isn't that a hell
of a thing?" Cullinane leaned forward. "I was on a PT boat
in the Philippines when I was their age. What's wrong with
these kids? It's as if they got the short end of the stick. I don't
get it."

"Well, I'm glad we had the manpower in there," Munroe
said.

"Yeah. Was the only way that was going to end. And I'm
glad it was one of them and not us."

Munroe pulled over a chair and straddled it backwards
with his arms resting on the top. "Autopsy's done."

"Let me guess," Cullinane said. "Cause of death, a bullet to the brain."

"Doc King says he found a hole near the top of William's skull. 'Bout the hairline. Dug out a large chunk of misshapen lead."

"A large chunk, huh?"

"Yeah like from a .45."

"Who was shooting a .45?"

"No one. But the entry hole is large enough you could stick a number two pencil into it."

"So, what are you saying?"

"The bullet penetrated William's forehead near his hairline and it mushroomed by bone and tissue. Caused a skull fracture and massive damage."

"Hmm." Cullinane rocked back in the chair. "What're you thinking?"

"None of the guys directly involved in the shootout had anything larger than a .38."

"Soft lead then?"

"Yeah."

"Hollow point?"

"I'm thinking wadcutter," the captain said.

"Anything else?"

"He also had two smaller holes in his buttocks, entrance and exit wounds. Same bullet, consistent with department issue. Probably a different shooter because of the angle."

"Have those guys been interviewed?"

"Yes."

"And?"

"No one is claiming the kill shot," Munroe said. They all say they don't know who fired the fatal round."

"Circling the wagons?"

"A lot of lead flying around that cranberry bog, Mike."

Cullinane drank the coffee.

"Is there a need for an inquest?" the captain said.

"I'll speak with the D.A., but I don't think so. The Philadelphia PD doesn't care."

Munroe stood. "Then, that's that."

31

A quiet bus ride back to Framingham, whispered conversations and then they were dismissed. The eighteen of them stood awkwardly on the hardpan, expecting something more. Then the gradual realization that it was over. They loaded up their gear and found their way to a local bar, assembled there, huddled in subdued conversations. And as time wore on, a few members of the detail posed with stiffly controlled role-playing postures, some were reflective, others bellowed, some just laughed for no good reason. And some of them hoped that the others had missed them tucked away in the quagmire, crawling and tilting away from the bullets and the death that flew about them. At the back of the room, there were columns of empty beer cases and other things stored, upturned tables and chairs stacked against the wall. There in the semi dark those closest to the firefight, like Frank and Lenny Von Fursten huddled privately and spoke with lowered voices. There were five of them. Bobby Clark got quiet and Paul Samuelson tapped his foot on the floor repeatedly. Sy Abramson with a cigar between his teeth sat with his chair tipped back. "Damn, that was fast," he said.

One of the detail from the front of the room approached the table. "So, which one?"

"Which one what?" Sy said. "What are you talking about?"

"Who got Coyle?"

The five men looked away or continued to talk privately. And when he didn't leave, Bobby Clark looked up and said, "What do you want?"

"Come on," he said. "When I'm shooting from that distance, I sure as hell know whether I'm in the ring or not."

Lenny stood. "Get lost," he said.

"What?"

"You heard me."

"What's wrong with you guys?"

"Take a hike," Bobby Clark said.

"Take it easy. I was just saying you never know, huh." He walked away and rejoined the others at the bar.

In time, most of them reverted to their original condition. And by the end of the day, they celebrated their training. They celebrated their traditions and their place in history. They celebrated their lives. "Oh man, I had to take the worst shit." They became crude, cursed more than usual, laughed meanly and then they left to return to their homes as fathers and sons and husbands.

Darkness arrived by the time Frank got out of his classmate's car at the bottom of the street. He exchanged few words with the driver and watched it speed away, followed it up the hill between the double row of houses. He stood there alone, frozen in place, as if he had no good reason for being there with the anxious and impatient temperament of a child and the compelling desire to scream. A low pitched buzzing hummed in his ears and he had a headache so severe he thought he could vomit. He was sore. One of his legs twitched involuntarily. And he had the overwhelming sensation that he had lost something.

He could smell the woods. The rotting decay burned in his nostrils. He heard the shouts of their voices. Gunshots and bullets ripping the air. Trails of smoke drifting over him like garlands and falling to rest in the cranberry bog. The

251

acrid odor hanging on him like a shroud, the sudden finality of it and the uncertain discovery of being alive. The euphoria of capture, its adrenaline rush and the haughty swagger of alcohol all gone. Now he questioned his memory. There was confusion and an emerging insecurity, the worm of self-doubt burrowing in. It was that boy's face that haunted him, frozen in an expression of despair, the bullet wound prominent, gaping like an open eye.

Sheila opened the door and the light from the kitchen fell out onto the stairs. Their oldest son stood behind her and the boy leaned out of the doorway to see him. Frank struck his boots against the pavement to remove the mud, the broken lacing hanging away from the tongue and gouges in the leather deep as knife wounds. He carried his uniform over his arm. It was soiled and stained and it had a rotting stench to it. Prickly burrs were stuck to the breeches. He saw his wife and his son and their smiles, an affirmation that everything was okay and it encouraged him to take the first few steps to home. When he reached the landing, she said to their son, "Alright, you saw him. Now, get to bed. We have a big day tomorrow." She took Frank's bag and directed him to a chair. She could smell the odor of alcohol amongst all the other odors that he carried in from the night.

"Are you alright?" she said.

He sat down heavy at the table.

"I went about my business," she said. "I didn't want to upset the kids." She locked the door and pulled the shade. "But you know good meaning people, they talk, so they found out anyways."

"Where are they?"

"They should be asleep."

He left the room. Then she heard him walking above her. Ten minutes later he returned.

"You didn't wake them, did you?" she said. "They'll be cranky for the trip tomorrow."

"I kissed them goodnight." He looked at her as if to pose a question, but didn't.

"They're still asleep?"

"Jack stirred. But he's out like a light."

She dropped his bag by the washing machine. "I wish you had called, Frank."

He sat down again at the table.

"Frank?"

"It happened fast."

"I thought I'd miss the telephone, I was afraid to go out."

He hung his garrison cap off the knob of the chair.

"You could have called afterwards. Just so I knew."

"I guess so."

"What happened? I heard one of them is dead."

"Can we talk about this later?"

"Don't you feel well?"

"Yeah, I'm fine. Hunky dory."

"Jesus, Frank." She lifted her apron and wiped the corner of her eye.

"Hell of a day, Sheila," he heard himself say.

She opened the refrigerator door and looked inside. "You want something to eat?"

He stretched his legs out in front of him, leaned back and closed his eyes.

"WBZ said that the gunshots coming out of the cranberry bog sounded like a battle zone. You weren't in there? Were you? I mean . . . Where were you?"

"Yeah, I was."

"I thought they already had troopers in there."

"They did."

"Did they shoot at you? How many times did they shoot at you?"

253

He pondered the question as if he was a witness to something.

"Frank?"

"I don't remember." He stared at the table. "Couple of times, I guess."

"Are you alright? How did you end up in there?"

He looked over at her. "I'll have a cup of tea."

"What? Okay, do you want some eggs too?"

"No." He placed the contents of his pockets onto the table. A single cartridge rolled off and it fell to the floor. It went across the linoleum and stopped near the refrigerator.

She picked it up and handed it to him. "That's odd looking."

"I'm lucky I got this vacation," he said. "Another week or two and I would have been screwed."

"What are you talking about?"

"Get me away from all of this for a while."

She filled the kettle with water and put it on the stove. "Well, the kids can't wait."

"They're awful quiet," he said. "Where are they?"

"What?" She turned back to him. "They're in bed."

"I'll have them scrambled."

"I thought you just said?" He had his elbow on the table and was holding the cartridge by the rim, turning it with the tips of his fingers.

"Don't jump up in the morning," she said. "We don't have to leave that early."

32

Middleborough, Massachusetts
June 18, 1959

Troopers sat on either side of John Coyle in the back seat of the cruiser and he shared a pair of handcuffs with both. The driver turned into the parking lot of the Egger Funeral Home. "How did you sleep, Coyle?" he said.

"Like a baby."

Detective Lieutenant Cullinane and Captain Munroe met the cruiser and walked John to a small room in the basement of the funeral home where they met three other men. Will's body lay on a table covered to its neck with a sheet. John stood there for a moment before he approached the body, his face without expression and the police behind him. Then he lifted the sheet by a corner and exposed his brother's side, it was the color of limestone. He stood there holding the white cotton sheet and he recalled the letters he wrote to him. How he convinced him that they had been left behind and how they could prosper as rebels. At the end of the table, Will's clothing lay in a neat pile and he picked up one of his shoes. It had a hole in the bottom and he probed the hole with his finger.

Cullinane said, "John, this is District Attorney Victor . . ."

He continued to examine his brother's clothing.

"John?" Cullinane said. "This is Philadelphia District Attorney Victor Blanc, and these other two gentlemen are Philadelphia detectives."

255

Coyle bent closer to examine the body.

"For their purposes, is that your brother?"

"That's him," he said.

"And are you declaring here that William killed Officer Kane in Philadelphia two weeks ago?"

"Yeah."

"And the other crimes to which you confessed yesterday, did he accompany you in the commission of them?"

He placed his fingers on his brother's forehead where the bullet had penetrated. He traced the outline of the hole, lingering there for a long moment.

"John?" Cullinane and Captain Munroe exchanged glances. "John?" the lieutenant said.

He shifted to one side and allowed room light to fall on his brother's face.

"Did Will accompany you during these other crimes?"

He held his brother's hand.

"John? Did Will participate in the other crimes?"

"I told you yesterday," he said.

"I know you did, but I need you to say it again in front of these men from Philadelphia."

Coyle looked back. "How many times do you want me to say it? Yes."

Cullinane stepped closer to him. "No one has claimed your brother's body. The Air Force denies any responsibility for his burial because since January, he has been classified as a deserter. We haven't heard from anyone else. What do you want us to do?"

Coyle remained engaged with his brother's body for several more moments. Then he turned and faced them. And he said it to all of them, "You killed him. You bury him, best you can."

WHILE JOHN IDENTIFIED his brother's body at the funeral home, troopers created a human barrier around the Wareham District Court to keep back a large crowd that had gathered to catch a glimpse of the young killer. Something about 'those rebels' that resonated with them. And when Coyle arrived a half hour later, some of them applauded. At his arraignment, the judge impressed with his overall condition, said to him, "You look pretty good, Mr. Coyle. Did you get any sleep?" and John responded, "Maybe, I got more than you did, Judge." And while John appeared before the court, Betty Schmidt opened a letter in Middleborough postmarked in Boston shortly after Coyle's capture. She read it and then sat down in a chair. Her husband asked her what it said. "You'll be dead before they get to court," she said. And in Pennsylvania as Thelma Sedgwick and her two sons celebrated the safe return of her husband, the telephone rang. She held the receiver away and stared into the room. "Who was that?" her husband said. "A woman. She told me, 'You better watch your boys or something will happen to them.'"

John pleaded guilty to seven charges, including Assault with Intent to Murder and being A Fugitive from Justice, he waived extradition, left in the custody of the Philadelphia police and arrived in the city seven hours later. Shortly after, he voluntarily participated in a filmed reenactment of the killing of Patrolman Jimmy Kane. He pointed out the place where Kane confronted his brother and where he'd hid during the murder. And as the filming continued, he grew eager in his role as director and became animated and confident. He spoke through a microphone with authority and grew in rebellious stature, instructing the actors to this thing or that. He yawned when asked to repeat a direction.

He played to the crowd of over a thousand onlookers who stood behind barricades and an affinity was developed with him. So when the man who represented William Coyle

257

shot the 'patrolman', blank rounds popped like fireworks on Sydenham Street, the policeman-actor fell and some of the crowd gasped. Some of them applauded. John Coyle seemed pleased.

33

A lazy breeze moved across the water apologetically, the morning light reflecting off the surface like the hard glimmer from broken glass. Frank looked out over the rim of his cup to the end of the beach where his younger son ran, the kite skipping along the sand behind him. The coffee splashed up and the hot liquid burnt his lips. He swore and held his knuckles against his mouth. Sheila came out of the cottage and she stood next to him. Their daughter sat at one corner of a blanket reading. He dug out a hole in the sand with his shoe, dumped out the remaining coffee and lit a cigarette. He exhaled the first deep breath and waved the smoke away from his daughter.

"You're smoking again," Sheila said.

He ignored the remark and continued to look up the beach.

"Let's go for a hike, today," she said. "We'll have a picnic."

He held his arm away and flicked the ashes. "I've got to rake out the sand before I do anything. It's full of weeds."

"We can help you." She also looked up to where their son ran. "What time did you get to sleep?"

"I'm not sure."

"Was it light?"

"I don't know."

"What were you doing?"

He didn't answer.

"What were you doing, Frank?"

259

"I was checking the cottage, making sure the kids were okay."

"Why?"

"I heard a noise outside."

"I didn't hear anything."

He turned to her. "I heard something."

"I'm just saying . . ."

"Do you think I'm nuts?"

"I'm not saying that."

"I'm telling you I heard someone out there."

"What's going on? You've been up every night since we've been here."

"Nothing."

"I can hear you pacing from one end of the cottage to the other."

Frank drew down on the cigarette, exhaled and waved his hand again to clear the smoke. She stared at the hard stone muscle in his jaw. "We only have this place for two more days," she said. "Do you think you can enjoy it?"

He turned away and looked back at the lake.

She sat down on the blanket next to their daughter. "Go in and have your cereal." After the girl left, she said, "I'm just trying to help."

"I'm fine, Sheila" he said.

"You're not fine. You're hearing people in the middle of the night. You drove to town the other day and had to drive back to ask me why you went there in the first place."

He looked over at her. "You don't forget things?"

"That's not the point."

"What is the point, huh? What-is-the-point?"

"Stop it, Frank." There was a trace of desperation in her voice. "I've never seen you like this. I had to call my sister yesterday to tell her not to come to the lake because all the kids were sick. I lied because you didn't want anyone around."

"Is there something wrong with spending time alone with my kids?"

"No. But . . ."

"But what?"

"You're closing yourself off. Ever since you came home from that swamp. Cranberry bog." She turned and faced him. "What happened in there?"

"You know what happened. The papers are full of it."

"I want to hear it from you." A tear formed in the corner of her eye. "I can't help you if you don't talk to me."

"I'm just sick of people judging me. Let them live their own miserable lives."

"Who's judging you, Frank?"

He turned away. Took a drag from the cigarette and crushed it in the sand. He went to where she sat clutching her knees. "I heard someone pounding the side of the cabin last night," he said. "That's why I was up."

"There was no one out there."

"I saw him. He was standing on the beach."

"Who?"

"Just standing there, waiting. Just waiting."

"There was no one out there, Frank."

"And how would you know that?"

"Because I was up too, standing at the window and watching you pace the beach in the middle of the night. By yourself. There was no one out there, Frank. You were alone. No one, but you."

"I heard it!"

"Stop it!"

He knelt down on one knee and scooped up a handful of warm granular sand. He let it sift through his fingers until his hand was empty. "I'm not crazy."

261

She ran her hands down the tops of her thighs. "Would you please stop saying that?"

"I'm not."

"Please. Please stop."

Frank stood and walked away to the end of the beach looking about the sand like he had lost something. An elderly man sat at the end and the man tried to strike up a conversation, but he looked away without acknowledging him. After several minutes, he came back to the blanket and stood there like he was vibrating. She looked up at him and gave him a thin desperate smile.

"It's like you're ready to fight the world." She reached out to him. "You're upsetting the kids."

He combed his hand through his hair and held the back of his neck.

"Sit down," she said. He sat and pushed his heels into the sand. She took his arm and leaned against him. They watched their son, running towards them, the kite bouncing along the beach and then lifting into the sky behind him. "He was determined to get that thing in the air," she said.

"He's got a lot of determination."

"Like someone else I know." She leaned against him.

"I'm alright, Sheila."

"Nightmares?"

He ignored her.

"Please, answer me."

"Yeah."

"They're not real, Frank." She pointed to their son. "He's real. I'm real."

"He just stands there."

"Who?"

"Coyle. I pull the trigger and I hear click, click, click. And he stands there, waiting for me to drop the bullets into the chamber. And I try again and again and again."

"In time, it'll go away," she said.

He looked at her. "It's funny, I can remember some things and others, they're just blanks. This woman comes out of nowhere, she's just there, must have been from one of the houses. And she's screaming at us because the older brother is naked. So, I put my raincoat around him. She's upset 'cause he's got no clothes on. No clothes on? He would have shot her dead nine times if he thought he could have escaped."

She took his arm. "It's over, Frank. It's over."

"Not for the second-guessers."

"Who's second-guessing you?"

"A lieutenant from headquarters says to me, 'Hey Mahan, I heard you might be the guy who put one in his head. Nice shooting.' Then he wanted to know how close I was to him."

"To Coyle?"

"Yeah."

"Why did he want to know that?"

"I don't know. Maybe he thought my life wasn't in danger. I told him both Coyles shot at me. He says, 'That's good enough for me. But you know the brass, they may ask questions.'"

"He probably didn't mean anything by it," she said.

"Then he says, 'What did you hit him with?'"

"What's he talking about?"

"Ammunition. What kind of ammunition did I use."

"Was he there?"

"No."

"So, who cares what he thinks. He wasn't there."

"Because once the dust settles, the second-guessing begins."

"He shot at you?"

"Yeah."

"So?"

"But then he just stood there. Like he was waiting for me to shoot him. Just me and him." Frank looked out to the lake. "And I lined up my sights right in the middle of his head."

"You defended yourself."

"I killed him."

"He had a choice. He could have surrendered, but he chose not to. He chose the outcome."

He put his hand down on the sand and ran it back and forth until it was smooth. He told her about the bus ride from Framingham and the arrival in Middleborough. The sudden command to form up while some of them were still in their seats. He told her how he ran, weighed down by the raincoat in the heat, the air thick and wet and breathless, charging through the brush and sprinting the woods, stumbling over a rise and leaping over fallen timber until he reached the bog where he collapsed against a tree, breathing in a heavy crushing respiration, wheezing from not enough air. Gunshots and commands echoing throughout the bog. The smell of gunpowder, the metallic odor hanging like the acrid stench of fireworks. The weight of the revolver in his hand, shaking so terribly he couldn't control the barrel, squeezing it in a death grip, jacking the rounds, and firing blindly in desperation. The Coyles returning fire and the click—click—click of his empty weapon. How he fumbled the bullets and how they fell. And when he stooped down, a round hit the tree above him. How he cringed under the death that spun in the air.

Then suddenly clarity and calmness. All things, the volume of life turned down and the world laid out before him in tableau. Sounds now like whispers, he no longer heard the firefight or calls for surrender. Time slowed and it froze to a snapshot. Smoke hung like decorations and insects became suspended in flight, winged arthropods pressed into the day's background. The bog became still. He began to reload with an unconscious exactness. And in the last moment, he found old familiar comfort again and dropped the wadcutter round into the last empty chamber. He didn't hear the cylinder close or see his thumb cock the hammer. He didn't remember supporting his weight or steadying the weapon. He looked down the six-inch string and sighted on William Coyle, a ten-ring target in the butts eight yards away. And he pressed his finger against the trigger and squeezed until he couldn't squeeze any longer. The shot, he never heard.

"His head snapped up and he fell over backwards," he said. "Sat there propped up on one side with his legs splayed out in front of him. 'You got me,' he said like he didn't believe it. Then he looked up as if he was seeing something. He was so close I heard him gasping for air and swallowing his words. 'John?' he called to his brother. He began to gag on his own blood like he was drowning. Then the ammo belts he was wearing pulled him home dead weight to earth, and his terrible burden was finished.

"This kid," Frank said. "This stupid kid, waiting for me to shoot him. Waiting for me to align my sights and end his miserable life."

"Don't torture yourself, Frank."

"You know the real shitty part? I don't feel any compassion, just anger. For squeezing the trigger on a dumb stupid kid. For loading unauthorized ammunition. Anger for being there for Christ's sake. Why did he stand there like that?"

"I don't know," she said. "But I'm glad you did what you did. For my sake and the kids."

They sat there in the shimmer of late morning, the day nearing its apex, brilliant and the shadows disappearing around them. And she looked out over the water. "Ask that cop in the grave in Philadelphia, was it fair? Or better still, ask his wife." She turned to him and saw him grinding his teeth. "Maybe, if you talk to someone."

"No one's interested, Sheila. They don't talk about things like that."

"Someone."

"Who?"

"I don't know. Someone you feel comfortable with."

"I wouldn't even know what to say."

"What've you got to lose?"

SHE CAME TO him early that night. He could smell her in the room before she joined him and he tried to remember the days and nights he lay with her. To the tiny bunkroom at the front of the cottage. After the three kids had totally exhausted themselves in and on the water. When the room was dark and the windows smoky with last light. He lay there awake, his boyhood scruples torturing him, accusing him until they left him wired like unfettered electricity. She slipped her brown summer legs within and without his own, the legs that turned strange men's heads and made him sullen. She touched him and it was as if she was an open flame.

"Don't," he said

She slipped her hand between his thighs.

"I can't."

"Yes, you can."

He wanted to love his wife, wanted to just love again. But felt neither passion nor the energy to engage, could not experience pleasure nor sought its companionship. He looked into the cool dark corners of the room, where no shadows existed nor accusations made and closed his eyes. "I'm sorry," he said.

"Don't be." She directed him to his side, facing the cabin wall and closed herself around him. "Don't ever be sorry."

He heard the lake and the water lapping the shore. Her body a vessel of strength.

34

Along the turnpike the convoy of cruisers raced at maximum speed to another prison disturbance. They were tense and geared up, wired for battle. PK Cunningham drove and Frank hung onto the ceiling strap with one hand, his other hand around the barrel of a 12-gauge shotgun. Cunningham in time with the moment flushed and stained in an alcohol sweat. Frank mired in the Middleborough swamp and the waters of a New Hampshire lake.

"Just like old times, mi amigo, saddled up and riding with the posse. How was the vacation?" Cunningham said.

"Could have been longer," he said.

"Hell of a way to come back."

"Yeah, shit."

They took the ramp for 128, the siren whining, the bubble gum machine grinding on the roof above them.

"One way or the other," Cunningham said. "One way or the other."

"I don't know if I'm ready for this."

"No time, Priest. Leave the vacation in the rearview mirror, this is the real deal. Better check your gas mask."

"It should be alright."

He had found some relief from the constant memory during his last two days at the lake. He became less angry and he fished with his boys and played checkers with his daughter. He had slept some. Another day and he would have made love with his wife. The memories, the anxieties lifting

267

away like wisps of the white smoke that drifted over the bog. The terrors had become less frequent and less frightening, not quite whole, not quite accurate. And for the first time in weeks, he nearly laughed.

But now he realized that he had never found an emotional release, no overwhelming sadness, no sorrow, no tears that would allow him to make an acceptable peace. He returned to the job and the loop played again. Will Coyle stood and waited for him, and he should have, could have, wished he had, the fucking wadcutter dropping down into the chamber again. *But they shot at me! And you killed him.* His hands began to shake and again the terrible feeling that he, not the Coyles, had become the hunted prey.

"Here we go, Priest."

They left the highway, the radio crackled, the siren wailed and the gray walls of the prison rose up in front of them like some great and terrible leviathan.

Massachusetts Correctional Institute at Concord
Concord, Massachusetts.
THE COOKS SAW them first. Shirtless savages, their bodies decorated with fruit juices and crude prison tattoos, biblical messages written into their flesh with pens dipped in their own blood. They armed themselves with knives pounded out of pieces of sheet metal and wore homemade corkscrews taped between their knuckles. Wild crazed men, running towards them. A terrible stampede straight out of hell. Rebel inmates, crazed on prison liquor and amphetamines exploded into the kitchen. Captured guards, civilian employees and non-participating inmates, fifteen hostages in all driven like beasts by these violent desperate men. They screamed savage threats as to what they would do if they weren't released, many of them carrying blankets, pillows, mattresses and

homemade weapons for the eventual siege. They scavenged knives, a fire extinguisher, a removable door handle, table legs and chair legs that they fashioned into clubs. And shards of glass, any kind of glass. At the lead, Charles Bull Martin pulled a guard shackled by a chain that chattered against his body like Sanctus bells, the maniacal convict waving a pistol in the air and pointing it to steer the mob. They "wanted out" and prepared for battle, hoping to secure a strategic advantage before the state police mustered on their doorstep. They concluded as did other American inmates that freedom, even in its most limited form attained through violent escape attempts, was an improvement over their present condition. From Massachusetts to Montana to California and back, prison unrest, riots and escape attempts swept the country. A deputy warden lost his life, shot by an inmate, guards were stabbed and assaulted and two inmate ringleaders died. And there were numerous kidnappings, hostages held and threats of mayhem. Thus, a few months after the assault on the Walpole institution, troopers mustered outside the Massachusetts State Prison at Concord.

Martin collared the captured guard, held the pistol to his head and directed him out of the kitchen. He yanked him back and the guard walked limbo-like on his heels. He herded the hostages down a narrow corridor. The drunken leader stumbled, intoxicated on lemon extract, corrected himself and regained his swagger. Behind him, sixty other rioters shoved and bullied the hostages as Martin maneuvered his bargaining chips into a play for freedom. They carried boxes of food taken from the kitchen and made preparations for a long protracted standoff. At the end of the corridor, only a station gate separated the growing parade from the large open-spaced dining area.

"Open the gate," Martin said to the guard.

"I can't." He saw the terror in the eyes of the captured officer. "I don't have a key."

Martin fired a round at the station guard's head. The bullet passed his face, it struck the bulletin board on the wall and fell away into the large open space behind him. "Open the gate!"

"I don't have the key."

He pressed the pistol against the captured guard's temple and pulled the trigger. The hammer fell and the sound of the metallic click filled the space like a blow to the end of a chisel. The misfire enraged the convict more. "We want out! Now open the goddam gate or I'll kill him right before your eyes."

"Don't shoot him." The guard opened the desk drawer, took out a key and unlocked the gate. It blew open from the force of human weight and he was struck in the face and pinned by it until one of the convicts seized him and claimed him for his own personal bargaining chip. Martin locked the gate behind him and led the rebels and the hostages into the spacious dining room. There, they pulled the pins from the hinges of several doors and used the doors to barricade the large steel entrance. He called out and demanded a meeting with the superintendent. Then settled in and waited.

They came from everywhere. The Berkshires and the Worcester hills, Cape Cod and the North Shore, one hundred and twenty-five came. And with each succeeding prison uprising, the time for negotiations lessened and the time for counter assault increased. The state police came and they optioned for a different strategy, deciding against a surgical strike by a specialized squad, instead employing a superior force to crush the rebellion, swiftly and savagely. So when the superintendent of the prison refused to meet and Bull Martin threatened to send out bodies, riot-equipped troopers came in the blue and white light of acetylene torches. They cut the bars from the windows and the hinges from the large steel door. Sledge hammers drove the bars from the windows and freed the main door, the dining room assaulted by a firestorm of tear gas. Rebels covered themselves in blankets, sheets and clothing in an attempt to shield themselves from the nauseous agent. Troopers and guards climbed through the windows and blew down the barricade, charged out of the smoke and the cloud of CS into the room with gas masks secured and riot batons at the ready. Any aggression greeted with wood, a brutal incursion. Rioters fell in bunches and some were attacked by inmate hostages who welcomed the force, submitted gladly and accepted the safety of the tier one cells.

Mired in the debris created by retreating rebels, troopers stumbled and some fell. The heat and the gas laid claim to the police, rioters and hostages all, and more bodies teetered and fell, strewn about the floor blinded, drooling and writhing in tears and gasping in the noxious cloud. Bull Martin and other ringleaders used blankets to cover their heads and low crawled across fallen bodies scattered about the dining room and escaped to the metal stairway. They climbed to the third floor and hid away in the Maximum Security Unit.

In the center of the dining room, Frank sat stunned, kneeling back on his heels and unable to breathe, the skin on his face afire, a scorching in his nose and throat, hiccupping and one spasm from throwing up in his mask. He sneezed and mucous oozed out of his nose and he thought he had soiled himself. Gas penetrated the mask and he panicked, lay down on the floor and tore at the straps. Then suddenly lifted and pushed out of the area, into the corridor, bandy-legged and wretched and not a clue as to whom or what controlled him. His impaired vision prevented him from navigating the room and he stumbled.

"You alright, Priest?" Cunningham said.

271

Frank looked about and saw the others assembled and ready to run the stairs. PK pulled off his mask and helped him to the steps. "You've got a leak," he said. He handed him a towel and gave him a canteen. "Come on. Let's finish these bastards." The others started up the stairs and he watched them. Cunningham propped him up and pushed him forward.

A prisoner yelled something religious, an Old Testament psalm, and there on the first floor, a murmur began. The locked-down prisoners hit the bars and began to hum as the troopers started their climb, a rhythmic primal sound like an old prayer offered, a petition, a mournful supplication. And as they climbed, the sound grew louder and magnified in the steel and cement building. The inmates struck the metal bars with books and shoes and wooden soup spoons, soap containers and pencils. Anything that created noise. They stood back and kicked the bars and threw their forearms into the cell walls. A rhythmic drumming continued to build with each level they climbed, the sound growing and filling the house, a disturbing message, a long ago beginning, the drum of primitive man. And by the time they reached the third tier and came upon the rioters, the noise was deafening.

They found the remaining rebels standing with their faces turned to the wall, their hands high above their heads. Bull Martin knelt on the floor, his head buried in his hands. Gas tears leaked from between his fingers and dripped from the end of his nose. They stripped down the rebels and locked them in the stand-alone units in the Maximum Security section and the prison became quiet again. The troopers left the floor, pulling off their protective gear as they descended. Frank stood, the last man at the top of the stairs and a strange mood enveloped him without warning or by invitation. He heard that sorrowful wail somewhere before, the one coming from Bull Martin's cell, a soulful lament that he recalled from many years ago when still a child of the brick and the mortar.

CUNNINGHAM FOLLOWED THE parade of cruisers out of the parking lot. "You back with the living?" he said.

"Yeah." Frank blew his nose and wiped the moisture from his face. "Thanks."

"Nothing like a prison riot to get you back on the horse and help you forget your other life." He raised his nose and sniffed. "Jesus Priest, you smell like shit."

Frank coughed and made a small gasp.

"Did you?"

"No. Well, maybe a little."

Cunningham pulled out onto the road. "That was a mistake in there," he said. He put a cigarette into his mouth and offered the package. Frank shook his head. "You know what I mean, right?"

"Yeah."

"It could have been fatal."

Frank looked out the passenger window.

Cunningham lit the cigarette, put his arm on the door rest and steered with one hand. He looked over at him. "Are you the guy who shot Coyle?"

"Where did you hear that?"

"You know, one thing or another. Besides, it's all over your face. You're as pale as an Easter lily and you look like crap."

"I don't look that bad."

"Uglier than usual."

His face brightened and he smiled.

"I'd be hell of a lot less concerned with that. Could have been your family planning a funeral."

"I guess I should be grateful."

"It happens. You're minding your own business at the end of a shift and bang, bang, bang. And now you going home in a different way than when you arrived."

"Yeah, I know."

"No, I don't think you do."

"What do you mean?"

"You getting any sleep?"

"Some."

"What's that mean?"

"I shut my eyes and the next thing I know I'm trying to figure it out again."

"You're not God."

Frank looked over at him.

"If you're looking for justice in this life, there is none. Just levels of hurt." Cunningham picked up the radio mic. "607 to C-2 on a signal seven."

"Received," the desk man said. "Is Trooper Mahan with you?"

"Yes, he is."

"There's a teletype message from headquarters in his box."

He looked over at him. "He's got it." He turned back to the road. "I once went and saw a doctor and told him I was having nightmares."

"Did you tell him about . . ?"

"Dachau? No, just kept it general."

"Army doctor?"

"Army? They're the last ones you want to talk to about that stuff. No, a regular doctor."

"What did he say?"

"He said think of something positive. Concentrate on the good stuff."

"Did it help?"

"On a good night, and there's not a lot of them, it's like a door opens and I can see for miles. Lately though, they've been downright hellish. I guess that's the penance I've been given." He paused. "You know which ones are the worst?"

"The bad nights?"

"No, the good ones. Those sinister bastards make me think I've finally beaten it."

Frank leaned against the cruiser door.

"This is serious business, Priest. Today's little misstep could be the start of something bad. I don't want to see you get hurt." They drove through the toll booths and entered the turnpike. "You didn't kill him, his brother did." He lifted his chin. "The people out there may not understand that. But every cop who walks out there must. Live your life, Priest."

"I wonder if it will ever completely let go."

"You did it, live with it. I told you about my stain, it did something to me. You don't want to go down that road. It happened and all the replaying is not going to make it go away. You've got your wife and kids. That always helps."

They walked into the barracks and they checked their mail boxes. Frank removed a teletype message. "Trial's been postponed again. We won't be going to Philadelphia."

"You need to get that behind you."

35

Philadelphia, Pennsylvania
November 1959

John Coyle rose to take the stand. In the third month of one of the longest prosecutions in Pennsylvania history, the Commonwealth rested. Several troopers testified and Frank too. Witnesses said that they saw John the morning of Officer Kane's murder running from the scene and some identified him as the killer. Detective Lieutenant Cullinane read John Coyle's interrogation verbatim at the objection of his attorney. To the circle of characters who made their living off the miserable wretches who regularly beat a path to the courtroom doors, the trial should have been a home run, an open-and-shut case. But when considering Coyle's defense counsel, they checked their projections knowing she had a knack for earning acquittals in some of the bleakest of cases. Attorney Mary Alice Duffy or MAD, as she was affectionately known by the court regulars, and her sister, Sara, had the reputation of giving no quarter or conceding the time of day, contested every witness, every argument, every objection. She just plumb wore out her opponents and could earn her most desperate clients a better outcome than they should have ever expected. A master of the melodramatic, she petitioned the court for several trial postponements claiming a variety of illnesses for both herself and Coyle. She described the Commonwealth's case as a fabrication and when Captain Howard Gatter of the Philadelphia police testified that

John Coyle told him, 'I'm guilty, let's get it over with,' Duffy bolted out of her seat and requested Judge David L. Ullman to move for mistrial. When the court ordered a medical examination of Coyle's injured leg, she vigorously opposed the order and threatened to sue both Judge Ullman and the physician who conducted the examination. And she demanded that a bench warrant be issued for a prosecution witness for failure to support her five children. For Coyle, he sat contented and pleased, enjoying the drama being played out on his behalf.

He moved to the bench with an exaggerated limp, gingerly stepped up to the witness stand and faced the jury. She asked him if his leg was a handicap and he said that he had difficulty walking, never mind running. He proceeded to bow to each juror, continuing this exaggerated display of respect until the prosecutor objected and the judge instructed him to stop. "He's not bowing," Duffy said, "he's nodding as any gentleman would do. And this admonishment is another example of the court's prejudice against my client." John swore to "tell the truth, the whole truth and nothing but the truth, so help me God," and then proceeded to testify to an entirely different set of facts known to the police. He spoke in a voice so soft and delicate that a cough at the rear of the courtroom caused the stenographer to ask him to repeat what he had said. Judge Ullman instructed him frequently to speak up. He denied being present when Jimmy Kane was murdered and testified that he told police that his brother had shot Kane in self-defense. He said that he was asleep in his apartment when wakened by gunshots at about 4:30 in the morning. He dressed and was about to go out when his brother returned. Coyle insisted he made statements implicating himself because the troopers threatened to kill him and let his brother die without medical treatment if he didn't cooperate. "If you want your brother to get medical care, there's a long way and a short way to the hospital," he reported. Coyle said his brother died two hours before he was told and that he didn't believe the cops until he saw his body at the funeral home. He described his capture in the Middleborough bog as savage, troopers coming upon them, firing hundreds of bullets and shooting Will, his brother mortally wounded, crying out in the most soulful way and him screaming at the police to stop. "I've had nightmares," he said. Then he said that he was stripped naked and threatened by a trooper with a machine gun. He was denied water and the use of the bathroom until he gave a statement. And threatened that if he had insisted on saying that his brother had shot Kane in self-defense, the cops would cut his wrists and let him bleed to death. In desperation, he confessed to anything they told him to say. Laughter erupted from the benches where Officer Kane's widow, family and friends sat. Attorney Duffy demanded that the court remove those responsible for the breach of decorum, but the judge said he heard no laughter and told her that if he did hear such disruption, the persons responsible would be removed.

Duffy complained about corruption of the judicial process and police brutality. She cited instances where the judge had erred, noting that they were all causes for appeal and requested that her exceptions be entered into the record. "This isn't a prosecution," she roared, "it's a persecution." Judge Ullman rose out of his chair and pointed with dramatic flair to where the Massachusetts troopers sat and said to Coyle, "Which of these officers, threatened you." Coyle looked out to the benches. He stood there for a long few moments, fixed on the troopers' faces and when he didn't respond, the judge asked him again. He remained silent and the judge continued with the trial.

On November 20, 1959 after the three-month comic-drama came to an end, the jury convened and deliberated for eleven hours. During this time, they asked Judge Ullman seven questions to assist them in rendering a verdict and then they voted. And though he had instructed them to consider Coyle's background, age and the fact that he had no prior criminal record and that he "may have stepped into a quagmire of crime and became more deeply and desperately engulfed," they came to a conclusion on the fifty-seventh day of trial after just one ballot. When the Court Crier asked for their decision, the foreman responded, "Guilty, murder in the first degree." And when asked for the penalty, he said, "The penalty is death." Upon request by Attorney Duffy, each juror was polled and the same verdict and punishment given. And so after he had testified that he "wasn't even there" referring to Kane's murder and after he suggested that troopers killed his brother in cold blood in the Middleborough bog, John Coyle stood there with his hands clasped in front of him. The verdict was read, he looked into the gallery. And he smiled.

"YOU GUYS EVER need anything in Philly, you let us know," Captain Gatter said.

They sat or stood around in a small meeting room in the basement at the back of the building, underneath the main courtroom and halfway down the hall from the prisoner holding area. The door was constructed with reinforced steel and the room built out of cement blocks. It had a rectangular double-plated glass window at the front that looked out onto the hallway. The district attorneys used the room to prepare witnesses, make last minute deals and receive last minute confessions. And it served, from time to time, as a temporary holding area. Frank sat facing the window, watching a steady stream of characters, players in the court's pageantry, pass in the hallway. A group of shackled prisoners and guards walked by the window on their way to the lockup. John Coyle passed in the group, hopping with an exaggerated limp, the smaller man lost amongst the larger and taller prisoners and guards. He moved with them in concert and yet without them, his eyes sweeping the layout of the hall, the doorways, the rooms and the exits.

"Ready to go, Frank?" Lenny Von Fursten said.

"Give me a couple of minutes."

"The bus should be here pretty soon."

"Okay."

The others left and Frank sat alone at a metal table in the room. He removed his suit jacket, pulled at his tie and opened his collar. Then he leaned back, stretched his legs and closed his eyes. In the end, the use of an unauthorized round never became an issue in the proceedings and no one claimed the fatal shot. Witnessing the spectacle that was the Coyle trial allowed him to begin to accept the fate that fell upon him. He started to daydream and soon gave way to a pattern of dozing and sudden wakefulness. After a while, he let himself go.

"DID YOU HAVE the nuns?" he said. "They really tried. Tried to teach us manners and make us into decent human beings. They must be heartbroken over me, one of their lost lambs."

"Shut up, let the man alone."

Frank heard the vibrato of their voices. And the harsh clamor of chains. He heard his own breathing, felt a chill and shivered, blinked his eyes open. One of them sat at the end of the table, opposite from him. And the other stood behind the first. A rush went through him and he snapped up. His hand struck the edge of the table.

"What about that family in Kansas, lived on a farm? The Clutters, four of them I believe. It was reported that they were just simple country people, I read about them in the newspaper. Two young killers murdered them in cold blood. Now those boys . . . the police have the goods on them. If they went to Catholic school. Do you see what I'm saying? The nuns must be besides themselves. What a terrible calling."

"Shut the hell up, Coyle," the young prison guard said as he finished securing him. "Excuse me sir, I didn't mean to disturb you." Frank looked up at the guard and studied his face. Then he turned to the man sitting at the table. John Coyle, his hands cuffed to a manacle with a chain and shackles on both legs, faced him, the chain looping through a ring that was bolted to the floor. He sat there chewing gum with no expression.

"Do you mind if we use the room?" the guard said. "The lock-up is full and we're waiting for the prison bus."

"Yeah, sure." Frank said.

"You ought to be in Kansas," Coyle said. "Four innocent people. Now there's cause for a proper accounting."

Frank stood and took his jacket from the back of the chair.

"Shut up Coyle," the guard said. "I'm sorry sir, I can't take him anywhere else."

"It's alright, I'm leaving," Frank said.

The guard took up a post by the door.

"How do we measure a man?" Coyle said. "Every day men enter our lives and in an instant, the universe pauses and we evaluate. We judge each. Friend or foe, aggressor or peacemaker, attracted to or repulsed by, lover or enemy." The chain dragged against the edge of the table as he rested his arms. "And some are dangerous and some can emit the most vile of lies, worse still, others are sinister and lust for control. What is it that attracts us to one while the other requires preparation for battle? What causes these supposedly random meetings?"

"Coyle!" The young guard took a step towards him. Coyle turned and the chain rattled through the ring and it snapped tight. The guard stopped. "Knock it off," he said. "This man don't want to hear your crazy shit."

"This man does," Coyle said.

Frank tightened his tie.

"I know him."

"You ought to know him," the guard said. "Him and his friends are the reason you're sitting here. It's all over, but the electric chair. You can give up the act."

He buttoned his jacket and turned to leave. He started out the door when Coyle said in a loud singing voice, "I remember you from the beach. You and your boy." Frank paused and Coyle brightened. "And the ball."

He and the guard stepped out into the hall.

"Lex talionis," Coyle said. "I knew who you were that day."

"Asshole, don't mind him," the guard said.

Frank looked into the room. "Can you give me a minute?"

"Geez, I don't want to get in any trouble."

"There'll be no problem."

"Alright, but be quick," the guard said. "Just don't mark him up where it can be seen."

Coyle folded his hands together on the table as Frank re-entered the room and stood opposite him. "I saw you then," Coyle said. "And I see you now." His voice strained with casualness.

In the hall, the guard glanced into the room and then turned away.

"I marked you that day."

"What do you want?" Frank said.

"You saw me also. Did you not?"

"I saw all of you. You, your brother and the man you kidnapped."

282

"But you didn't act."

"I wasn't sure."

Coyle nodded in agreement.

"You've got something to say?"

"I saw something with you and your boy that was missing from mine." Coyle paused. "I could have killed you that day on the beach. But it wasn't our time."

"Time?"

"We were destined to meet in that bog."

"Is that why you double backed rather than escaping?"

"You knew that."

"My sergeant told me you had made it outside the perimeter. But you decided to double back, all the way back to the beginning."

"Maybe I was lost. You can get turned around in the woods."

"You weren't lost. You hunted those woods, you knew every tree in the swamp. Knew them like the back of your hand."

"This is true."

"You made a choice."

"Choice?" Coyle laughed. "There is no choice."

"Then what would you call it?"

"Destiny. I saw Will's head wound, put my finger on it. Special bullet?"

"Your arrogance caused your brother's death."

Coyle turned his face up. "Do you ever wonder how you got there? The bog?"

"I didn't choose to be there. It just happened."

"You don't believe that, do you?"

"I don't know what I believe anymore. But I'm left with it."

"Millions of bits of energy play into what appears to be random chance encounter, including the exact place and

283

time. One day two bodies pass unnoticed to one another and on the next, the synergy changes and the ball tumbles into place."

"I don't know what you're talking about. "

"You don't? You were meant to be there. Not your sergeant, not the other 399 police in the swamp and the woods. The slightest change in energy, the results might have been different. We might have escaped. We might have surrendered."

"What's your point?"

"It might have been you who died in the bog. Your body on the slab at the funeral home instead of my brother's."

"All I know is that you and your brother killed that cop while he pleaded for his life. Over a bottle of milk. You had your chance to surrender and you chose . . . wrongly." Frank turned to leave, but stopped. "How can you be so sure it was destiny and not just pure coincidence?"

Coyle leaned forward. "We all have our roles as if we were chosen by lottery. From our born days, we marched to that bog, you and I. And you were there, ready to pull the trigger. It was my destiny, Will's destiny, your destiny."

Frank looked out to the hall where the young guard stood fingering a ring of keys.

"You realize. We're not that much different," Coyle said.

"It's over," Frank said.

"Now that I'm in jail and my brother dead?" He began to turn the manacle on his wrist. "Remember, men lust for wealth. Men lust for power. If they are denied these things, men must hunt. It'll never be over."

"You'll soon be out of the spotlight, left alone with the executioner. So, what do you think now?"

"I'll remember that I hunted."

"Goodbye, Mr. Coyle. Nice knowin' you."

"There is no goodbye. Our place, our time, you and I, it's indelible. I will hunt and you will be there to exact a proper accounting."

Frank turned and left the room and the courthouse. He walked down the long granite stairs, out to the day and made his way to the bus. Ribbons of brown slush lay in the street and blackish dirty snow was piled against the gutter. The wind blew in a steady gale without taking a breath blowing straight up the avenue from the Delaware and he shivered as he climbed aboard. He stood by the driver and looked for an empty seat and noticed that all the other troopers stared back at him. He sat next to Lenny Von Fursten.

Lenny looked over at him. "Sorry about your buddy," he said.

"What?" Frank said.

"Your coach."

"PK Cunningham? What about him?"

"One of the guys called into the station and they told him."

"Told him what?"

"He's dead."

36

When he arrived at the barracks later that day, the desk officer told him that Sergeant McGreevey was waiting to see him. Frank knocked on his door and heard the dog's whimper. He entered and the sergeant invited him to sit. The dog stood and he came to him, his head and shoulders stooped, the way a weary old man moves when he no longer has the strength to hold himself erect.

"He left this," McGreevey said and he passed a handwritten note to him. In it, PK Cunningham described the burden of killing and the terror of carrying it with him all the years since that day at the concentration camp. How as he aged and the bullet-proof veneer of youth wore away, he became afraid and lonely. How he never became totally disengaged, keeping a loaded weapon close at hand, locking and re-checking locked doors. And nailing all of the windows shut in his apartment. How the black of night rose up against him, hideous vaporous spirits and shaggy demons. How he could see and describe each of the wretches that he lifted out of the Death train and the faces of the German tower guards that he killed. He said he hadn't slept a full night's rest in years and that the weight of life like running water over stone just wore him down. He thought that had he had someone in his life to love, he might have survived. But he wasn't entirely sure. He thanked him for resurrecting a renewed dedication to the job. He left him his record collection. And he ended by telling him that he was more of a priest than most.

And finally, "The dog is yours if you'll have him." Frank paused. "I hope I haven't disappointed you. I guess I was better at giving advice than taking it."

McGreevey told him that Cunningham had checked into one of the fly-by-night motels out on Route 146. He sat on the floor with his back to the bed and consumed enough booze to drunken several men. Placed the heel of a shotgun between his legs, held it still with his knees. Placed his mouth around the muzzle and pulled the trigger.

Frank looked down at the dog. The dog stood next to him and he rested his head against his leg. Frank knew that the dog realized in some mysterious way that his companion was gone and would not return. He stroked his head and spoke calmly to him, telling him that he would care for him all of his days. He massaged the back of his neck and behind his ears. He rubbed his arthritic shoulders. Then he nudged the dog closer to him and the dog sat.

"Looks like the funeral service will be at the end of the week," McGreevey said. "If you don't mind, I'd like that letter back."

He passed the note across the desk.

McGreevey took the letter and set a match to it. Let it burn until the fire began to lick his fingers. Then he dropped the remnants into the wastepaper basket, the ember of fire flaming like a slender taper. Until it smoked and smoldered and disintegrated into black flakes, until all of his words finally disappeared. When all that remained were ashes, the sergeant handed the basket to him. "Take this outside and empty it into his garden. Turn over the soil and mix it in real good."

He took the basket and walked to the door with the dog beside him.

"Frank."

"Yes, Sergeant."

"The official report of Trooper Pearly K. Cunningham's death will be out tomorrow. It will read that he died while cleaning a malfunctioning shotgun. An accidental discharge."

Frank looked down at the dog. He looked up and he nodded.

On Friday morning, he stood in the ranks of hundreds, troopers and police officers from across the state and beyond and he thought about his first encounter with PK Cunningham, the image of him large and foreboding, his bald head prominent, sitting at the end of the kitchen table and holding court like a Silurian prince.

An academy D.I. gave a command and they turned and he called cadence. The bass drum sounded, there was a roll of the snares and the bagpipes whined to pitch, the music carried them, wave after wave of blue for as far as he could see bending with the curve of the road and climbing the hill to the spires of the basilica.

37

A thunderous double boom sounded in the night sky as a jet broke the sound barrier above him, a shaking of the earth's dome, two monstrous claps heard for miles. The windows in the house rattled and he awoke. He stared at the ceiling in the darkened bedroom, mottled with shadows created by the street lights and waited for the quiet. He listened for her breath. She lay asleep beside him, naked and curled on one side, partly covered by the sheet. He pulled it over her and slid one of his hands under his head. The other he rode along the slope of her shoulder and over the curve of her hip. Sheila murmured and she turned into her pillow. She spoke from out of the folds of bed coverings and asked him if he was okay.

"Yeah," he said. "Go back to sleep."

With time, he had learned to live his life and accept his fate. A new crop of troopers graduated and some new boots took up residence at the Grafton barracks. They assumed the shit duty and Frank and his classmates were awarded a few minor benefits, a room with only one other occupant and cruisers with less than two hundred thousand miles on the odometers. The dog died shortly after he had brought him home. He tolerated the children and showed great patience with them. He had him cremated and he brought his ashes to PK's garden, dug up the soil in a place off the perimeter and planted them where he could watch over his master while he worked. On some days, he would take one of PK's albums out of its paper sleeve, hold it up reverently by its edges and blow his breath across the surface. Place it on the spindle and set the needle down and grieved the only way a cop can grieve. In the deep dark well of his soul.

He thought about John Coyle, his certainty of their moment in place and time. The claim of destiny that he thrust upon him and the indelible mark on his soul. PK called it carrying the stain. He thought about the bog and the swamp, full of life and the spectacle of nature. How violence is sewn into its fabric and the fabric of the human condition, every living thing. And how the letting of blood is eternal. And for those who would invoke the name of God in order to refute this claim, he thought only that they should look up and turn to the hill of Calvary.

THE END

Epilogue

Fairview State Hospital for the Criminally Insane
Waymart, Pennsylvania

A nurse sat in a chair inside the glass and she watched the men in the room. There were five of them. All occupied with one thing or another. An orderly sat across from her in the office and he wrote his answer in the crossword puzzle of the day's newspaper. John Coyle stood near a barred window in the open recreation area and he was looking out. After a few minutes, he turned and faced into the room and began to speak to no one in particular.

"Games of death cannot be ignored. Do you see that man standing there? The one tossing the ball with the boy. You can feel him as certain as one feels rain. And it comes on you in a rush and a shiver."

The nurse leaned forward in her chair and the orderly looked up from his puzzle.

"It is the universal existential flirtation, the lifting of the face to the sky and the beating of the drum. I've seen where we all end up. Time passes, codes written, but the drum persists. The drum beats loud."

John turned back and resumed gazing out the window while the other men remained occupied. Two of them played cards, one of them watched the new color television and the last shot pool by himself. The orderly turned the page of the newspaper.

"Do you think he's psychotic?" he said.

"I don't know," said the nurse. "But the court sent him here."

"If I was facing the electric chair, I'd be dreaming up all kinds of shit to say."

The nurse began to type into the shift's log. She stopped and looked out through the glass again.

"He's pretty convincing though," she said. "Very convincing."

Acknowledgments

An Appointed Time is a work of fiction. The circumstances in this book are based on actual historical events. During a six month period in 1959, the Massachusetts State Police responded to several dangerous and violent actions, including two prison uprisings and the Coyle brothers' manhunt. During this period, the state police performed at an exceptionally high level of professionalism and established itself as an elite police organization with unique capabilities. And while this period in the Department's history is recorded, all scenes, incidents and characters are intended to be fictional and any semblance to actual events or persons is coincidental.

With deepest respects, this book is dedicated to Denis J. Donoghue, Jr., 47th RTT, Massachusetts State Police, Robert W. (Skip) Scofield, 55th RTT, Massachusetts State Police and William E. Mulvey, 232nd Regiment, 42nd Infantry, the Rainbow Division, 1942-1945.

This book would not have been possible without the support and generosity of the following: The Massachusetts State Police; former members Leonard F. Von Flatern, 40th RTT and Robert A. Enos, 41st RTT; Janice McCarthy, C.O.P.S.S.; and the Town of Middleborough Conservation Commission.

I thank the following who took the time from their own busy lives and careers to read and review all or some portion of the manuscript: Lt. Colonel John Kelly, 58th RTT; Sergeant Jerry Galizio, MSP Bomb Squad; Linda Sperling, editor; Larry Rothstein, author and editor; Maxine Rodburg, author and Harvard Instructor; and Jordan Rich, Chart Productions. Lastly, I thank my wife, Gail, without whose support, this work just wouldn't exist.

The following source material provided invaluable details of the prison riots, the Coyle brothers' manhunt, and 1950's America: *Enforcement Odyssey: Massachusetts State Police* by William Powers; "E.G.& G. Inc. History" from *International Directory of Company Histories*, Vol. 29; *The Press, The Rosenbergs and the Cold War* by John F. Neville; "Blackstone River Valley" by Blackstone Corridor, Whitinsville, MA; "A Brief History of Outlaw Motorcycle Clubs" by William L. Dulaney; "The War on the Home Front" from *Americans at War* by Stephen E. Ambrose; *The Autobiography of Malcolm X* by Malcolm X and Alex Haley; "The Shape of Jazz That Was" by Nat Hentoff, *Boston Magazine*; *God's Country: America in the Fifties* by J. Ronald Oakley; *Grand Expectations: the United States, 1945-1974* by James T. Patterson; *Surrender of the Dachau Concentration Camp 29 April 1945: The True Account* by John H. Linden; *1959: The Year Everything Changed* by Fred Kaplan; *The Outlaw and The Gangster: Similarities and Defense* by Joseph O'Keefe, PhD. News accounts from *The Boston Globe, Boston Daily Record, Boston Herald, Philadelphia Bulletin, Fall River Herald News, and Bangor News*. And *Commonwealth v. Coyle, 415 Pa. 379 (1964)*.

CPSIA information can be obtained
at www.ICGtesting.com
Printed in the USA
LVHW09s1823040918
589117LV00001B/274/P

9 780983 996019